The Fortune Teller

La Voisin stared into the ball for a long while. Finally she spoke, in a tone so bleak and ominous that it made me shudder. "I see," she said, "that you will come into a fortune."

Sam's face took on a look of surprise and indignation. "That's the same thing you told *me!*"

"Not so," said La Voisin. "What I said was, 'You will receive more money than you imagine.'"

"That's the same thing, isn't it?" When the cunning woman made no reply, he fished out another coin and clapped it into her palm. "Tell mine again."

"As you wish." While she peered into the ball, I sat weighing the words she had directed at me. A fortune? How could I possibly come into a fortune? I could hardly inherit it. My mother had died in the poorhouse, and I had no notion who my father was.

La Voisin lifted her head but said nothing. "Well?" Sam prompted her.

"You are certain you wish to hear it?"

"Of course. What is it? What did you see?"

The cunning woman turned toward him, and I caught for the first time a glimpse of her visage. The skin of her face was as thickly covered with warts as a pox's victim's is with scars. "I see that you will turn traitor."

OTHER BOOKS YOU MAY ENJOY

Shakespeare's Spy

GARY BLACKWOOD

PUFFIN BOOKS

PUFFIN BOOKS

Published by the Penguin Group

Penguin Young Readers Group, 345 Hudson Street,
New York, New York 10014, U.S.A.

Penguin Group (Canada), 10 Alcorn Avenue, Toronto,
Ontario, Canada M4V 3B2 (a division of Pearson Penguin Canada Inc.)

Penguin Books Ltd, 80 Strand, London WC2R 0RL, England

Penguin Ireland, 25 St Stephen's Green, Dublin 2, Ireland
(a division of Penguin Books Ltd)

Penguin Group (Australia), 250 Camberwell Road, Camberwell, Victoria 3124,
Australia (a division of Pearson Australia Group Pty Ltd)

Penguin Books India Pvt Ltd, 11 Community Centre,
Panchsheel Park, New Delhi - 110 017, India

Penguin Group (NZ), Cnr Airborne and Rosedale Roads, Albany, Auckland,
New Zealand (a division of Pearson New Zealand Ltd)

Penguin Books (South Africa) (Pty) Ltd, 24 Sturdee Avenue,
Rosebank, Johannesburg 2196, South Africa

Registered Offices: Penguin Books Ltd, 80 Strand, London WC2R 0RL, England

Published in the United States of America by Dutton Children's Books,
a division of Penguin Young Readers Group, 2003
Published by Puffin, a division of Penguin Young Readers Group, 2005

1 3 5 7 9 10 8 6 4 2

Copyright © Gary Blackwood, 2003

CIP Data is available.

Puffin ISBN 0-14-240311-3

Printed in the United States of America

For Emily, who is partly insane
and totally great

Shakespeare's
Spy

1

Of all the dozens of tasks a fledgling actor is called upon to perform, surely the two most difficult are dying and falling in love.

As a prentice with the Lord Chamberlain's Men, I was called upon to do both, sometimes on a daily basis. Not in earnest, of course; I was expected only to approximate them. This is not as simple as it may sound. I could feign sadness well enough, or fear, or loneliness, for growing up an orphan as I did, I had known more than my share of such things. But my experience with love and death was more limited. Though I did my best to persuade the audience that my groans of mortal agony and my melancholy, heartbroken sighs were real, they always seemed to me to lack a certain conviction.

Most of the stories we acted out were rife with romance, but in our ordinary lives it was sadly absent, and no wonder. Since women were not permitted to appear upon the stage, all the parts were played by men and boys. As a result, I seldom came in contact with anyone of the fairer gender, aside from Good-wife Willingson—who kept house for my mentor, Mr. Pope—and Tetty, a young orphan girl who lived with us.

Foul murders and duels to the death were also an important part of our repertoire. But, though we spent several hours each day hacking at one another with stage swords, either in practice or in performance, our lives were seldom truly in peril. Unless he fell victim to the plague, the worst a player could ordinarily expect was that he would misjudge his position and tumble off the edge of the stage, into the arms of the groundlings.

But Fate cares little about our expectations. In the winter of 1602, the Lord Admiral's company were performing *Palamon and Arcyte* at the royal court when the stage, hastily built and loaded down with heavy scenery, suddenly collapsed. Five of the actors were injured and three were crushed to death.

Now, if the truth be told, there was no love lost between our company and theirs; in fact, in the ongoing struggle for ascendancy in the world of London theatre, the Admiral's Men were our chief rivals. Still, not one of us would have wished such a calamity upon them. Though they might be the enemy, they were also fellow players, and we were saddened and sobered by the tragedy—especially when we considered that we might easily have been its victims, instead. Only a week before, we had presented Mr. Shakespeare's play *The Merry Wives of Windsor* upon those same treacherous boards.

Fortunately for the Admiral's Men—though not for us—all their principal players were spared, and within a fortnight they were once again competing with us for the playgoers' pennies—and there were far fewer pennies than usual to go around that winter.

Ordinarily we played outdoors at the Globe Theatre right up until Yuletide, when we peformed at Whitehall for the queen and her court. But this year, winter had forgotten its cue and come on early. The groundlings were a hardy lot, willing to stand uncomplaining in the drizzling rain and the baking sun for hours on end, asking only to be rewarded with a bit of fine ranting, a reasonable number of laughs, and, from time to time, a limb or two being lopped off and a few guts spilled upon the stage. But we could hardly expect them to risk having their ears and toes bitten by frost for the sake of art.

So in the middle of December we had forsaken the Globe and begun performing indoors, in the long gallery at the Cross Keys Inn. Though the audience was grateful, we players were not. The Cross Keys lay on the north side of the Thames, a long, cold walk from Southwark, where most of the company lived. The smaller confines of the inn meant smaller profits as well; no matter how tightly we packed them in, we could accommodate only half the number of playgoers that the Globe held.

In January, the royal court made a move of its own, from the damp, drafty palace at Whitehall to warmer quarters upriver at Richmond. It was there that we gave our second command performance of the season for the queen.

We were always a bit anxious when appearing before Her Majesty. After all, it was mainly thanks to her that the London theatre managed to flourish as it did. Without her support and protection, we would be at the mercy of the Puritans, who insisted that the stage was a breeding ground of sin. If something about the play displeased her—and, according to her master of revels, she had lately become even more difficult to please than usual—she might be more inclined to listen to the mounting protests of the Square Toes, and let them close us down.

We had worried very little about how *Merry Wives* would be received, for it was an old favorite of Her Majesty's. In fact, Mr. Shakespeare once told me that he had written it at her behest. After seeing *Henry IV*, she was so taken with the character of Sir John Falstaff that she insisted he must have a play of his own.

Our second show, *All's Well That Ends Well*, had no such favorable history. Mr. Shakespeare had composed it only the previous summer, while we were on tour to escape the plague. Thanks to a broken arm, he had been forced to dictate most of it; I had put the words on paper for him, using my system of swift writing. Though the script had been approved by Mr. Tilney, the master of revels, and given a trial run at the Globe, the queen would be seeing it for the first time.

For my part, I was seeing the palace at Richmond for the first time. A year earlier, I had performed in the banquet room at Whitehall, playing Ophelia in *Hamlet*, and been awed by its magnificence. The great hall at Richmond was even larger and more lavish. When we entered, Sam, the youngest of the prentices, gave a low whistle. My other companion, Sal Pavy, glanced about with a rather bored expression, as though he were wholly accustomed to playing such places.

"Widge." Sam elbowed me and pointed upward. I followed his gaze. The entire ceiling was covered in great billows of muslin, painted with fanciful figures representing the constellations of the night sky. "I hope they fastened that up there really well," said Sam. "If it lets go, we'll all be smothered."

"Perhaps," I said. "But I'm more concerned about the stage." Mr. Tilney's men had constructed a platform for us at one end of the hall. The three-foot-high trestles that supported it looked far too flimsy and widely spaced to suit me, especially considering the amount of furniture, properties, and painted backdrops the Office of Revels felt was necessary for the production. "I don't ken why we must ha' so much stuff. We did well enough at the Globe wi' naught but a few chairs."

Sam shrugged. "Perhaps royal folk don't have much imagination."

"Well, I like it," put in Sal Pavy, rather haughtily. "We always had elaborate sets at Blackfriars."

Sam groaned and rolled his eyes. Sal Pavy had said this same sort of thing so often about the theatre at Blackfriars, where he had belonged to the company called the Children of the Chapel, that it had become a standard jest. Sam would surely have had some choice comment to offer had not Mr. Armin, our fencing master, called out just then, "If you're quite done gawking, gentlemen, there are costume trunks to be carried in."

One thing I had learned about royalty, in my few brief encounters with them, was that they kept later hours than us ordinary wights. Because our stage was in the banquet hall, we could not begin our performance until after supper—a meal that did not commence until eight o'clock or so, and might drag on for hours.

While the queen and her court dined, we players donned our costumes, wigs, and face paint in an anteroom, then waited about anxiously for our summons. When Mr. Tilney, the master of revels, strode into the room, we all got to our feet, but he motioned for us to sit again. "Not yet, gentlemen, not yet," he said brusquely. "Where is Mr. Shakespeare?"

"P-pacing back and f-forth in the hallway, most like," replied Mr. Heminges, our business manager. "I'll f-fetch him."

When he returned with our playwright in tow, the master of revels approached them hesitantly, clearly embarrassed about something. "Ah, Will. I . . . I meant to tell you this earlier, but . . . you see, I've been so busy with—"

"Tell me *what?*" interrupted Mr. Shakespeare.

Mr. Tilney shifted about uncomfortably and cleared his throat. "Well, just that . . . that you must . . . or, rather, that it would be in your best *interests* if you were to delete from the play any reference to the King of France's illness."

Our entire company stared at him incredulously. Mr. Armin was the first to find his voice. "For what reason?" he demanded.

Mr. Tilney glanced about, as though afraid of being over-heard, and then explained, almost in a whisper, "Since you performed for her at Yuletide, Her Majesty's health has declined considerably. The last thing she will wish to see is a monarch with a mortal disease."

Mr. Heminges, who played the king, scowled and shook his head. "I'm n-not sure it c-can be done, it's such an essential p-part of the play. After all, if I'm not d-dying, Helena can hardly g-go to Paris to c-cure me, can she?"

"How long before we go on?" asked Mr. Shakespeare.

"Oh, half an hour, at least," Mr. Tilney said blithley, as though that should be ample time to compose a whole new play.

Mr. Shakespeare nodded grimly. "We'll manage it somehow."

When Mr. Tilney was gone, Mr. Heminges cried, "We'll *m-manage* it? How?"

"I don't know, exactly. But if I hadn't said so, we'd never have gotten rid of him." Mr. Shakespeare turned away and began toying with his earring, as he habitually did when deep in thought.

Sam could be counted upon to offer some harebrained solution to nearly any problem, and he did not disappoint us now.

"I have it! The king has really bad hair, and so he sends for the best hairdresser in all of France—Helena!" He clapped me on the shoulder. The role of Helena, of course, belonged to me.

Mr. Shakespeare either did not hear Sam's proposal, or chose to ignore it. Finally he looked up and said, "Here's what we'll do. We'll keep the illness, but instead of the king, it will be Lafeu, the king's lifelong friend, who is dying. Can you reword your lines accordingly, Widge?"

"Aye, I wis." There was a time when such a request would have sent me into a panic, but in my year and a half with the company, I had become quite adept at thribbling—that is, improvising new lines when something went awry on the stage. It took a fairly serious calamity to throw me out of square.

One was not long in coming. The first two scenes of *All's Well* did, indeed, go well enough—except that the most important member of our audience seemed to be missing. Then, halfway through the third scene, Her Majesty made her entrance. We actors might as well have stopped speaking altogether, for the attention of everyone in the room turned to her.

Had it not been for the red wig and the dozen or so maids of honor who clustered about her, I might not have recognized her, so changed was she. I knew well enough that Her Majesty was getting on in years; after all, Mr. Pope, who was nearing sixty himself, told me that he had been a mere boy when she took the throne. But never before had I seen the years hang so heavy on her.

When we performed *Merry Wives* for her, she had looked remarkably well preserved. This was due in part, of course, to the thick mask of white lead and cochineal with which she concealed the ravages of time and to the well-made wig, which was far more natural looking than those we prentices wore. But her behavior, too, had belied her age. She had laughed at Sir John's antics, flirted with her male courtiers, and consumed a prodigious amount of ale.

Though she still wore the makeup and the wig, she seemed to have forgotten how to play the part expected of her, that of the ever-youthful Gloriana. Mr. Tilney had warned us that her health was poor, but I had not expected to see her shuffling along, head bowed, like an old woman. In one hand she carried a rusty sword, which she used as a cane to support herself. When she reached her chair, she had trouble gathering in her skirts so she could sit properly. One of the maids of honor rushed forward to help, but she brushed the young woman irritably aside.

So taken aback was I by Her Majesty's condition that I dropped my lines, forcing Sal Pavy, who was playing the countess, to repeat his: "'Her eye is sick on 't; I observe her now.'"

"'What is your pleasure, madam?'" I replied.

Before Sal Pavy could get out his next line, he was interrupted by the queen's voice; despite her illness, it had lost little of its power or its sting. "It is our *pleasure*," she said, "that you speak up! We can scarcely make out the words!"

Though we put on our best Pilate's voices, we got no more than twenty lines in before she berated us again. So exasperated was she that she neglected to use the royal *we*. "Can you hear me up there?"

Sal Pavy and I glanced at each other. Though it was considered bad form for a player to break character, he turned to the queen and bowed. "Yes, Your Majesty."

"Then why can *I* not hear *you?*"

"I beg Your Majesty's humble pardon. We will try harder."

But try as we might, we could not speak loudly enough to suit her. Finally she rose and, grumbling, laboriously dragged her heavy chair forward, fending off all attempts to assist her, until she sat only a few feet from the stage. I wished she had not. At that distance, no amount of paint or dye or elegant clothing could conceal the painful truth: the queen was wasting away.

A blow that is struck without warning is always the most telling, and at that moment it struck me for the first time that Her Majesty was mortal, the same as ordinary folk—that she might not, in fact, live through the winter.

I shuddered to think what effect her passing might have on England, which had known no other monarch for nearly half a century, and on our professsion in particular. What would become of us poor players when we no longer had her powerful presence standing like a breakwater between us and the swelling tide of Puritans? At that moment I had an inkling of how the Admiral's Men must have felt when the stage gave way beneath their feet.

2

Every member of the company was, I think, unnerved by having Her Majesty so close at hand. But we were accustomed to adversity. After all, we had acted in inn yards while the ostlers led horses back and forth; we had put up with conceited wights who took seats upon the stage in order to be seen; we had been pelted by hazelnuts and leather beer bottles when we failed to please our audience.

Though our performance before the queen was not the best we had ever given, neither was it the worst. We recalled a reasonable percentage of our lines, and for those we forgot, we usually substituted something fairly sensible. We even managed to remove the king's deadly fistula and give it to poor Lafeu.

By the time we took our bows, it was past midnight, and we were, to a man, exhausted. Luckily the next day was Sunday, which meant we could sleep late. Ordinarily I went to morning services at St. Saviour's, along with Mr. Pope and the orphaned children who shared our household. All Her Majesty's subjects were, in fact, required to attend church, or risk paying a substantial fine. But when I woke, it was nearly noon. Mr. Pope, as I later learned, had taken pity on me and told the priest that I was indisposed.

I scarcely had time to eat before Sam and Sal Pavy came to fetch me for our Sunday outing. In truth, after six long days in the constant company of my fellow players, I would have welcomed a bit of solitude. But I also welcomed the opportunity to see something new, and it was not the best idea to go wandering about London alone, especially those parts of London that appealed most to us.

Though Sam was not the most reliable or the most responsible member of the Chamberlain's Men, he could be a good companion—provided he was expected to be neither serious nor silent. I had even learned to like Sal Pavy to some degree. Well, perhaps *like* is too strong a word. There were things I liked about him: he was talented; he was dedicated; he was determined. He was also vain, quarrelous, and ungrateful. But one of our many duties as prentices was to keep peace among ourselves. So I did my best to overlook his numerous and glaring faults and appreciate his few feeble virtues.

He and Sam and I got along well enough. Still, I could not imagine us ever truly being friends, in the way that I had been friends with our other prentices, Sander and Julia. It had been six months since the plague claimed Sander, but the thought of his death still made me feel as though I had been struck soundly in the ribs with a blunted sword, and not a day passed that I did not think of it.

Julia had not gone to paradise, only to Paris, where she could fulfill her desire to be a player. But there was little hope that she would return, unless the queen suddenly declared that women would henceforth be allowed to act upon the London stage.

Her Majesty was as likely to do that as a gib-cat was to sing sweetly. Though she might ignore the protests of the Puritans, she listened closely to the voice of the common people. And their voice said unmistakably that though any woman was free to watch a criminal get his neck stretched on Tyburn Tree or a toothless bruin be savaged by dogs in the bear-baiting ring, or to dress in rags and beg for alms in the street, or to sell her favors to men for a farthing, she must not be corrupted by taking part in a play.

I had not lost touch with Julia altogether. Every few months a French sailor turned up bearing a letter from her. These were usually brief and disappointingly impersonal, devoted mainly to what roles she was playing at the Théâtre de Marais. But now and again she let slip some line that made me suspect she was not as happy with her lot as she would have us think. The letters I sent in return were as carefully cheerful as hers; if she was pining for home, I had no wish to make her burden heavier by reminding her of how much she was missed.

Though the premature winter had hurt our company's profits, in the city as a whole commerce seemed unaffected. Shopkeepers went on displaying their goods in the street before their shops; St. Paul's churchyard still swarmed with vendors and buyers; beggars still pleaded with passersby on every corner; ballad-mongers and sellers of broadsheets still waved their printed wares aloft and called or sang out enough of their contents to whet the appetite for more; and we prentices, on the one day of the week that we could call our own, still strolled through the streets, looking for an excuse to part with a bit of our weekly wage of three shillings.

Sam, the most daring among us, usually led the way, and Sal Pavy and I were content to follow after. On most Sundays, he led us first to the area of St. Paul's churchyard where the agents of the royal lottery had their booths. And on most Sundays I tried to talk him out of it.

"You ken, do you not, that these wights must sell half a million chances at the least. That means the likelihood of you winning even one of the fourteen-shilling prizes is . . . um . . ."

"One in fifty," put in Sal Pavy.

I cast him a peevish look. "I was about to say that."

"No," said Sam, "it's one in twenty-five."

"How's that?"

"Because I intend to buy two chances."

"At a shilling each? You noddy! If you kept the two shillings instead, you could save up the same amount in—" I held up a restraining hand in front of Sal Pavy's smirking face. "Don't tell me. Seven weeks."

"Very good, young man," said Sal Pavy, in a schoolmasterish voice.

Sam made a scoffing sound. "You don't really imagine that I'd be content with fourteen shillings, do you? I've got my eye on the *big* prize." He leaned forward, his eyes wide, and whispered as though it were a secret known only to him, "Five . . . thousand . . . pounds!" Sal Pavy and I burst into laughter, but Sam was unperturbed. "Go ahead and laugh, like the clapbrained coystrels that you are; I care not a quinch. You know what they say: Let him laugh that wins the prize. You see, I've been told that I am to win, and very soon."

"Ah!" Sal Pavy said. "He's been *told!* That's different!"

"Told?" I said. "By whom?"

"By a soothsayer."

"You mean"—I lowered my voice—"a *witch?*" Where I came from, witches were not openly discussed, for fear one of them might overhear.

"No, just a cunning woman."

"What's that?"

"You know," Sal Pavy said. "Someone who finds lost valuables, and tells your future, and so on."

"Oh. I thought the city had a law against practicing that sort of thing."

"It does. It also has laws against cutpurses and moneylenders—and, if it comes to that, against performing plays within the city limits."

"How does it work, then?" I asked Sam, still half whispering.

"What?"

"How does she tell your future?"

He shrugged. " I don't know, exactly. She has this ball, made of something black and shiny, and she stares into it."

"And it tells her the future? I'd like to see that."

"Well, come on, then." Sam strode off abruptly, heading west on Fleet Street.

Sal Pavy was staring at me rather contemptuously. "Surely you don't believe in all that?"

"Not really," I replied softly. "But it's got him away from the lottery, hasn't it?" I hurried after Sam, calling, "You might wait for us!" The last word, though it was but one syllable, covered two octaves, for my voice broke, as it had been doing lately with alarming frequency.

Sam turned back with a mischievous grin on his face. "Was that your voice cracking, or were you attempting to yodel?"

"Neither," I said sourly. "I'm—I'm coming down wi' something, I wis." To support my contention, I coughed a few times, the same pitiful cough I sometimes used on the stage when dying of a chest wound.

"A likely tale," put in Sal Pavy. "I can spot a cracked voice as easily as a cracked coin." He directed an aside to Sam. "Have you noticed he has little hairs sprouting from his chin as well?"

"Nay!" I protested, feeling my jaw. "I got them all, I'm sure—"

Sam snickered. "So, you've been doing a bit of plucking, have you?" He reached out and gave my face a pat in supposed sympathy. "Poor babby. Did it hurt?"

I knocked his hand aside. "You two striplings are envious of me manliness, that's all."

"Envious, is it?" Sam said. "Much!"

"Striplings, is it?" Sal Pavy stood next to me and pulled himself up to his maximum height. "I'm nearer to fully grown than you by a good three inches!"

"Oh, aye," I replied. "Only most of it is hair." Sam and I had taken to cropping our costards closely so that the wigs we donned for our female roles would go on and off more easily. But Sal Pavy refused to part with his golden locks, which were so abundant that he could scarcely contain them beneath his woolen prentice's cap.

"You know, I do believe Widge is gaining on you, though," said Sam. "And small wonder. Did you notice how many helpings of beans he shoveled in last night at supper?"

"No," said Sal Pavy, "but I noticed them later." He pinched his nose and made a face.

I gave him a look of mock reproach and clucked my tongue. "Master Pavy, I seem to recall when you were too refined to speak of such vulgar matters."

His cheeks, already ruddy from the cold, turned a brighter shade of red. "That was before I fell under such bad influences," he murmured.

"Talking of food," I said, "I'm hungry as a hawk. Let's find a sweetmeat seller."

Sam rubbed his gloveless hands together. "A roasted-potato seller, more like. Anyway, you've got to wait until we've seen the cunning woman."

As we continued along Fleet Street and passed through Ludgate, Sam and Sal Pavy went on talking, but I was occupied with my own thoughts. Though I had managed to brush off their jests concerning my chin hairs and my uncertain voice, secretly I considered them no laughing matter. Rather, they seemed to me an unsettling omen, a reminder that I could not go on playing girls' parts forever.

In terms of physical development, I had always lagged well behind most boys my age—thanks, no doubt, to a lack of proper nourishment. Now that I was provided with good food and all I cared to eat of it, my body seemed bent on making up for lost time. For an ordinary wight, this was a source of pride, a sign of approaching manhood. But I was no ordinary wight; I was a player, and any pride I felt was overshadowed by a sense of apprehension.

I had been assured by other members of the company—and even by the queen herself—that I was a capable actor. In most of the parts I was praised for, though, I was impersonating a girl. It wasn't that I minded doing female roles; I was only acting, after all. But I could not shake the nagging fear that once my voice deepened and my beard began to show, the company might no longer have any use for me.

I half hoped that the cunning woman truly could see into

the future. Perhaps she could give me some hint of what lay in store for me so that I might either put my mind at ease or else prepare for the worst—and I could not imagine a fate much worse than being turned out of the only family I knew, or had ever known.

Sal Pavy was asking Sam what he meant to do with the five thousand pounds he had been assured of winning. Sam ignored the snide quality of the question. "Actually," he said, "I've given that a good deal of thought. I believe I'll buy a ship."

"A *ship?*" I said.

He nodded smugly. "A big three-master. I'll sail her to India and return with a hold full of spices and silk. I've always wanted to go to sea."

"Oh, aye," I said. "That's why you prenticed to an acting company."

"Well, I wasn't old enough to be a sailor, and it seemed like more fun than sweeping chimneys or tanning hides."

Sal Pavy gave him a disparaging look. "What a good reason to go into the theatre."

"Is there a better reason?"

I thought of Julia, and how desperate she had been to be a player. "Because you love it?" I suggested.

He shrugged. "It's all right. But doesn't it ever strike you that there's something a bit odd about what we're doing? I mean, if you think about it, we're not really *doing* anything, are we? We're just *pretending* to do things. Sometimes I could do with a bit less acting and a bit more action, that's all."

We crossed the stone bridge that spanned Fleet Ditch. Though it lay outside the walls, Salisbury Court was still part of the city proper, and it had its share of legitimate businesses—

taverns, printers, booksellers. But it was also headquarters for a considerable number of less respectable concerns—bawdy puppet shows, sleight-of-hand artists, palm readers, astrologers, and the like.

Sam led us to a tattered, grimy tent set back a few yards from the edge of the road. Before it stood a folding wooden sign that bore no words, only a crude and rather unsettling painting of a huge eye, with rays of what was presumably meant to be light shooting out from it in all directions.

I had rarely seen Sam appear anything but cheerful and cocky, even in those moments when we stood behind the stage waiting to go on, and when I was trying hard to hold down my dinner. But now he was clearly a bit out of square. He seemed to find it necessary to screw up his courage a bit before he called, in a voice that might have been more steady, "Madame La Voisin?"

There was no reply. Sam glanced at us rather sheepishly, shrugged, and called out more loudly, "Madame La Voisin!"

A low, hoarse voice from within commanded, "Be silent, fool!"

Clearly startled, Sam took a step backward, treading on my foot. "Sorry. She—she must be in the midst of a reading already."

"Perhaps we should just go," I suggested, feeling not a little uneasy myself now.

"No, no!" Sam said heartily, and then, glancing toward the tent, spoke more softly. "It's all right. It'll be worth the wait, you'll see."

3

We stood shivering in the cold for several minutes before the flap of the tent lifted and a woman emerged. She looked utterly out of place here, with her richly embroidered gown, her starched neck ruff, and her elegantly coiffured hair. Lifting her skirts a little, she brushed past us, leaving a sweet scent from her pomander hanging in her wake.

"I take it," said Sal Pavy, "that was not Madame La Voisin."

"No." Sam lifted the flap and motioned us inside. The interior of the tent was dim, and so thick with acrid smoke that I could scarcely see, let alone breathe.

"Be seated," said the same rasping voice we had heard before. Stifling a cough, I eased myself onto a rickety three-legged stool. Sam sat on the one remaining stool. Sal Pavy stood just inside the tent flap, shifting about restlessly, as though ready to make a run for it if necessary.

When my eyes adjusted to the lack of light, I could make out a hunched figure whose head was swathed in a number of dirty, moth-eaten scarves. On her hands were a pair of equally soiled kid gloves with the fingertips cut off, allowing the ends of her fingers to protrude. When I wiped my stinging eyes, I could see that her knuckles were clustered with a multitude of small warts.

On the wooden table before her, cradled between her palms, was a surprisingly clean cloth that concealed something spherical. On the ground next to her sat a black iron kettle—the source of the smoke that threatened to suffocate me. I leaned forward and peered into the cauldron, half expecting to find some eldritch brew of newts' eyes and adders' tongues, but saw only glowing chunks of Newcastle coal, with no purpose more sinister than to warm the tent.

La Voisin's hoarse voice issued again from the folds of her several scarves. "And what do you young ladies wish of me?"

Sam gave a feeble laugh. "Ladies? We're no ladies, madame."

"Perhaps not today," she replied slyly. "But sometimes, yes?"

Sam glanced my way and lifted his eyebrows slightly. "How did you know?"

"It is my business to know things."

"Could you—could you tell our futures, then?" When La Voisin made no answer, Sam shifted uncomfortably in his seat and seemed about to repeat the question. Then the soothsayer laid one of her hands on the table, palm up. "Oh." Sam dug in his purse for a penny, which he dropped into her worn glove.

"I have told your fate before," La Voisin said. Then she pointed a finger in my direction. "I will tell *his*." She laid aside the cloth, revealing a globe perhaps six inches across, fashioned from some substance that was black as coal; it had been polished until it gleamed darkly, like the pupil of an enormous eye.

She stared into the ball for a long while. Finally she spoke, in a tone so bleak and ominous that it made me shudder. "I see," she said, "that you will come into a fortune."

Sam's face took on a look of surprise and indignation. "That's the same thing you told *me!*"

"Not so," said La Voisin. "What I said was, 'You will receive more money than you imagine.'"

"That's the same thing, isn't it?" When the cunning woman made no reply, he fished out another coin and clapped it into her palm. "Tell mine again."

"As you wish." While she peered into the ball, I sat weighing the words she had directed at me. A fortune? How could I possibly come into a fortune? I could hardly inherit it. My mother had died in the poorhouse, and I had no notion who my father was. Perhaps, as Sam implied, the cunning woman gave more or less the same prediction to everyone. After all, folk were more likely to come back, and to bring their friends, if she told them what they wanted to hear.

La Voisin lifted her head but said nothing. "Well?" Sam prompted her.

"You are certain you wish to hear it?"

"Of course. What is it? What did you see?"

The cunning woman turned toward him, and I caught for the first time a glimpse of her visage. The skin of her face was as thickly covered with warts as a pox victim's is with scars. "I see that you will turn traitor."

Sam gaped at her for a moment before he found his voice. "That's not a prediction! That's an accusation!"

"You said you wished to hear it."

"And now I wish to have my penny back! I didn't pay good money to be insulted!"

"I am not responsible for what the future holds; I merely say what I see."

Sam got to his feet, grumbling under his breath, "Yes, well, if you ask me, you need spectacles." He waved Sal Pavy toward the stool. "It's your turn."

"I—I don't believe I—" Sal Pavy started to say.

Sam cut him off. "Come, now, stop your whingeing and take it like a man. Your future couldn't possibly be any worse than mine." Reluctantly, Sal Pavy perched on the edge of the stool. "You've got to give her a penny," Sam reminded him. "Though perhaps you'd do well to make it tuppence; you might get a better reading." He turned to me. "Not to forget, you owe me a penny. You can well afford it," he added, with a secret wink, "seeing as how you're coming into a fortune, and all."

"Silence!" hissed La Voisin. She gazed into the ball even longer than before. I nearly strangled, trying to keep from coughing as the coal smoke wafted about me. When the cunning woman spoke at last, she sounded puzzled. "I see . . . I see *nothing*."

Sal Pavy laughed. "What does that mean? That I have no future?"

La Voisin gave him a look that erased his skeptical smile. "Perhaps," she said. "I will look again."

"That's not necessary." Sal Pavy started to rise. "You may keep the penny."

"*Sit*," said the woman. Sal Pavy's knees seemed to bend of their own accord. "I will look again." She hunched over the ball, her nose nearly pressed against it. After a long minute or two, her voice broke the silence, but only barely. She seemed to breathe the words, rather than speak them, as though they came forth without her willing them to, or even wishing them to. "I see . . . a rough hand gripping you . . . a knife . . . at your neck . . . " She sat back abruptly and, snatching up the cloth, draped it over the globe. "It has gone dark."

"But . . . what did all that mean?" Sal Pavy demanded.

"I do not interpret. I only see."

Sal Pavy got to his feet, obviously angry, but just as obviously shaken. "What a lot of bilk! I know what you're trying to do! You believe that if you make only half a prediction, I'll give you money to hear the rest! Well, you're not as good at seeing the future as you imagine for, by my troth, you'll have not so much as a brass farthing from me!" He spun about and pushed through the tent flap.

Sam cleared his throat and, with uncharacteristic meekness, said, "I—um—I'd like to apologize for our friend's behavior. He's a bit of a hothead, is all. While I'm at it, I apologize for anything I might have said that . . . that might have . . . "

"You need not bother with your false contrition," said La Voisin. "I am not going to call down a curse upon your heads. That is Fate's task, not mine." She pointed toward the flap of the tent. "Go now."

We did not need to be told twice. There was no sign of Sal Pavy outside. "Now, where do you suppose 'a's got to?" I said as we walked back toward Ludgate.

"If I was him, I'd go find another soothsayer, and get a second opinion."

"So should you, I wis. What could she have meant by that—turning traitor?"

Sam waved a hand dismissively. "Who knows? Who cares? Obviously she's just making it all up."

"When she predicted you'd win the lottery, you believed her."

"Well, wouldn't you like to believe that you're going to come into a fortune, the way she said? Speaking of which, where's my penny?"

I gave him a hurt look. "Don't you trust me to pay you back? I thought we were friends."

Sam hung his head. "Of course we are," he said. "That's why I'd really hate to have to pound you to a pudding if you don't give me the bleeding penny."

With a sigh, I tossed him a coin from my purse. "We'd best find Sal Pavy now, afore some scanderbag pounds *him* into a pudding and takes all his money."

"Some *scanderbag?*"

"Aye. What's wrong wi' that?"

Sam shook his head. "How long have you been in London?"

"Nearly two years. Why?"

"You still sound as though you'd arrived from Yorkshire yesterday. How do you manage to keep from sounding like such a lob when you're on the stage?"

"I don't ken, exactly. The same way Mr. Heminges manages not to stammer, I suppose."

Sam laughed. "One of these days you're going to forget your lines and have to thribble, and it's going to come out in Yorkshire-ese." He put a hand to his brow, in a parody of the way I played Ophelia in *Hamlet*. "'Gog's blood! I wis some scanderbag has brast his noble costard wi' a waster!'" He yodeled the last word in imitation of my uncertain voice.

I tried to scowl at him, but my features kept wanting to break into a grin. "You sot! I'll never again be able to do that scene wi' a straight face!"

Unexpectedly, Sam's own expression turned from silly to sober. "Whist! Did you hear that?"

I halted in my tracks and listened. From a dark, narrow alleyway between two buildings came the sounds of a struggle, then a frantic cry that was cut off abruptly.

"Oh, gis!" I breathed. "That's Sal Pavy's voice. I'm certain of it!"

4

Like all prentices, Sam and I were armed only with short daggers that were designed for dining, not for defense. But we drew them and hastened to the mouth of the alleyway.

Within its gloomy confines I could make out three figures, bunched together. One was, as I had suspected, Sal Pavy. A bald, burly wight with a wooden leg had Sal's arms pinned behind him with one huge hand; the other was clamped over the boy's mouth. The scoundrel's scrawny companion was clutching Sal's long blond locks and sawing at them with a knife twice the size of ours.

"Let him loose, you dog-bolts," I shouted, "or we'll carve you into collops!" My voice chose that moment to break like a biscuit.

The underfed fellow laughed. "With those toothpicks? Law, I'm so afeared, I'm trembling!"

"Stay back now, the both of you," warned his one-legged friend. "We've no wish to harm anyone."

"Nay, nor do we," I said.

I picked up a good-sized cobblestone, and was set to launch it at him when Sam cried, "Let it be! All they want is his hair!"

"Smart lad." The skinny brigand severed the last of Sal Pavy's golden hair and held it aloft, like Jason holding the Golden Fleece. "Some grand lady will pay a pretty price for this, to make up for what nature failed to give her."

The one-legged fellow released Sal Pavy and gave him a shove. The boy stumbled toward us, holding his shorn head between his hands and sobbing. As the two thieves sauntered off down the alley, the burly man said, "Perhaps we should have taken his leg as well. I could have used it."

"You'd have more use for a wig," replied the other man, and cackling with laughter, draped Sal Pavy's curls across his companion's bald head.

I tossed the stone aside. "Stupid sots. We shouldn't let them get away wi' this."

"There's no point in getting ourselves killed over it," Sam said. "There's little point in calling a constable, either. Those two will get rid of the hair at the nearest wig shop, and even if we found it, we can't very well put it back, can we?" He retrieved Sal Pavy's cap and carefully covered the ragged remnants of the boy's hair with it. "I don't see any wounds. Did they hurt you?"

Sal Pavy had ceased sobbing and was fiercely wiping away his tears with the hem of his cloak. "You might have done more to try and chase them off!"

"What would you have us do? If we'd come any closer, they'd have cut your throat, not just your hair. Besides, we didn't dare let them get a look at *our* luxurious locks." Sam pretended to stroke his nonexistent tresses. "They surely would have cast you aside and snatched us instead."

This attempt to coax Sal Pavy out of his foul mood failed miserably. "I might have expected you to make a jest of it! You've always made fun of my hair, both of you! I suppose you think it serves me right, getting it chopped off!"

"Well, you know," Sam replied, "if you'd had it cut sooner, you could have sold it for a good price yourself. As it is, you've neither the currency nor the curls."

I took Sam's arm and drew him aside. "Can't you see how upset 'a is? Don't make it worse."

"Well, he behaves as though it's *our* fault, for not saving his wretched hair!"

"Perhaps it was. Perhaps we should have done more. In any case, it's not *his* fault. Let's get him home now."

"Home? It's not even nones yet! We have half the afternoon ahead of us!"

"Well, do as you like. I'm taking him home."

"When did you become so concerned about his welfare?"

"When 'a became a part of our acting company," I said.

He scowled. "You're beginning to sound the way Sander used to—like an older brother."

"I consider that a compliment. Now, are you coming wi' us or not?"

Sam sighed heavily. "All right, all right. It's no fun going about by myself."

Sal Pavy walked well ahead of us, his cloak pulled tightly about him, his shoulders hunched to shelter his newly bare neck from the cold.

I said softly to Sam, "Did you notice that things happened back there just as the cunning woman said they would?"

30

"Of course I noticed."

"Can she truly see into the future, then, do you wis?"

He sniffed skeptically. "More likely she was in league with those two louts, and she let them know somehow that there was a good head of hair to be had."

"I suppose you're right." I couldn't help wondering, all the same. I was not so naive as to suppose that everything La Voisin said could be counted on to come true. Even so, was it not possible that occasionally she got a genuine glimpse of things to come?

Sam tried his best to talk me into taking a shortcut home, across the Thames. Ordinarily, that would have been a sensible enough suggestion; we need only have paid a wherryman to row us across. But the winter had been so unusually cold that the river was frozen over from London Bridge to Whitehall, so solidly that folk had begun to venture out upon it to skate or to fish through the ice. Some parts were less solid than others, though, and the unfortunate souls who found them often ended up in the land of Rumbelow—that is to say, a watery grave.

Though Sam seemed to think that it would be a great lark to cross on the ice, I insisted on using the bridge. "Ha' you never heard the saying: Wise men go over London Bridge; fools go under?"

"I had no intention of going under the bridge," Sam grumbled, "only across the ice."

We came to the spot on Cheapside where the public pillory stood. Despite the cold, the authorities had sentenced some poor wight to stand there with his arms and neck imprisoned. He appeared more prosperous and respectable than the usual occupant of the pillory. He twisted his stiff neck to give us a beseeching look. "I don't suppose I could prevail upon you to do me a small favor?"

"Such as setting you free?" Sam suggested.

The man tried to grin, but it was more in the way of a grimace. "I wouldn't refuse. But what I'd really like is for someone to wipe my nose. There's a kerchief in the pocket of my cloak."

Sam retrieved the kerchief and then swiped the man's cold-reddened nose several times. "You don't look like a vagrant to me. What did you do to earn this?"

"Nothing wicked, I assure you. I'd move on now, if I were you. You don't want to be seen talking to me. They may think I'm attempting to convert you."

"What do you mean?" I asked.

Sal Pavy spoke up unexpectedly, and his voice still carried a load of spite. "He means he's a Papist."

"A Catholic? I didn't ken they punished a wight just for that."

Sam leaned in close to him and whispered, "You're not a *priest*, are you?"

"Hardly. Only a printer who was unwise enough to publish a few rather harmless pamphlets defending the old faith."

Sam gave the man's nose a last wipe and returned the kerchief to him. As we turned down Fenchurch Street, Sam said, "It doesn't seem right, does it, him being put in the stocks just for printing a few pamphlets?"

"Not just any pamphlets," Sal Pavy pointed out. "*Papist* pamphlets."

Sam snickered. "I'll wager you can't say that quickly three times in a row."

"Yes, yes, make a jest of it, as always. You've not been exposed to Catholics, as I have."

"Oh, you've *exposed* yourself to them, have you?"

"Stop it, Sam," I put in. "Can't you tell when you've touched a sore spot?" I turned to Sal Pavy. "What crow do you have to pull wi' them, then?"

He scowled at me. "*What?*"

"I mean, what's given you such a poor opinion of them?"

"I'll say no more. You'll only mock me." Yanking his cloak tightly about him, he again put several paces between himself and us.

5

I had no strong feelings about Papists, one way or another. In truth, I knew very little about the old faith except that it had fallen out of favor many years before, when Queen Mary, a staunch Catholic, died and left the throne to her half sister Elizabeth, the present queen.

My personal experience with Catholics was limited as well. In fact, I had known but two. One was Jamie Redshaw, who for a time had claimed to be my father. He had later done his best to convince me otherwise. As with La Voisin's predictions, I was left wondering what the truth was. Reason told me to believe one way; hope inclined me in the other.

My other Catholic acquaintance was the playwright Ben Jonson. Mr. Jonson had been working mainly for the Admiral's Men, but the company's manager, Philip Henslowe, had refused to produce his latest play, *Sejanus*, on the grounds that it was full of pro-Catholic sentiments. Mr. Jonson had proceeded to offer the play to the Lord Chamberlain's Men. Our company's sharers had agreed to perform it, provided that he tone down the Papist propaganda. Mr. Jonson had spent the past week or so resentfully revising it.

When we set out for the Cross Keys on Monday morning, Sam tried again to talk me into crossing on the ice, and again I insisted on going by way of the bridge. He shook his head in disgust. "You know what your trouble is? You've no sense of adventure."

As we entered the courtyard of the inn and climbed the stairs to the rooms our company rented, Will Sly leaned over the railing above us. Will was one of our hired men—a step above us prentices, and a step below those who owned shares in the company. "Widge, Mr. Shakespeare's been asking after you. He's in the dark parlor."

"Oh, law!" Sam exclaimed in mock dismay. "What have you done now?"

"Naught that I ken."

"I wouldn't fret," said Will Sly. "He didn't seem angry, just out of sorts. Where's your friend Sal Pavy, by the by? I hear he got his curls cropped."

"Sulking somewhere, I expect." Sam stopped at the door of our makeshift tiring-room. "Ah! I know why Mr. Shakespeare wants you!"

"Why?"

"He means to give you that fortune you've got coming!" Laughing, Sam ducked inside the room before I could assist him with the sole of my boot.

I descended to the main room of the inn. Though it was by tradition called the dark parlor, it was in fact well lighted by a bank of windows that looked out upon the street. Along one wall was a row of tables with wooden dividers between them, providing a degree of privacy for those who desired it.

I discovered Mr. Shakespeare in one of these booths. Before him sat several sheets of paper filled with scribbles. At the moment he was adding nothing to them, only gazing out at the traffic on Gracechurch Street. I stood there, still and silent, for a passing while, unwilling to interrupt his reverie lest I put to flight some idea or snatch of dialogue that he was attempting to lure into the net of his thoughts.

When two or three minutes went by and he still took no notice of me, I cleared my throat softly. Absently, he lifted his earthernware tankard and set it at the edge of the table, as though to be refilled with ale. "Um," I said. "You wished to see me?"

"What?" He turned to me with a puzzled frown. "Oh, it's you, Widge. I thought you were the tippler."

"Nay. But I can fetch you more ale, an you like."

"No, no, sit down. I have a more demanding task for you."

I noticed that he was rubbing his right forearm, the one that had been cracked by a catchpoll's club the previous summer. As I had been the one to mend the arm, I took a sort of propri-etary interest in it. "It looks as though your arm is paining you."

He nodded and flexed his hand. "It doesn't like the cold, and when I work it for any length of time, it begins to complain. Actually, it reminds me a good deal of my brother Ned."

I couldn't help laughing at the apt comparison, though in truth Ned's habits were more annoying than amusing. If he had been anyone but Mr. Shakespeare's brother, the company would surely have given him the chuck long ago. As an actor, he was competent enough, even engaging given the right role; it was the way he acted off the stage that kept him in constant trouble.

"However," Mr. Shakespeare went on, "I did not bring you down to listen to me rail about Ned. I'd like your help."

I glanced at the papers spread before him. "Transcribing, I wis."

"Do you mind? It'll give my arm a rest."

"Nay, I don't mind." I pulled the pages to me and peered at his unruly handwriting. "What's this play about, then?"

"An excellent question. Would that I had as good an answer for you."

"You might reply, 'Oh, Lord, sir,'" I suggested. This was an all-purpose answer Mr. Shakespeare had devised for the clown in *All's Well That Ends Well.*

He smiled faintly. "Perhaps I should." He toyed with the ring in his ear. "The truth is, I'm not at all certain what the play is about. So far, it appears to be about a wealthy man who is overly generous with his wealth, and when he loses his money he finds that all the friends he imagined he had are no longer his friends."

"Does 't ha' a name? The play, I mean."

He gave me a rather peevish glance. "I did not bring you here to ply me with questions."

"I'm—I'm sorry. I'll just . . . get me pencil, then." I dug into my wallet for the plumbago pencil I used when I needed to write rapidly.

Mr. Shakespeare sighed. "You needn't apologize, Widge. I'm not upset with you, only with the play."

"Oh. It's not going well, then?" Realizing I'd asked yet another question, I added quickly, "An you don't mind me asking."

"If 'not going well' is the Yorkshire way of saying 'a total shambles,' then yes, I'd say that's an accurate assessment." He lifted his tankard and, finding it empty, rapped it on the table. When the innkeeper had filled it, Mr. Shakespeare took a long draught of ale and then sighed again. "At this point the play has no title. I suppose I could name it after the main character, Timon, but that seems a bit dull."

"You called *Hamlet* after the main character," I pointed out.

"Yes, well, this is not *Hamlet*. More's the pity."

"Most of the wights seem to ha' Roman names: Lucius, Sempronius, Flaminius. Is that where it's set, then?"

"That was my plan, originally. But considering how cold the climate is these days for Catholics, I thought it would be wiser to choose some non-Papist country."

At a nearby table, a quartet of well-dressed wights who had clearly swallowed too many tokens, as they say, had been trading drunken insults for some little while. Now their dispute suddenly turned physical. It might have escalated into a duel with rapiers and daggers had not one of their number suddenly been seized by the urge to bring up all the ale he had consumed, even more quickly than it had gone down.

When the cursing innkeeper had chased them out and set about mopping up the mess, I said, "I don't ken how you manage to write anything down here, wi' all the hurly-burly."

"I seem to work better where there's life going on about me. It's far too quiet in my lodgings—not to mention cold. Besides, I like to read the dialogue aloud. My landlord disapproves of theatre folk enough as it is; if he were to catch me ranting to an empty room, he'd likely call a constable and have me evicted. But here"—he gestured at a table across the room, where a grizzled man in a dyer's apron was apparently having a spirited discussion with a meat pie—"no one even notices." Mr. Shakespeare took another swig of ale. "All right, then. Where did I leave off?"

I did my best to read his scrawl. "*Flavius:* 'The greatest of your having lacks a half to pay your present . . . belts'?"

"*Belts?*" echoed Mr. Shakespeare. "Where does it say 'belts'?" I pointed to the word in question. "Oh. It's *debts.* Go on."

"*Timon:* 'Let all my land be solid—*sold.*' That's where you stopped."

He stared out the window again, fingering his earring. "*Flavius:* ''Tis all engaged, some forfeited, some . . . ' No. 'Some forfeited and gone. And what remains . . . and what remains will hardly stop the mouth of present dues; the future comes apace.'" He glanced at the paper. "Am I going too rapidly?"

"Nay, I've got it. See?" Though Mr. Shakespeare's hand was difficult for anyone but himself to decipher, mine was impossible, for I had used the system of swift writing taught to me by Dr. Bright, my first master. The passage I had put down looked like this:

Mr. Shakespeare waved the paper away. "I'll take your word on it, Widge. Let's proceed." But before he could dictate another word, a slim, beardless fellow with black hair that was pulled back into a horse's tail strode up to the table and, without a by-your-leave, blurted out, "Will! I must speak to you! At once!"

6

Mr. Shakespeare turned to his brother with a look that would have made anyone with an ounce of tact apologize and return at some better time. Instead, Ned glared accusingly at me, as though I were the intruder. "Don't you have something else to do, Widge?"

I, in turn, looked to Mr. Shakespeare. "Shall I . . . ?"

"Yes, yes, go on," he said. "We'll work some more this afternoon."

I slid from the booth and Ned took my place, so impatiently that he trod on my foot. As I headed upstairs, I heard Mr. Shakespeare say wearily, "What is it *this* time, Ned?"

I did not linger to listen to Ned's reply. I was already more familiar with his troubles than I cared to be. They were predictable, in any case, nearly always involving either a game of chance, a drunken brawl, or an insult to someone's honor—very often a woman's. Occasionally he managed to combine all three. The most predictable thing was that Ned himself was never at fault. He was, he insisted, a mere victim of circumstances, condemned by Fate forever to be in the wrong place at the wrong time and in the wrong company.

I made for the tiring-room, meaning to unpack and examine my costume for that night's performance of *The Two Gentlemen of Verona*. I found Sam rummaging through a costume trunk like a badger digging a den. The floor was strewn ankle-deep with gowns and cloaks, doublets and breeches. There was no sign of our tiring-man. "Where's Richard, then?" I asked.

"At home," Sam replied without looking up from his task. "Sick with the ague."

"Oh," I said. "That's good. I was afeared 'a might be buried under all this. I thought you were supposed to be straightening up this room."

"I am!"

"Well, an this is your notion of straightening up, I'd hate to see you make a mess."

He paused from his pawing to wave his arms about despairingly. "I can't find my costume for tonight! I've looked everywhere!"

I placed a hand on his shoulder. "Calm yourself, Sam. It's certain to be here somewhere—beneath all this, no doubt." I picked up several items of clothing, smoothed them out, and hung them on one of the many hooks that lined the walls. "You've made a mingle-mangle of these. Help me sort them out."

Grumpily, Sam left off digging and set about separating the costumes into lots, according to the name tags that were sewn inside them. "This gown says *Julia*. Does that mean Julia the character, or Julia the real person?"

"Julia the character." I picked up the dress labeled *Silvia* and held it up near the window to catch the dull winter daylight.

There was a ragged hole under one arm. "Oh, gis. A rat's been gnawing at me gown. It'll ha' to be mended."

"Never mind that now," Sam said. "Help me find Lucetta's costume. If it doesn't turn up, they'll take it out of my pay."

"Surely they wouldn't blame *you*, would they?"

"That's the rule. We're each of us responsible for our own stuff."

"Oh. I thought it was up to the tiring-man to take care of the costumes."

Sam shook his head. "The sharers made the rule several years ago, when costumes started disappearing. As it turned out, one of the hired men was making off with them and selling them for several pounds apiece."

"Gog's nowns! They're worth that much?"

"Why do you think I'm so frantic to find mine? Even if they held back my whole wages, it would take me months to pay it off."

"Unless, of course, you win the lottery," I said.

"Well, I was hoping you'd help me out, once you come into that fortune."

"I might. For now, let's keep looking."

Between us, we shook out and hung up every piece of clothing from the trunk. There was no sign of Sam's costume for *Two Gentlemen*. Sighing, he sat on the trunk and put his head in his hands. "It's no use. I'm in the briars."

"Perhaps it got put i' some other trunk by mistake?"

"Well, we don't have the time to go through them all. I'll just have to wear something else." He eyed my gown, which was spread out on the windowsill. "Perhaps I'll wear yours. As much as you've grown in the past year, I'll wager it no longer fits you."

"I'll wager it does."

"A penny?"

"A penny." I began unhooking the front of my doublet.

Sam picked up Sal Pavy's gown and studied the tag that read *Julia*. "What do you hear from the real Julia, then?"

I tossed my doublet aside and started on my linen shirt. "Naught, for three months or more. I hope she's not fallen ill or something."

"It's possible. I hear the plague took nearly as many lives in Paris as it did here."

The mere suggestion that Julia might have met the same dismal fate as Sander sent a shudder of dread through me.

"I'm sorry, Widge," Sam murmured. "I wasn't thinking."

I forced a smile. "It's all right. I'm sure there's naught amiss wi' her. Most likely she's busy, that's all." I was down to my underclothing and about to slip into the gown when the door to the tiring-room swung inward and a face appeared in the opening. To my surprise and dismay it was not one of the men from the company. It was, in fact, not a man at all, but a very attractive young woman.

I quickly covered myself with the gown, my face hot with embarrassment. The intruder, however, was apparently neither very embarrassed nor very apologetic. More than anything else, she seemed amused. Her eyes, which were strikingly blue in contrast to her milk-white skin, gave my gown an appraising glance, as though I had held it up for her approval. "Very fetching," she said. "But the hem is several inches too short."

"There, I told you!" crowed Sam. "You owe me a penny!"

I was having some difficulty finding my voice. When I finally did, it betrayed me by breaking dramatically. "What—" I cleared my throat, and blushed even more deeply. "What did you want then, mistress?"

Her only difficulty seemed to lie in keeping a laugh from escaping her. She succeeded by biting her lower lip—which, I could not help noticing, despite my discomposure, was red as a rose petal. "I was looking for my father, actually."

"Oh." It was all I seemed able to come up with.

Luckily, Sam was not so tongue-tied. "If you tell us *who* he is, perhaps we may tell you *where* he is."

"Mr. Shakespeare."

"Which one? Ned or Will?"

She laughed a very charming laugh. "Does it seem likely to you that Ned Shakespeare would have a daughter of seventeen?"

Sam shrugged. "He may have gotten an early start."

"I'm sure he did. But not *that* early."

The tiring-room had no heat save what little crept in from adjacent rooms, and in my scantily clad state I had begun to shiver. "An you gi' me a moment," I said pointedly, "I'll be happy to take you to your father."

"All right." She added mischievously, "I suppose you'd like me to wait outside."

"Aye."

She had started to leave, but this brought her back. "*Aye?* You're not from London, are you?"

"Nay. No. Yorkshire."

"Really? How did you happen to come to London?"

My teeth were fairly chattering now. "Do you mind an we discuss this another time?"

"*An* you insist." She closed the door at last. I scrambled into my breeches, shirt, and doublet.

"I never knew Mr. Shakespeare had a daughter," Sam said. "He so seldom speaks about his family. She's a lot better looking than he is, don't you think?"

"I can't say that I noticed," I lied.

Sam laughed. "Much! That's why you were gaping at her so dumbly, as though she were some Gorgon whose gaze turns men to stone."

"I was embarrassed, that's all." I sat on the trunk and put my hand to my chest.

"What's wrong?"

"I—I don't ken, exactly. Me heart's pounding and I'm—I'm all out of breath, as though I'd been dancing the Spanish panic. And just feel me forehead." Despite the chill in the room, my face felt like a live coal.

Sam's face grew grave. "I've seen these same symptoms before, Widge. They're unmistakable."

I tried to swallow a rising sense of fear, but my throat was dry and tight. "What do you wis it is, then? It can't be—it can't be the plague, surely. I've shown none of th' other signs."

"I'm afraid it's even worse than that. Unless I'm sorely mistaken, you've a bad case of lovesickness."

For a moment I stared incredulously into his face, which now wore a broad grin. Then I shoved him away. "You huddy-peak!" I got to my feet and straightened my doublet. "Love's not an illness!"

As I exited the tiring-room, Sam called after me, "I wouldn't be so sure!"

7

Mr. Shakespeare's daughter was waiting just outside the door. I suspected, in fact, that she had been eavesdropping. If so, she showed no sign of shame. "Well, at last!" she said. She turned to her companion, a tall, fashionably dressed fellow with a curly black beard, a swarthy complexion, bushy eyebrows that nearly met over a nose like a hawk's beak, and eyes as dark as lumps of coal—or Madame La Voisin's scrying ball. "And I thought," the girl went on, "that it was only women who were so slow in dressing themselves."

"I—I was only—" I stammered.

"Instead of trying so hard to embarrass the lad," said the stranger, "you might introduce us."

"I can't," the girl said, a bit petulantly. "I don't know his name."

"It's Widge," I offered.

"*Widge?* What sort of name—?"

"My name is Garrett," the man interrupted, and offered his hand to me. His grip was so firm that my finger bones ached for some time afterward. "And this is Mistress Judith Shakespeare. You'll have to pardon her if she seems a bit lacking in the social graces. She's from Warwickshire, you know, and doesn't get out much."

I was accustomed to such good-humored jesting, but the indignant look on Judith's face told me that she was not. Though I was not schooled in the social graces myself, I knew how well-bred folk sounded from having played them so often. "As Aristotle says, 'Beauty is a greater recommendation than any letter of introduction.'"

The man named Garrett laughed heartily. "Well-spoken, lad."

A smile stole across Judith's face, making it even more striking. "You know, I think I'm going to like you, Widge."

Even had I had another suitable line at the ready, I could not have found the breath to utter it. All I could manage to do was look at my feet.

"You promised to take me to my father," Judith reminded me.

"Oh. Aye. Yes. This way." I led them down to the dark parlor, where Mr. Shakespeare and Ned were still engaged in a heated discussion.

"Our father would have helped me out readily enough!" Ned was saying.

"Perhaps so. Unfortunately, he's dead." When Mr. Shakespeare saw us approaching, his face took on a curious expression that seemed composed equally of astonishment, delight, and disapproval. "Judith! What in heaven's name brings you here?"

"Why, a horse, Father." She curtsied to Ned. "God you good day, Uncle."

"Yes, hello." Ned seemed to be not so much pleased to see his niece as he was peeved by the intrusion.

Judith gave her father a kiss on the cheek. Mr. Shakespeare smiled rather wanly and patted his daughter's hand. "What an unexpected surprise."

"You don't seem very happy about it."

"Of course I am; of course," Mr. Shakespeare said, not very convincingly. Clearly, her sudden appearance had put him out of square, and thinking about it later, I could see why. Mr. Shakespeare's world was divided into two hemispheres. One centered around his hometown of Stratford and his family, the other around London and the theatre, and the two seldom intersected. To have someone arrive unannounced from his other life must have been jarring, as though he had been performing in *Hamlet* and a character from *The Comedy of Errors* had suddenly strolled onto the stage.

Though Judith pretended to be put out, I had the feeling that she rather enjoyed seeing her father so disconcerted, just as she had enjoyed catching me unclothed. "As you see, I've brought someone with me. This is Father—" She broke off and cast a sidelong glance at Mr. Garrett. She appeared flustered, as though she had said something improper. "That is . . . I mean . . . Father, this is John. John Garrett. He was kind enough to accompany me all the way from Warwickshire, providing me with both companionship and protection."

Mr. Shakespeare shook the man's hand. "My thanks, sir." He turned back to Judith. "But why—"

"Have we met before, sir?" Ned interrupted. "I don't recognize the name, but your face seems familiar to me."

"It's possible," said Mr. Garrett. "I travel about a good deal."

"Do you? For what purpose?"

"Uncle!" Judith said. "You're being rude!"

"Why?" Ned asked innocently. "Does he have something to hide?"

"Ned!" Mr. Shakespeare put in. "A gentleman's business is his own."

Ned glanced irritably at his brother, then made a slight, ironic bow in Mr. Garrett's direction. "My apologies, sir. And now I must take my leave. I have business to attend to."

"Do you?" said Mr. Garrett. "What sort?"

Ned gave a quick, sharp laugh. "Touché. Your point."

"Will you not stop and talk awhile, Uncle?" Judith said. "I've only just arrived."

"You'll be here a few days, won't you?"

Judith turned to her father with a look that seemed to carry a subtle challenge. "Longer than that, I hope."

"Then we'll talk later." He placed a swift kiss on her pale cheek and departed.

"Now," said Mr. Shakespeare. "We will all sit down and have a drink, and you will tell me why you came to London."

"I—I'd best see to me costume," I said. "I'm afeared it will ha' to be let out."

"You're keeping it prisoner?" said Mr. Garrett.

"Nay. It will need altering, I mean. It's grown too small."

"I suspect it's you who have done the growing," said Mr. Shakespeare.

"Oh, don't you rush off as well, Widge." Judith patted the seat next to her. "Come. Sit with me." She gave Mr. Shakespeare that challenging look again. "My father is about to chide me, I suspect, for being so impulsive, and he may go easier on me if I've a friend at my side."

"You've Mr. Garrett," I pointed out.

49

"Oh, he's an *adult*. He'll side with Father."

"You may as well sit, Widge," said Mr. Shakespeare. "If we don't let her have her way, she's liable not to speak to me at all."

Judith clucked her tongue. "You make me sound as though I were a spoiled child!"

"I'm sorry. It's—it's difficult sometimes for me to realize that you've become a young woman."

"Perhaps," she said, "that's because you see me so seldom." There was an awkward silence, then Judith went on, more brightly, "Anyway, that's one reason I've come to London—so that we may spend some time together."

"Oh. Of course. I'd like that. Unfortunately, I don't have a great deal of time, what with the demands of putting on existing plays, and the constant need to turn out new ones, and . . . "

Judith nodded, as though this was precisely what she'd expected to hear. "That's just what Mother said. But I don't ask for much—an hour or so in the evenings, that's all, and I could come to the plays and see you perform. That would be all right, wouldn't it?"

"I suppose so . . ."

"And Widge could show me around the city, couldn't you, Widge?" When she turned to me, I caught the scent of cloves, which ladies sometimes chew to sweeten their breath. It worked.

I looked to Mr. Shakespeare for my cue; he shrugged rather helplessly. "I—I don't ken," I said. "We prentices don't have many hours free, either . . ."

"Well, it's time you did, then."

"Have you given any thought to where you'll stay?" said Mr. Shakespeare.

"Wherever you lodge, I suppose."

"Oh. Well. The Mountjoys do have a daughter near your age. Perhaps she would be willing to share her room . . . for a *short* while."

Judith clapped her hands. "Good! It's all settled, then! Now. I believe that Mr. . . . Garrett"—she stumbled over the name like an actor who is uncertain of his lines—"would like to speak with you in private. I'll just go help Widge with his costume. I'm not a bad hand with a needle, you know." She slid sideways, nudging me out of the booth. The fleeting contact between our bodies turned my knees so weak that I could scarcely stand.

"Wait one moment," said Mr. Shakespeare. "You said that a desire to spend time together was *one* reason you came to London. What was the other?"

"Oh. I'm to try and persuade you to send more money home."

8

Sam had managed to put the tiring-room in order, or as near as one could expect from a wight who once cleaned the sheep's blood from his costume by giving it to a dog to lick. "Did you find your gown for tonight?" I asked him.

He shook his head in disgust. "I suppose I can say farewell to my wages for the next several months."

"Not to worry; I'll lend you half of mine."

"Thanks. And don't forget—you owe me a penny."

"Nay! I paid you back!"

He held up the gown that no longer fit me. "Our wager, remember?"

I drew a penny from my purse and threw it to him. "I'm surprised you haven't asked for interest on 't."

He grinned. "Well, now that you bring it up—"

"Don't you have something else to do?" I suggested.

"Yes, and so do you. It's called rehearsal."

"Aye, all right. I'll be along."

"Take your time. I'll just tell Mr. Lowin that you're already busy rehearsing . . . " In a sugary, fluttering voice, he added, "A looovvve scene!" At that moment I longed for something far larger and more dangerous than a penny to throw at him. As he went out the door, he could not resist a parting shot—a line from *Two Gentlemen:* " 'I think the boy hath grace in him; he blushes!' "

"I'm sorry," I murmured in Judith's direction. " 'A's such a swad."

"Oh, he's young, that's all. He'll fall in love himself one day, and then he'll sing a different tune." Taking my gown by the sleeves, she held it up against my shoulders and surveyed it critically. She seemed wholly unaware that, only a few inches from her right hand, my heart was doing its utmost to leap out of my chest. "If we let down the hem a bit and move the hooks and eyes out, you may get by with it—provided you don't make any sudden movements. Where can I find a needle and thread?"

"I'll—I'll just get them." Reluctantly, I pulled away and went to seek out the sewing box.

"Sam mentioned someone named Mr. Lowin. I don't recall my father ever speaking of him."

" 'A's new to the company. When Mr. Pope retired, John Lowin took his place."

"Oh? When did Mr. Pope retire?"

"Well, when we toured last summer, 'a stayed behind, and 'a's never performed since." I handed her the sewing box. "It's his health, you ken. 'A no longer has the strength for it."

She set about threading a needle. "That's a pity. He must miss being on the stage."

"No more than we miss him, I wis. I've naught against Mr. Lowin, but it's just not the same. Of course, I still see a good deal of Mr. Pope, as I lodge wi' him." I stole a glance at Judith, to find that she was regarding me with open amusement. "What?"

"Your speech." She proceeded to mimic me. "'I wis.' 'I've naught against him.' 'I lodge wi' him.'"

I felt my face flush again. "And I suppose in Warwickshire they all sound like princes, do they?"

She laughed. "Far from it." She laid her hand—the one not holding the needle—on mine. "I'm sorry, Widge. I wasn't trying to hurt your feelings. I just find it . . . quaint."

I had been called many things in my life—a poor pigwidgeon, a lazy lout, a liar and a thief, even a horse—but no one had ever considered me *quaint* before. I was not certain how I felt about it. I would have preferred to be thought of as courageous or clever or handsome. Still, I supposed that being quaint was better than being a liar or a thief.

I would also have preferred that Judith go on resting her hand on mine for the foreseeable future. But at that moment the door of the tiring-room opened and Sal Pavy entered. It was clear that he had been to a barber. His hair, which had been ragged and unsightly after his encounter with the hair bandits, was now evenly cropped. He still seemed self-conscious, though, tugging at the back of his cap as though to conceal as much of his head as possible.

"You're missing rehearsal," I said, not very cordially.

"So are you." He looked Judith over rather suspiciously, eyeing her yellow tresses in particular, as though he suspected her of being the receiver of his stolen hair. "Have we hired a seamstress?"

Judith gave him a swift, sarcastic glance and then said to me, "Have you hired a new fool?"

I suppressed a smile. "Nay. Sal has been wi' us for some time now. Sal Pavy, this is Judith, Mr. Shakespeare's daughter."

"Oh?" Sal Pavy's manner changed at once. "Well, that explains how the lady came by such a sharp wit. It certainly served to cut me down to size. Mistress Shakespeare." He bowed to her, and she half rose from her stool to perform a cursory curtsy.

Though Sal Pavy was often disagreeable, he could put on the trappings of charm, like a new suit of clothes when it suited him. The other members of the company had long since ceased to be fooled by his performance, but Judith was seeing it for the first time, and she was an appreciative audience.

"Never fear." Smiling, she held up the rat-chewed sleeve of my gown, which she had nearly mended. "I am also very good at making *amends*."

I got to my feet. "We'd best get ourselves upstairs." Though I had no wish to quit Judith's company, I wished even less to quit the Lord Chamberlain's company. I was not likely to get the chuck merely for being late to a rehearsal, of course. But I had worked hard to earn a reputation for being trustworthy and conscientious, and I didn't mean to compromise it.

Judith looked hurt. "You're not going to leave me here all alone, are you?"

"I'm certain no one will mind if you attend the rehearsal," said Sal Pavy, and offered her his hand.

"What a good idea!" Judith tossed aside my gown and slipped her arm through Sal Pavy's. "Coming, Widge?"

"Aye," I replied miserably—but quaintly.

For the past week, our morning rehearsals had been devoted to getting that ancient, creaking vehicle called *The Spanish*

Tragedy into suitable shape to go on. Like my gown, it needed extensive alterations. But rather than letting it out, we were taking it in, so that it would fit into the two hours between evening prayers and curfew—the only time of day when the city fathers grudgingly permitted us to present our plays.

Though *The Spanish Tragedy* was set in a Catholic country, of course, our audience loved it so that we were obliged to resurrect it at least once a year. Perhaps its appeal lay in the fact that so many of its Popish characters were killed off. Despite the script's many flaws, I had a certain fondness for it; it was the first play in which I appeared at the Globe. I had played a messenger, with a total of three lines to say. Now I had the part of Bel-Imperia, and two hundred and twelve lines—as every aspiring player does, I had counted them. I had made a good deal of progress in less than two years.

No one would have guessed it from the performance I gave that morning. I had long since grown accustomed to spouting speeches before a crowd of several hundred rowdy playgoers. Aside from the irrational fear that always seized me just before I stepped onto the stage, it no longer bothered me. Yet I found myself reduced to a blethering, nowt-headed noddy by an audience of one well-mannered girl who neither offered her opinions of my acting at the top of her voice nor pelted me with hazelnuts.

Though I prided myself on my excellent memory, I could not say two sentences together without consulting the side, or partial script, I had tucked in my wallet. Despite daily lessons in graceful footwork, I found myself stumbling over the other players' feet, and occasionally my own. To make my mortification complete, my voice reminded me regularly of how unreliable it had become.

My one consolation was that none of the sharers was there to witness the debacle. They customarily went over their lines on their own, while the prentices and hired men practiced under the eye of a seasoned player such as Mr. Lowin. Very often our first performance before an audience was also the first time the entire ensemble was on the stage together.

From the the way the company clustered about Judith after rehearsal, anyone would have thought that she had been the one performing and that we were all complimenting her. I knew that, with all the attention being paid her, she would pay none to me. Heaving a melancholy sigh, I slunk off to the tiring-room.

Just as I reached the door, it opened and a tall, unfamiliar figure emerged, dressed in the apothecary's robe from *Romeo and Juliet*. "Here!" I cried, my voice breaking yet again. "Who are you, and where are you going wi' that costume?"

The man raised his hands, as if to show that he was unarmed and harmless. "It's only me, Widge. John Garrett, remember?"

"Mr. Garrett?" He looked very different from the man I had met a few hours earlier. His hair was cut nearly as short as my own, and it was now an odd brownish hue. So were his mustache, his beard, and his eyebrows, which no longer met in the middle. His beard had been trimmed into a neat spade shape. The only feature I recognized was the coal-black eyes. Even his swarthy complexion seemed to have grown several shades lighter.

There was one other peculiar thing about him—he gave off a rank smell that I could not quite identify but that put me in mind of a stable somehow, one that had not been cleaned lately. Grimacing, I stepped back. "What—why are you wearing one of our costumes?"

"Mr. Armin will explain. Do you by any chance know where I might find Mr. Jonson?"

"Try Mr. Heminges's office, two doors down. 'A may be there, working on his script."

"Thank you. And thank you for being so polite as to not mention my offensive odor. Mr. Armin will explain that as well."

In the confines of the tiring-room, the awful odor was so strong that I could scarcely keep from gagging. Mr. Armin seemed not to notice. He was busy gathering up barber's tools, sponges, and jars of makeup. "What reeks so badly?" I demanded.

"Horse urine," Mr. Armin said matter-of-factly. He handed me an earthenware mug—clearly the source of the smell. "Will you empty that outside for me, please?"

"Horse urine?"

"Yes. You know, the yellow liquid sometimes known as—"

"Aye, I ken what it is well enough. What I don't ken is why you'd want a mug of 't."

"For bleaching purposes."

"Oh. Mr. Garrett's hair and beard, I wis."

"Exactly."

"I don't suppose 'a will be performing in a play wi' us?"

"No."

"So it's a disguise?" I took Mr. Armin's silence as an affirmative. "I expect that Garrett is not his true name, either." Mr. Armin remained silent. "Has 'a done something wrong, then, that 'a must conceal his identity?"

"That's a matter of opinion," Mr. Armin said. "I happen to think not. Still, it would be best if you do not inquire further into the matter. Can I depend on you?"

"Aye."

"Good. Now empty that mug, will you?"

9

I dumped the horse urine into the ditch that ran down the center of Gracechurch Street. The ditch had been designed to carry rainwater—and, along with it, household wastes and the contents of slop jars—downhill into the Thames. It did not fulfill its function very well, mainly because home owners tossed into it all sorts of inappropriate objects, some too large to be washed away by anything short of a flood—animal hides and guts, dead dogs, broken crockery, moldy straw from bed ticks, and the like.

Some folk felt that the plague was caused by corrupted air; if they were correct, then the city's gutters must be the prime breeding ground for the disease. But the corrupted air theory was only one of many. Astrologers blamed some particular alignment of the stars. Others, depending upon their own religious convictions, claimed that the contagion was part of a Popish plot, or a Jewish one, or even a Protestant one.

I had my own tentative theory about the plague and how it spread. I had noticed how often the illness was preceded by a rash of tiny red marks on the victim's limbs, like so many insect bites. My old master Dr. Bright believed that the contagion passed from person to person by means of invisible "plague seeds"; though he was not a particularly good physician, I suspected that, for once, he had stumbled upon the truth. Perhaps, then, the seeds could be conveyed not only through the air, but also through the bites of mosquitoes, fleas, bedbugs, and the like, that carried the seeds within them. After all, these insects were at their worst in the summer months, when the plague was also at its peak.

I had converted our housekeeper, Goodwife Willingson, to my way of thinking, and she had begun a crusade against all manner of bugs. So far her tactics had worked; since Sander's death, no one in Mr. Pope's household had been stricken. It remained to be seen whether or not they continued to work once the hot weather returned.

Just to be safe, Goody Willingson insisted that we have our daily spoonful of sage, rue, and ginger steeped in wine, and that we take the time-honored precaution of wearing about our necks small pomanders filled with wormwood and rosemary. I wondered whether she might know of some such measure one might take to avoid being stricken by love.

But perhaps it was too late for that. Perhaps I needed not a preventive but a cure. Each time Judith's face entered my mind—though, in truth, I don't believe it ever quite left—a curious feeling came over me, not unlike the one that always gripped me just before I was due on the stage. It was impossible to define, it was such a mingle-mangle of conflicting emotions—anticipation and uncertainty, eagerness and dread, pleasure and pain.

A rapping sound brought me out of my reverie. I turned to see Mr. Shakespeare beckoning me from within the dark parlor. I scoured out the mug with snow and went inside.

Mr. Shakespeare had obviously continued working on his unnamed play—or at least had attempted to. The booth was littered with wads of crumpled paper. The stack of completed pages, though, seemed no thicker than before. He was not writing now, only staring into his ale pot as though, like Madame La Voisin's scrying ball, it might tell him how to proceed.

"Did you want me to transcribe for you, then?" I asked.

"Not really." His voice echoed a little in the empty tankard. "Unless you can think of something yourself to set down. I certainly can't—nothing that isn't a pile of putrid tripe, at any rate."

I perused the few uncrumpled pages. "Perhaps . . . perhaps an you found somewhere quiet . . ."

"What I *need*," he replied sharply, "is not somewhere quiet. What I *need* is a decent story to work with—something with a bit of life to it. Plays should not be about *money*." He flicked the pages contemptuously with one finger. "They should be about . . . about madness and betrayal, about love and death."

"Like *Hamlet*."

"Yes. Like *Hamlet*." He rubbed his high forehead as though it pained him. "Unfortunately, money is the thing that is uppermost in my mind these days. Perhaps I was trying to purge myself by writing about it." He gathered up the wadded papers. "But that's not your concern. The reason I called you in was to ask another sort of favor."

"Gladly. What is 't?"

"I want you to escort my daughter to my lodgings. You know where I live?"

"Aye. The corner of Silver and Monkswell Street in Cripplegate."

"I've sent her trunk on ahead, along with a note to the—"
Mr. Shakespeare broke off as someone approached the booth.
The scent of cloves infused the air around us.

Judith slid in next to me. I kept my eyes on the table, certain
that the expression on my face must be a foolish one. "You
were saying, Father?" she prompted.

"I was saying that I've sent your trunk to my lodgings, along
with a note to Madam Mountjoy, asking if she will kindly put
you up for a few days."

"I would rather you had said a few weeks." Judith picked up
his tankard and peered into it to see whether any ale remained.
I snatched up the mug that had held the horse urine, lest she
decide to examine it, too. "In fact," she said, "I'm not at all
sure that I won't decide to stay in London indefinitely."

Mr. Shakespeare appeared alarmed by this prospect. "Oh?
Have you discussed this with your mother?"

"Of course not. She'd have had a seizure." Judith gave a
long-suffering sigh. "Oh, Father, you know what Stratford is
like. Aside from mother, there's absolutely no one and nothing
there that holds the slightest interest for me." She gave an imp-
ish smile. "And, honestly, sometimes even Mother can be a bit
tiresome."

Mr. Shakespeare did his best not to look amused. "All the
same, I don't think it would be wise to stay in London. What
would you do with yourself?"

"I don't know. Be a gatherer for the Globe, perhaps. I'm good
at managing money. On what you send us, I've had to be."

"That's enough of that!" Mr. Shakespeare snapped. Judith's
smile faded and she looked down at her lap as though a trifle

ashamed of her impudence—but only a trifle. "Now," her father continued, "I've asked Widge to accompany you to the Mountjoys'."

Judith's gaze met his again, and it seemed puzzled, reproachful. "You've asked Widge? I thought that *you* would . . ."

Now Mr. Shakespeare was the one to look away. "I'm sorry. As I've told you, I'm very busy just now. We have a sharers' meeting shortly. We must come to a decison on whether or not to raise the admission price of the plays."

"Oh. Well. I can see how that would be more important than squiring me about." She slid from the booth and held out a hand to me. "Come, then, Widge. You'll no doubt be better company, anyway."

Though Mr. Shakespeare pretended to ignore his daughter's barbed remark, I could tell from the way he stiffened slightly that it had struck its mark. As I got to my feet, Judith said to her father in a voice as cool as a cowcumber, "I trust you were able to make some arrangements for Mr. . . . Garrett?"

"Yes. Ben Jonson has volunteered to take him in."

"Good." She slipped her arm through mine. "I suppose I'll see you after the performance this evening, Father?"

"Yes. You needn't wait up for me, though. I may be late."

"Of course." She swept out of the parlor, hauling me with her. After fetching our cloaks, we passed through the courtyard and onto Fenchurch Street. Judith drew in a deep breath of the cold air and put on the semblance of a smile. "Parents can be so vexing. Particularly fathers. Don't you agree?"

"I . . . I wouldn't ken," I murmered.

"What do you mean?"

I was not anxious to reveal how little I knew of my mother and father and their station in life. Mistress MacGregor, who ran the orphanage where I grew up, had given me a crucifix my mother once wore, inscribed with the name Sarah. Jamie Redshaw had told me a few more things about my mother, but whether or not any of them were true I could not say, any more than I could say whether anything he had said about himself was true.

Judith peered into my downturned face, making me so flustered that I missed my footing and very nearly sent us stumbling into the path of a costermonger's cart. "Sorry," I mumbled.

"Never mind. I want to know what you meant when you said you wouldn't ken."

"It means I wouldn't *know*."

"I ken that. But why would you not know?"

"Because." I would have left it at that, but the way her bright blue eyes were fixed upon me somehow made me wish to tell her everything that was in my mind and in my heart, all in one great rush. "Because me mother died borning me, and me father . . . well, I'm not exactly certain who me father was."

She bit her lip. "I see. You're an orphan, then?"

"Aye," I admitted mournfully, half expecting her to pull away, as though I'd confessed to being the bearer of some dread disease.

To my surprise, she drew even closer and patted my arm. "But that's not such a bad thing, is it? I mean, if you don't know who your parents are, then they might be anyone, mightn't they? Who knows, perhaps you're the illegitimate son of some great lord with piles and piles of money."

"Would that were so," I said fervently. "Then I might hope to—" My voice broke then, and perhaps it was just as well, for I had been about to say something I had no business saying, or even thinking: that if I were rich and of noble birth, and not a poor prentice with no prospects beyond my next role, then there would be some chance, however small, that I might win her affections.

"What?" she urged. "What would you hope for?"

"Nothing," I said. But the knowing smile on her face led me to suspect that she had guessed my thoughts.

She tossed her yellow curls. "Well, in any case, I believe it doesn't matter whether a man is born high or low, not in this day and age. If you work hard and use your wits, you can make of yourself what you will. Look at my father, or Mr. Jonson. They're the sons of tradesmen, both of them, and yet they've earned both renown and respect."

"I didn't ken that anyone had much respect for theatre folk—even for playwrights."

"Of course they do. My father's name and work are well regarded all over England."

"It sounds as though you're very proud of him."

"I am. I may not always show it, I grant you. Even though he's a genius and all that, he can be a bit of a dolt sometimes. My mother says that it's not just him, it's men in general." She shook my arm playfully. "Tell me, Widge, are you a dolt sometimes?"

"Aye. More often than not, I expect," I said glumly.

Suddenly aware of how dismal her image of me must be, I rummaged through myself, as Sam had rummaged through the costume trunk, searching for some admirable quality or uncommon skill that I might bring to her attention. My acting? No, she had seen a sample of that this afternoon, and I did not care to remind her. In my desperation I resorted to a deplorable habit I had foolishly thought I was rid of: I lied. "I am writing a play, though."

10

A lie is like an arrow: once you've let it fly, there's no calling it back; the damage is done. And telling a single lie is like
loosing a single arrow at an angry bear: one is seldom enough;
it must be followed by another, and another.

"You're not!" she said.

"You doubt me?" I managed to sound indignant.

"No, of course not. What's this play of yours called, then?"

I pulled a title out of the air, a phrase I had once heard. "It's
called *The Mad Men of Gotham*." There was a certain perverse
satisfaction in finding that my talent for fabling had not grown
rusty from disuse.

"And what is it about?"

I had asked Mr. Shakespeare the very same thing that morning, and, like a good player, I recalled the line he had given me
in reply. "An excellent question. Would that I had as good an
answer for you."

"Oh." She smiled slyly. "I see what you're doing."

I swallowed hard, fearing my lie was so transparent that she had seen through it. "You do?"

"Yes. You're putting me off, because you don't want to discuss it. Father does the same thing. I think he's afraid that if he talks too much about a play in progress, it will put a curse on it somehow, and he'll never complete it."

"That's it exactly. I don't wish to put a curse on 't."

"Well, will you let me read it, at least?"

I wanted to say, *Aye, at the last Lammas*—meaning never. Instead I shrugged and said, "I might. When I'm further along wi' 't."

"I can't wait." She shook my arm again. "Perhaps it'll be performed, and become wildly popular, and make a fortune for you!"

Her words brought to mind Madame La Voisin's prediction that I would come into a fortune. I let out a nervous laugh. "Much! I've never heard of a play making its author rich."

"Oh, I don't know. Father does well enough with his."

"'A does?"

She nodded. "He never lets on to Mother and me how much he makes, of course; he doesn't want us demanding more of it. But"—she leaned in close to me, nearly stopping my poor heart—"it's enough to allow him to buy a hundred acres of land in Stratford, and the largest house in town—three stories, it is, with ten fireplaces!"

"Gog's blood! I never would ha' thought it. 'A lives so modest a life here, and 'a's always fretting about money."

"I know. To tell the truth, he's a bit of a miser. He won't even consent to loan money to his nearest friends. I think he's afraid of ending up like his father—my grandfather."

"How's that?"

"When Grandfather died, he was up to his ears in debt. Father says it's because he was too trusting, too ready to loan money to anyone who asked. But Mother says there's more to it than that. She says it's because . . . " She stood on tiptoe to whisper in my ear. "Because he was a *recusant*."

"A what?"

"A Catholic who refuses to attend the Anglican services."

"Oh. So 'a paid all his money out in fines, then?"

"That was part of it. But his business suffered because of it, too. No one but his fellow Catholics would buy wool or gloves from him, or rent his properties from him. He lost a good deal of property as well, in the rash of fires that Stratford suffered several years ago. Grandfather always claimed that the fires were set deliberately by Puritans. My mother has always staunchly denied it, but of course she would, being a Puritan herself."

"I take it you're not, then?"

"Not really. I suppose that when it comes to religion, I take more after my father. He says that the world is so full of ideas and customs and beliefs, each with its own merit, it seems a shame to place our faith in only one and rule out all the others." She turned her face up to me. "And what about you, Widge?"

"What about me?"

"Well, I assume you're not a Puritan, or you wouldn't be a player. But what are you? A good Protestant? A Church Papist? A skeptic? An atheist?"

"I don't ken, exactly. Is there a name for folk who can't make up their minds?"

"Yes," she said. "They're called women." Though she clearly expected a laugh from me, I was not in a laughing mood. In fact, my heart had suddenly turned as heavy as horse-bread.

My face must have given me away, for Judith said, "What is it, Widge? What's wrong?"

I nodded toward the house that lay just ahead of us. "We're here," I said grimly.

She laughed. "You needn't sound as though you're delivering me to the Tower."

"I'm sorry. It's just that—" I faltered, unable to give voice to the feeling that rose up in me—the feeling that, despite the cold, despite the fact that my shoes were soaked through with slush, I would willingly have gone on walking—in circles, if necessary— for another several days at least, as long as I had her company.

Once again she seemed to read my thoughts and, patting my arm, said, "Don't worry, Widge. We'll have lots more time together."

"Truly?"

"Of course. After all, we'll have to, won't we, if you're to read me your play?"

I left Judith in the care of Mary Mountjoy, a plump, rose-cheeked girl I had met several times before, when I carried some message to Mr. Shakespeare. I had always thought her attractive enough, but put up against Judith, she seemed as plain as porridge.

Reluctantly, I turned my steps again toward Cheapside, the most direct route back to the Cross Keys. My head was as full of thoughts as a hive is of bees. Like a player committing a new part to memory, I went over and over every word that had passed between Judith and me, relishing hers, deploring my own. My conversational skills were on much the same level as my acting skills had been earlier in the day. At least at rehearsal my lines had been written out for me, and so my speeches, when I could get them out, had consisted of something a bit less plodding and obvious than "I'm sorry" and "How's that?" and "'A does?"

I had often wondered why the wights in plays were forever composing songs or sonnets to their ladies, and not just saying straight out what was in their hearts. Now I understood. But, thanks to my lying tongue, Judith would never be content with a mere stanza or two of maudlin verse. She expected an entire play. When it came to stupid behavior, the Mad Men of Gotham—whoever they might be—could not possibly hope to compete with me.

And yet, as I mulled it over in my mind, the notion of writing a play was not really so preposterous as it seemed on the face of it. I had some little knowledge, after all, of how the deed was done, from transcribing Mr. Shakespeare's *All's Well That Ends Well* for him. I had even made a few modest contributions of my own, including the title.

Though I might be stupid, I was not so stupid as to imagine that I could come within hailing distance of a gifted poet such as Mr. Shakespeare, even at his worst. But not all the plays we performed were as accomplished as his. In fact, there were times, as I was mouthing some silly, stilted speech from *The Dead Man's Fortune* or *Frederick and Basilea*, when I swore that I could do far better without even breaking a sweat.

In truth, the notion of composing a play held a certain appeal for me. Though I found acting more gratifying than anything else I had ever done, I sometimes felt less like a player than like an instrument, a mouthpiece for someone else's words. The feeling was not an unfamiliar one; I had experienced it years before, when I was forced to copy down other rectors' sermons for Dr. Bright in the swift writing he taught me, and again when I was hired to set down the words of

Hamlet as it was being performed. All my life I had been compelled to do and say as others instructed me to. I wondered what it would be like, for once, to be the one telling others what to say and do, to be the craftsman, not the tool.

What I had told Judith might not be altogether a lie, then. Perhaps it was like one of La Voisin's predictions, instead. Sam had said that she was only telling her clients what they wished to hear. Perhaps I had merely been expressing some secret wish.

I was startled to my senses by the sound of the bells at St. Paul's tolling nones. For the first time I took a good look about me. Not only had I lost track of time, I had lost my way. I had come out not on West Cheap as I had meant to, but a good deal farther to the south and west, where Ludgate Street passed through the city wall. After two years of navigating London's crooked streets, I still had not fully mastered the maze, just as I had not completely mastered London speech.

I was but two or three minutes' walk from Salisbury Court, where we had visited Madame La Voisin the day before. I had missed dinner already and, if I did not hurry, I would miss scriming practice as well and be obliged to pay a fine. But such mundane concerns as food and fines seemed of little consequence at the moment. I had more weighty matters on my mind—my future, for example.

Folk who are contented with their lot in life tend not to give much thought to the future. Ever since I joined the Lord Chamberlain's Men, I had been more or less contented. My thoughts about the future had been limited mostly to wondering what would become of me if I lost my position with them. Now, suddenly, like a sailor who spies some green and welcome land on the horizon, I had been given a glimpse of new and unfamiliar territory, and I longed to know whether or not I had any hope of reaching it.

It took me some time to find the cunning woman's tattered tent, for the sign with the enormous eye no longer stood before it. I paused at the flap, uncertain whether or not to call out to her. To my surprise, a rough voice within said, "You may enter, young lady." When Sam and Sal and I came here together, she had called us young ladies. Did she know it was me waiting outside, then? Or was it simply that most of her clients were young ladies?

I ducked through the opening. The interior was even more smoky than I remembered. When my eyes adjusted to the gloom, I saw why. Instead of coal, she was burning a chunk of the wooden sign in her kettle.

"Sit," said La Voisin, and I obeyed. She peered at me from beneath the layers of woolen scarves. "I have already read your future."

"Aye. But I—I'd like to know more."

"Hmm. It is not wise to try to learn too much of what lies in store."

"I don't wish to know *everything* . . . "

She gave a hoarse, humorless laugh. "Only the good things, eh?" When I had placed a penny gingerly in her grimy hand, she unveiled her scrying ball and gazed into it, but only for a few seconds. Then she said matter-of-factly, "I see that you will make a name for yourself."

Though I suppose this should have pleased me, I was disappointed. It seemed to me a sort of all-purpose prediction, designed to appeal to anyone and everyone. "That's all?"

"It seems quite enough to me."

"Can't you tell me something more . . . well, *specific?*"

"Just what did you have in mind?"

"Perhaps something about . . . " I had no desire to discuss with this odd old woman anything as awkward and intimate as love. " . . . about other people?"

"Other people," she muttered. "I can try. But I see only what I see." She held out her hand and I dropped another penny into it. This time she stared into the ball, motionless, for so long that I feared she had drifted into some sort of daze, or fallen asleep with her eyes open. As surreptitiously as I could, I waved the wood smoke away from my face. The motion seemed to bring her out of her trance. When she spoke, it was in a monotone, without inflection, without emotion. "Because of you," she said, "someone will die." Before I had quite gotten my mind around this ominous prediction, she made a second that was even more startling: "But another will return to life."

11

"Return to life?" I said. "How is that possible?"

"I do not interpret. I only—"

"Aye, I ken. You only see." I leaned forward to get a closer look at the scrying ball. "I don't suppose you saw aught about someone . . . " I hesitated, embarrassed. " . . . someone named Judith?"

She pulled the cloth protectively over the black ball. "No." Then on her shrouded, wart-speckled face, I saw something approaching a smile. "But if you were to send this Judith to me, I could tell her future . . . and perhaps make certain that you appeared in it."

"For a price, of course."

"Of course."

So, not only did she tell her clients what they wished to hear, she would also tell them what someone else wanted them to hear. She was clearly a fake. And yet . . . and yet she had revealed to each of us one thing that we could not conceivably have wished to hear—that Sam would turn traitor, that Sal Pavy would lose his hair, that I would be the cause of another person's death. Those were hardly the sorts of predictions that were calculated to keep us coming back for more.

I got unsteadily to my feet, dizzy from breathing in the smoke—or from too many confusing thoughts buzzing in my brain. "I must go. God you good day."

"A good day," she said, "would be a warm one."

I glanced at the smoldering sign. "You've run out of fuel, then?" She nodded and pulled her scarves more tightly about her. Impulsively I reached into my purse, brought out my last shilling, and laid it on the table. "To buy coal with." As I left the tent, I thought I heard her murmur something in reply; I could not be sure of the words, but they might have been "May Fate be kind to you."

Only when I was halfway back to the Cross Keys did I realize how foolish I had been to give her that shilling. What would I use now to pay the fine Mr. Armin was sure to demand of me for missing scriming practice? And, as I soon discovered, that was not the only penalty I would be expected to pay.

In my preoccupation with Judith, I had forgotten all about my costume for that night's performance, and the fact that it had not yet been let out to fit me. With our tiring-man home ill and but two hours remaining before performance, it would have to wait. Perhaps no one would notice if I pressed into service my costume from *The Spanish Tragedy*.

But when I dug through the trunk of clothing for that play, there was no sign of Bel-Imperia's gown. Alarmed, I went through the lot again, piece by piece, and still failed to turn it up. "Oh, gis!" I sank to the floor, my head in my hands.

"S-something wrong?" said a voice behind me.

"Aye," I groaned. "Me gown for *The Spanish Tragedy* has come up missing."

Mr. Heminges crouched down next to me. "I hate to t-tell you this, W-Widge, but we're not d-doing *The Spanish Tragedy* this evening."

"I ken that. But me dress for *Two Gentlemen* no longer fits, and I thought I'd substitute this one, only it's gone."

Mr. Heminges sighed heavily, as though he'd heard this same tale before and was weary of it. "That's unf-fortunate. But I'm n-not surprised. It's the f-fourth item that's d-disappeared in as m-many weeks."

"Is someone stealing them, do you wis?"

"I'm afraid it's a p-possibility. Of course, it's also p-possible that they're st-still at the Globe somewhere, though I d-doubt it. Richard is always very c-careful in p-packing the costumes."

"I suppose it'll come out of me wages, then?"

"I'm s-sorry, but that's the r-rule. We c-can't make an exception for you. If we f-find out who the th-thief is—assuming th-there is one—we'll return the m-money to you." He got stiffly to his feet. "N-now, let's see about that other g-gown."

When I tried it on, the hem proved to be, as Judith had guessed, several inches too short, and no matter how Mr. Heminges tugged at the back of my bodice, the hooks and eyes could not be made to meet. "Well, we d-don't have much t-time. If you'll s-see to the hooks and eyes, I'll l-let down the hem—pr-provided you thread the n-needle for me; my eyes are n-not what they were."

Though, like all prentices, I had made my share of emergency repairs, I was no great hand with a needle. Before I had managed to move all two dozen hooks and eyes to their new positions, I must have dropped each of them at least twice; several were never seen again. Mr. Heminges's needlework, however, was swift and sure. When I commented upon this, he laughed. "When you have b-been on the road as many t-times as I have, without b-benefit of a seamstress or t-tiring-man, you learn to d-do for yourself."

"Will we go on the road again this summer, do you wis?"

He paused and rubbed thoughtfully at his graying beard. "It's hard to s-say, at this p-point. What we d-do will depend largely upon what the p-plague does. I hope it will not c-come to that. Our p-position is precarious enough as it is. If we had to c-close down the theatre for several m-months, it could be—" He broke off, then, as though he had said too much, and went back to his stitching. "Well, as I s-said, I hope not."

Though I did not wish to pry into matters that did not concern me, I had the uneasy feeling that this *did* concern me. "Are we—is the company in difficulty, then?"

Mr. Heminges considered for several moments before replying. "A bit. But we'll w-weather it. We always have." He gave me a rather worn smile. "In any c-case, there's n-no need for you or the other pr-prentices to worry. L-let us sharers do the w-worrying, all right?"

I would willingly have obeyed him; I had more than enough on my mind already. But worry is like the plague—or, it seemed, like love. It's no good at all ignoring or denying it; once the seed has found its way inside you, you are doomed.

Even had I succeeded in casting aside my concern, it would not have been for long. As we players stood in the cramped space behind the stage, listening to the audience arrive and trying to judge from the sound of them what mood they were in, Mr. Shakespeare, still dressed in his street clothes, burst through the door that led to the outside stairway, bringing with him a gust of frigid air. "Widge!" he called above the din of the playgoers.

"Aye!" I made my way toward him through the shifting mass of actors applying their face paint, adjusting their costumes, mumbling their lines to themselves, making all sorts of curious sounds meant to limber up their voices.

When I was within his reach, Mr. Shakespeare drew me to him. "The master of revels sends word that some men from the queen's Privy Council are out there tonight, checking up on us."

"Is there something amiss wi' our privy?"

He laughed. "The Privy Council is a body of Her Majesty's closest advisers. No doubt they hope to catch us feeding the masses some morsel of Papist propaganda, as a priest gives out morsels of the host at Communion. I imagine Henslowe has put them up to it."

Our sharers had long suspected the manager of the Admiral's Men of mounting various strategies to injure our reputation or our box—that is, the amount of money we took in—including attaching Mr. Shakespeare's well-known name to plays written by Henslowe's own committee of hacks, inciting Puritan preachers to stand outside the Globe railing at the playgoers, even planting his men in our audience, where they shouted insults at the actors.

"You have a line about confession, do you not?"

"Aye. Eglamour says, 'Where shall we meet?' and I say, 'At Friar Patrick's cell, where I intend holy confession.'"

"Yes, yes. I want you to replace that line."

"Wi' what?"

"You'll think of something. Are there any other Popish sorts of speeches that you can recall?"

"Nay. But—"

The sound of Mr. Phillips's hautboy signaled that the play was about to commence. Mr. Shakespeare glanced down at his everyday doublet and breeches. "By the matt!" he whispered. "I nearly forgot; I'm playing the duke!" He left as precipitously as he had come, leaving me to invent some new bit of dialogue for myself. Well, if I had any hope at all of living up to my boast of writing a play, surely I could conjure up a line and a half of passable iambic pentameter. If nothing else, the effort would give me something to do besides fret, which is what I was ordinarily doing at this point in the performance.

Mr. Pope had assured me that a certain amount of fear before going on was a good thing. "Without frets," he was fond of saying, "there is no music." But none of the other actors, not even the prentices, looked as though they were going to face the hangman, as I had been told I did. Sal Pavy was examining himself in a looking glass, touching the locks of his blond wig as though wishing they were his own. Sam, dressed in a gown borrowed from the *As You Like It* trunk, stood next to me at the stage-right curtain, whistling a tune under his breath and practicing a little jig step Mr. Phillips had taught him.

I took a deep breath—or as deep as I could manage, considering how tightly my ribs were bound by the bodice of my dress—and tried to compose a line to replace the censored one. *Where shall we meet? Ta tumpty-tumpty tum. Behind the abbey wall?* No. *Some nonreligious place?* When I glanced again at Sal Pavy, who played my romantic adversary, Julia, a clever though totally unsuitable possibility entered my head: *Let's meet in Julia's room, where I intend to strangle her with her wig.*

"What are you sniggering about?" Sam asked softly.

"Oh, nothing. I was just thinking of strangling Julia."

Sam nodded, as though this were a perfectly reasonable proposal. "May I help?" This set me laughing again, so violently that I had to cover my mouth to avoid being heard on the other side of the curtain. "Careful," Sam said. "You'll burst your bodice." When I had gotten my mirth under control, he said, "I hear you've lost a costume, too."

"Aye. Between that and the fine for missing scriming practice, I'm afraid I'll ha' no money to help you out."

"No matter. Mr. Heminges has promised to withhold only a shilling each week."

"We'll still receive two shillings, then? That's good. That's more than you imagined." Something about those words struck me as odd, or perhaps familiar. I had to mull it over for a moment before I realized where I had heard them before. "Sam!" I whispered. "The cunning woman's prediction!"

"What about it?"

"She said, 'You will receive more money than you imagine.'"

He stared at me. "No. That can't be what she meant. Can it?"

Out on the stage, Will Sly, our Proteus, delivered the last line of the scene: "I fear my Julia would not deign my lines, receiving them from such a worthless post."

Sal Pavy appeared beside us. "That's our cue!" he told Sam.

But Sam seemed not to hear. He was shaking his head in disbelief. "That can't be what she meant," he repeated. I had to plant my foot on his nether end and propel him onto the stage.

Though Mr. Shakespeare was disturbed at having members of the Privy Council in the audience, I much preferred their presence to Judith's. I was distracted enough just thinking about her in the abstract; to have her there in the flesh would certainly have undone me completely.

Just in case I should happen to forget my infatuation with her for a second or so, the play seemed specially designed to make certain I would not, from Sal Pavy's first speech—"But say, Lucetta, now we are alone, wouldst thou then counsel me to fall in love?"—to the end, when Mr. Shakespeare spoke the line with which Sam had teased me earlier in the day: "I think the boy hath grace in him; he blushes."

The one thing I did manage to forget was the need to think up a new line, until the very scene was upon me. When Mr. Armin, as Eglamour, asked, "Where shall we meet?" I froze. Seeing that I was speechless, he did as any good player would—he prompted me. "Shall we meet at Friar—" he began.

"No!" I interrupted frantically, my voice cracking. "Let's not! Let's meet . . . somewhere else! In the forest!"

Mr. Armin was too seasoned an actor to let this throw him. "An excellent idea, your ladyship," he said. When we met behind the stage later, he gave me a look of mock disparagement. "In the *forest?*"

"It was all I could think of," I protested. "At least I said *no* rather than *nay*."

"Why did you say it at all? I was about to cover for you."

"Mr. Shakespeare told me to cut the line about Friar Patrick. 'A says there's a wight from the Privy Council out there."

"A pox on the Privy Council!" muttered Mr. Armin. "They were here last week as well, for *Romeo and Juliet*. John Lowin had to amend his line about going to confession. No doubt they would have been even happier had we made Friar Laurence an Anglican priest." He smacked a fist into his palm. "They've never bothered us before. Why now? And why would they pick the very plays that happen to have references to Catholic rites in them?"

"Perhaps because the plays are set in Italy?"

"Perhaps," Mr. Armin said. "Or perhaps someone is keeping the Privy Council apprised of everything we do."

"You mean . . . "

"I mean," he said, "a spy."

12

By the time I returned home that evening, I was as bone weary as I had ever been, even the previous summer, when we sometimes slogged along a muddy road in the rain from dawn until dusk. Though for a prentice every day is a hectic one, this day had been without equal or precedent, as full of alarums and excursions and general hurly-burly as both parts of *Henry VI* put together.

As was their custom, the dozen or so orphan boys who lodged with Mr. Pope were waiting to pounce on me the moment I came through the door, yelling like wild Irishmen, rifling my wallet in search of the sweetmeats I sometimes brought them, begging me to play a game of Barley-Break or Rise Pig and Go. But when Goody Willingson saw how haggard I looked, she chased them off to bed and brought me a cup of what she called clary—warm wine with honey, pepper, and ginger—and a bowl of frumety—wheat kernels boiled in milk—which she had kept hot for me on the back of the cast-iron heating stove.

I was too exhausted to eat more than a few mouthfuls. "Has Mr. Pope retired for the night?" I asked.

"He's in the library."

I sighed, knowing that he was waiting for me, too—not so that I might play a game, but so that I might tell him all the day's news. I did not like to disappoint him, for I knew how much he missed being a part of the company, and how eager he was to hear what we were up to.

In warmer weather, Mr. Pope frequently made the short journey to the Globe, sometimes to watch a performance from behind the stage, sometimes simply to share conversation and a drink with his old comrades. But the combination of cold weather, ill health, and distance kept him from coming to the Cross Keys, so he relied on me to keep him abreast of things. We had a running jest about my being his informant, his spy within the company. Now, in light of Mr. Armin's deadly serious remark, it did not seem so amusing.

Mr. Pope had his feet propped up before the fire, a mug of clary in one hand and a woolen blanket draped over his ample belly. "Come in, Widge, come in. Sit down. You look as though you've had a long, hard day."

"Good. I'm glad I've something to show for it." Like the messenger in a play, who describes for the other characters and for the audience some action that took place off the stage, I proceeded to give him an account of all that had happened that day, in as few words as I reasonably could.

In truth, I did not include everything. I did not tell of my visit to La Voisin and what she saw in her scrying ball. Nor did I repeat what Mr. Armin had said about a spy, or what Mr. Heminges had said about the company being in difficult circumstances. The physician who attended Mr. Pope had cautioned us that any undue strain or stress could worsen his patient's condition, and I had no wish to fulfill the cunning woman's prediction that I would bring about another person's death, least of all his. I did describe for him the mysterious Mr. Garrett, thinking that they might have crossed paths before. But Mr. Pope had no notion who or what the man might be, or why he would feel compelled to disguise himself.

When I introduced Judith into my story, I did my best to sound nonchalant, but I was not a good-enough actor to carry it off. Though I confined myself to facts, carefully avoiding any mention of feelings, Mr. Pope was not fooled for a moment.

"I believe you neglected to clean all the rouge off your cheeks, my boy," he said mischievously. "Either that, or the frost has nipped them a bit."

I ducked my head sheepishly. "Aye, I expect that's it."

"I've met Will's daughters a time or two. Judith is the fair one, is she?"

"Aye."

"She is a pretty thing. I'm not surprised that you'd be smitten with her."

"I never said I was."

Mr. Pope laughed. "There's no need to say it. It's written all over your face." His smile slowly faded then, to be replaced by a look of concern, and he leaned forward in his chair. "Widge. I hope you don't mind my saying this. I know you haven't asked for my advice, but . . . well, I think of you almost as a . . . as a son, and . . . while I don't wish to meddle, or to say anything against Judith, I think you'd do well to be . . . careful."

"Careful?"

"Yes. I wouldn't like to see you hurt."

"What do you mean?"

"I mean that . . . On occasion Will has spoken to me about . . . about his family, and from what he's told me, I gather that Judith is . . . " He shifted uncomfortably in his seat. "How shall I put it? Well, you recall the duke's description of his daughter in *Two Gentlemen*?

"No, trust me: she is peevish, sullen, forward,
Proud, disobedient, stubborn, lacking duty;
Neither regarding that she is my child,
Nor fearing me as if I were her father."

I stared at him, unable to quite grasp what he was getting at. "Aye?"

Mr. Pope sighed. "Never mind, Widge. You're tired. We'll talk more in the morning."

"Aye, all right." On the last word, my weary voice broke.

Mr. Pope winced. "It sounds as though your pipes can't decide which octave to play in. Has that been happening often?"

I nodded despondently. "No one i' the company has mentioned it yet—except Sam and Sal Pavy, of course—but I'm certain they've noticed."

"Well, don't let it worry you. It doesn't mean you're through playing girls' parts; it just means we'll have to work a bit more to keep you sounding sweet. We'll get some oil of almond for you to gargle with daily, and I'll show you some vocal exercises that will keep your throat strings in tune. For now, go on to bed."

I got to my feet. "Before I do, can I fetch aught for you?"

"No, no." He lifted the blanket to reveal a thick book wedged in next to him. "I've a cup of clary and a volume of Rabelais. What more could a man want?"

My brain was not so befogged that I failed to hear the wistful tone behind his words. What he wanted, I suspected, was not to sit before a fire with a book in his lap, but to strut before an audience with a speech in his mouth. In the doorway of the library, I turned back. "Mr. Pope?"

"Yes, lad?"

"Ha' you ever tried writing a play?"

"Me?" He laughed heartily, as though the notion were ludicrous. "No, I'm happy to leave that task to Will. What makes you ask such a thing?"

"I—I only thought it might gi' you something to do," I lied.

"Thank you, but I believe I'd prefer to dig a ditch. Dirt is far more agreeable to work with than words."

As I started up the stairs, I discovered Tetty sitting halfway up them, clad only in her nightshirt, her thin arms wrapped about her knees. "Tetty!" I whispered. "Why are you sitting here? You'll catch a chill!"

"I was waiting for you to tuck me into bed."

"And not eavesdropping at all on me conversation wi' Mr. Pope, I suppose?" I led her down the hall to the room she shared with Goody Willingson, who was still cleaning up in the kitchen.

"Only a little," she said. "Who's Judith?"

Here it was dark enough to hide my blushes. "Mr. Shakespeare's daughter." I turned back the covers, and when she was done snuggling into her spot, I tucked them around her.

"Is she very beautiful?"

If neglecting to tell the whole truth counts as a lie, I was guilty once more. Instead of confessing that Judith was the most comely creature I had ever set eyes upon, I simply said, "I suppose so."

"Are you going to marry her?" Clearly Tetty was no more fooled by my show of indifference than Mr. Pope had been.

"Marry her? I've kenned her but a single afternoon!"

"After Romeo talks to Juliet for only five minutes they're exchanging their love's faithful vows."

"How is it you ken so much about Romeo and Juliet?"

"Mr. Pope told me. He acted out all the parts." She gave a soft, sleepy giggle. "He doesn't make a very good Juliet."

"No, I expect not."

Tetty yawned. "You mustn't marry her, you know." Her voice was growing drowsy now.

"Why not?"

"Because," she murmured, "you must wait for me."

13

Despite my exhaustion, I spent a restless night. I woke well before dawn, and as I could not force myself back to sleep, I rose and lit a candle. Then, wrapping my blankets about me, I sat at the small table by my bed and took up my plumbago pencil, determined to write something resembling a play—or at any rate enough of one to make the lie I had told Judith seem more credible.

It was more than just a matter of making good my boast, though. I wished desperately to do something that would impress her favorably. Heaven knew I had done little enough in that line thus far. I was very much afraid that if I remained in her eyes—her bright blue eyes—nothing more than Widge, the quaint prentice, she would have little time for me. If, on the other hand, I were Widge, the quaint playwright . . .

Well, she had said herself that she was more than willing to spend time with me in order to hear my play. The main problem, as I saw it, was that I had no play, not even the ghost of an idea for one—nothing more than a title, in fact, and a rather stupid one at that.

The *ghost* of an idea . . . Well, there was a possibility. The groundlings went wild over anything with a ghost in it. The only thing they relished more—as the undying popularity of *The Spanish Tragedy* attested—was revenge. Something about a ghost who demands revenge, then? It wasn't exactly clear where the Mad Men of Gotham would fit in, but I could always tell Judith I had decided to change the title. After all, it was a practice her father routinely indulged in; *All's Well That Ends Well*, for example, had begun life as *Love's Labour's Won*. I could redub mine something on the order of *The Madman's Revenge*. I rolled the title on my tongue: *The Madman's Revenge*. That wasn't bad; in fact it was quite good. Using my swift writing, I scribbled it down on the back of a broadsheet.

I rubbed my hands together, partly in anticipation, partly to warm them up a bit. This was beginning to look less like a chore and more like a lark. All right; I had a ghost. Whose ghost was it, then? Someone who had been foully and treacherously murdered, no doubt, since it was demanding revenge. A prince, perhaps, or a king—the penny payers liked to see royalty up there on the stage, not dull, ordinary wights like themselves. So, let us say that this prince—or king, if you will—is poisoned by some villain who covets the throne, only the prince's ghost—or king's, if you will—comes back, all mangled and bloody—let's have him hacked to death, then, instead of poisoned—and torments his brother, or his son, or someone, and . . .

I stopped scribbling. Wait a moment, I thought. This all sounds awfully familiar. It sounded, in fact, very much like *Hamlet*. Disgusted, I held the broadsheet over the candle flame and watched it burn. Then I snatched up another sheet of paper and smoothed it out before me.

What else would the stinkards flock to see, then? A rollicking comedy, of course, full of puns and pratfalls, misunderstandings and mistaken identities. But, though I knew next to nothing about composing a play, I knew enough to realize that a script of that sort would demand a wit keener than mine; even worse, it would require an involved and intricate story. I was better off sticking with something simple and straightforward, like death. Or perhaps love. If there was anything that appealed to the general playgoer as much as a tragic tale of murder and revenge, it was a tragic tale of star-crossed lovers.

Again, it was best if they were royalty, or at least nobility. What maiden in her right mind, after all, would waste her time pining away after a cob carrier, or a rat catcher—or an apprentice player? If the romance was to end tragically, there must be some obstacle, something to keep them apart. If they were both of noble birth, it could not be a difference in station. Or could it? What if one of the lovers—the boy, let us say—discovers that the man and woman he believes to be his parents are, in fact, not? What if they reveal to him that he was a foundling whom they took in and raised as their own? What if his true parents were, say, a cowherd and a milkmaid?

I groaned. That was not tragic; it was merely pathetic. What about the other way 'round, then? The lovers are simple country lobs—the groundlings might not mind that; they always cheered the rustics in *Midsummer Night's Dream*, and besides, I knew far more about rustics than I did about royalty—but then one of them—the girl, let's say—discovers somehow that she's actually the daughter of a duke or earl or something, who gave her to this cowherd and this milkmaid to raise, and . . .

As Sam was fond of saying: "Much!" What reason in the world would a duke or an earl have to hand his daughter over to a couple of poor peasants that way? Our audiences were often asked to accept the unlikely, but there were limits to what one could ask of them. When I was growing up in the orphanage, I imagined—as did most of my fellow orphans, I am certain—that I had been sent there by mistake, that someday my parents would come and claim me, and they would prove to be wealthy folk of high degree—or at least wealthy. But that was a child's dream, not the sort of thing that ever actually occurred.

The second sheet of paper went the way of the first. Though as a premise for a play it was hopeless, at least it served to warm my hands a little. I took up a third sheet and stared at it. There was something intimidating, almost mocking, about its blankness, as though it were daring me to fill the void with something of consequence. I was tempted to burn it as well, just for spite. Instead I pinned it roughly to the table with one hand and with the other held my pencil poised over it. Now. What else might keep these hypothetical lovers apart? Money? Religion?

When I first met Jamie Redshaw he told me a touching tale of how my mother's parents had forbidden her to have anything to do with him because they were Protestants and his family were Catholics. Though I now suspected that the whole thing had been a fabrication, a ploy to win my trust, at the time I had been utterly convinced by it. Might it not, then, convince an audience as well?

I had the page nearly covered with scribbled notes—names for the characters, possible titles (*The Mad Monk of Gotham; The Revenge of the Rosary*), thoughts on how I might work in a ghost of some sort—before it occurred to me how foolish, even dangerous, it would be to compose a play in which one of the protagonists was a flagrant Papist.

As I sat watching yet another idea go up in smoke, the bells of St. Bennet, directly across the river from us, began to ring prime. I sprang to my feet and flung off the blankets. I was due at the Cross Keys in half an hour. I pulled on my clothing as quickly as I could and sprinted downstairs. Before I had taken two bites of my porridge, Sam came to call for me.

As I hurried out the door, Goodwife Willingson snatched me by the cloak and thrust into my hand two thick slabs of bread with slices of cold beef packed between them.

"Overslept, did you?" said Sam, casting an envious eye at the bread and beef.

I broke it in two and handed half to him. "Nay, as a matter of fact I've been up for hours."

"Doing what?" he asked around a monstrous mouthful of food.

I was not about to tell him what I had truly been up to; then I would have two people pestering me for a look at my nonexistent play—and very likely far more than that, for Sam was not known for keeping his tongue in his purse, as they say. So, to avoid compounding the trouble my first lie had gotten me into, I was forced to come up with a totally new one. Was there no end to it? "I was working on improving me charactery."

"Improving your character? I don't see that getting up a bit early is all that virtuous."

"Nay, nay, not me *character*; me *charactery*—you ken, me swift writing." Well, that was not altogether untrue. Dr. Bright's system was, to put it kindly, imperfect. There were times when I grew so frustrated with its shortcomings that I swore I would devise my own set of symbols. One day I might even get around to it—when I was finished writing my play, perhaps, or at the last Lammas, whichever came first.

At the start of each day, it was the job of us prentices to put the tiring-room and property room in order again, after the two hours of disorder they had suffered the night before. When Sam and I arrived in the property room, Sal Pavy was already hard at work—at least until he saw that it was only us and not one of the sharers who had entered, at which point he reverted to his normal practice of doing as little as possible.

Sam cast him a look of disgust. A moment later, as he was putting a leather breastplate into its proper trunk, Sam suddenly stood stock-still, his eyes squeezed shut as though in concentration, a hand clapped to his forehead. "I've just had a vision of the future," he intoned, in a voice very like Madame La Voisin's. "I predict . . . I predict that Master Pavy is about to say—" He switched to a wicked imitation of Sal Pavy's rather nasal tenor. "'At Blackfriahs we were not obliged to pick up propahteeahs.'"

It was Sal Pavy's turn to express disgust. "If I sounded remotely the way your parody of me sounds. I'd quit the stage at once and become a hermit."

"Promise?" Sam said.

"Stop it, you two," I said. "We've work to do."

Sam picked up the rope ladder used by Valentine in *Two Gentlemen* and began winding it into a neat bundle. "I mean no offense, Sal, but if you had it so easy at Blackfriars, why didn't you stay there?"

I had a good idea what the reason was, for I had seen the stripes that decorated Sal Pavy's back—the result, I did not doubt, of frequent and severe beatings. Sam had seen them, too. But Sal Pavy, for all his talk of Blackfriars, had never talked of this. "You may tell us," I said. "We're all friends here."

Sal Pavy glanced warily at me, then at Sam. "He'll only make another jest of it."

"Not I," Sam vowed, and drew a cross over his heart.

"Don't do that!" Sal Pavy's tone was unexpectedly harsh. "It puts me in mind of *them*."

"Who do you mean by *them*?" I asked.

"Mr. Giles and Mr. Evans."

I recognized the names. "They're the wights i' charge o' the Chapel Children?"

Sal Pavy nodded. He looked about furtively, as if fearing that one of them might have infiltrated our theatre. Then he said, in a voice so low that I could scarcely hear him, "They're also Papists."

14

"Papists?" Sam said incredulously. "Running the queen's own company?"

"You sound as though you don't believe me!"

"I believe you, Sal, I believe you. It just seems a bit . . . risky, doesn't it?"

"Well, obviously they don't go about telling everyone. But we Children all knew. It would have been impossible for us not to. Every week we had to make a confession to one of them."

"A confession?" I said. "Were they priests, then?"

Sal Pavy shook his head. "They insisted we confess our sins to them, all the same. If we couldn't think of anything we'd done that was sinful enough to suit them, they accused us of holding out on them, so we'd have to make something up. Sometimes a number of us would get together the night before and share ideas for despicable things we could confess to."

"Why didn't you just refuse to do it?" Sam asked.

"I did," Sal Pavy replied defensively. "Several times. And then I got tired of being beaten, and decided it was better just to do what they wanted."

"Gog's nowns," I murmured. "Could you not simply leave?"

"I tried that as well, but my—" His voice faltered and he looked down at the floor as though ashamed.

"It's all right," I said. "Go on."

"My parents always sent me back. When I tried to tell them what went on there, they wouldn't listen. All they could think of was what a great honor it was for me to be one of the Chapel Children."

"They didn't object when you joined the Chamberlain's Men?"

He gave a thin, bitter smile. "They were willing to sacrifice a bit of honor in favor of the fee the company pays them for my services."

I placed a sympathetic hand on his shoulder. "Now I ken why you were so desperate to stay on wi' us."

He shrugged off my hand. "I didn't tell you all that in order to get your *pity*."

Sam gave him a peevish look. "Why did you tell us, then?"

"A few days ago you asked me why I had such a poor opinion of Papists. Now you know." With that, he stalked out of the property room.

"Well," said Sam. "Just when I was starting to think that perhaps he wasn't a complete ass after all, he began to bray again."

"Don't be too hard on him. 'A let down his guard for a moment, and now 'a's feeling a bit vulnerable, I expect."

"That may be. But I expect he's also feeling a bit smug."

"Why is that?"

"Well," Sam said, looking about at the still-cluttered room, "you'll notice that he's left us to clean up the properties without him."

We did not see Sal Pavy again until rehearsal. He seemed resentful toward us, as though, like his former masters, we had forced him to confess to us against his will.

I prayed that Judith would not turn up to torment me again and cause me to turn our Spanish tragedy into a French farce, with me as the principal clown. But then, when she did not appear, instead of being grateful, I was sorely disappointed, even desolate, as though I had been forsaken.

Fortunately my mood was perfectly suited to playing Bel-Imperia, whose lover, Don Andrea, has been slain in battle. Mr. Lowin even commended me on how convincingly wretched I sounded. If I had said a word to Sam about how I felt—which I did not—he would surely have seen it as yet another sign that I had contracted a severe case of lovesickness. There was one classic symptom, though, that I had not yet suffered—a lack of appetite. I had not had much in the way of food that morning, and by the time our midday break came around, I was ravenous.

For most of the company, going home for dinner would have meant a walk of a quarter hour or more in the cold, so we customarily dined downstairs, at a long trestle table set up specially for us by the innkeeper. As we would not have the leisure for another bona fide meal until after the evening performance, we made a feast of this one, often lingering at the table until nearly nones.

It was my favorite part of the day—a time for companionship, conversation, a congenial game of cards. Today we had even more companionship than usual, for Mr. Garrett had joined us. Before sitting next to him, Mr. Armin sniffed him warily, like a dog. "Just checking, to make certain you'd gotten the smell out."

"And have I?" asked Mr. Garrett.

"For the most part. You smell less like a stable now, and more like a brewery."

"That's because I rinsed myself with ale, at Ben Jonson's suggestion."

"Well, you have it from an expert, then," said Will Sly. "No one knows more about ale and its uses than Ben."

"Are you a c-cardplayer, sir?" asked Mr. Heminges. "We n-normally engage in a r-rousing round of whist after d-dinner."

"Thank you, sir. I'd be delighted to join you."

Mr. Garrett proved an entertaining dinner companion. Though he seemed to know little enough about the theatre, he had something intelligent, and often witty, to say about nearly every other topic on which we touched.

I watched him closely and listened to him carefully, looking for some clue to his identity and why he chose—or was compelled—to conceal it. He spoke with a slight lisp, but not the precious sort so often affected by fops. His seemed, rather, to be the result of some injury to his upper lip, where a thin scar was still visible beneath his newly bleached mustache. When he turned toward me, I could see traces of other old wounds on his neck and on his forehead. Whatever else his past life might have been, it had certainly been dangerous.

I was, I noticed, not the only one in the company who was taking Mr. Garrett's measure. Ned Shakespeare was regarding him with narrowed eyes and a furrowed brow, as though still trying to recall where he had seen the man before. Ordinarily Sam paid far more attention to the food and drink than to the conversation, but when Mr. Garrett began to speak of all the countries he'd traveled to and all the strange things he had seen, Sam hung on his every word, as though he hungered far more for adventure than for the mackerel and the parsnip fritters on his plate.

Mr. Garrett could also hold his own when the talk turned to such popular pursuits as hunting, falconry, and gardening. And, although he had been in London but two days, he was already knowledgeable on the subject of most concern to us all—the state of the queen's health.

"This morning," he said, "I spoke with . . . with someone in a position to know. He tells me that Her Majesty grows weaker with each day that passes. She often seems confused and forgetful, and will seldom speak except to complain that her limbs are cold. Yet she adamantly refuses to take any of the medicines prescribed by her physicians, apparently because she fears being poisoned."

The sharers glanced solemnly at one another. "What I fear, gentlemen," said Mr. Armin, "is that we players will not have Her Majesty's protection much longer." He turned to Mr. Garrett. "Do you know whether or not she has given any indication of who she wants to succeed her?"

"According to the man I spoke with, she has not. Everyone expects, of course, that her choice will be the Scottish king."

"Lord help us," said Mr. Shakespeare.

"Is that bad?" I asked. I knew nearly nothing about King James, except that he was the son of Mary, Queen of Scots, who once tried to claim the English throne and had her costard chopped off for it.

"Well," Mr. Shakespeare said, "let me put it this way: How many Scottish theatres have you heard of?"

I thought for a moment. "None."

"And how many famous Scottish playwrights are there?"

"None?"

He nodded grimly. "How well do suppose we players are likely to fare, then, under James's rule?"

"I understand, though," said Mr. Garrett, "that his queen, Anne of Denmark, often presents elaborate masques at court, and even performs in them."

"Oh, good," said Mr. Armin. "We'll all become courtiers, then, and prance about before a lot of fake scenery, pretending to be gods and goddesses, and spouting doggerel."

"P-perhaps it won't be as b-bad as you imagine," put in Mr. Heminges, always the optimist.

"And perhaps it will be a good deal worse," said Ned Shakespeare. "After all, His Royal Scottishness was raised by Puritans, and most, if not all, of his advisers are Puritans." He took a great gulp of ale and wiped his mouth on his sleeve. "If you ask me, we'd better all pray very hard that Her Majesty makes a miraculous recovery."

15

The congenial, companionable mood had vanished. It was as though a sneaping southerly wind had swept into the room, bringing on its wings a load of melancholy, which hung over the company like a dark and dreary cloud.

There was a long stretch during which no one spoke very much and everyone drank a lot. Then Mr. Heminges cleared his throat. "I w-was reluctant to bring this up b-before, but as we're all in a f-foul humor anyway, I m-may as well." He glanced at the other sharers as though for moral support, and then went on. "A short wh-while ago, it was discovered that yet another c-costume has d-disappeared from its trunk."

Murmured complaints and curses went up from one end of the table to the other. Mr. Heminges's voice rose above them. "Now, one or two m-missing garments may be chalked up to c-carelessness, but when the t-toll reaches half a dozen, we c-cannot help suspecting . . . " He paused and cleared his throat again. "Well, n-naturally we do not w-wish to accuse anyone, but—"

"If you're looking for someone to blame," put in Ned Shakespeare, "I'd begin with the tiring-man. He has the most ready access to the costumes, after all."

"P-perhaps. But R-Richard has always been v-very reliable. Besides, the trunk I m-mentioned was sent over from the Globe only t-two days ago, and Richard has b-been laid up for n-nearly a week. In any c-case, as I said, we d-do not wish to accuse anyone, so we've decided to t-take the following m-measure: From n-now on, the t-tiring-room and property room will be kept locked d-during the day, until an hour b-before the performance. That should leave sufficient t-time for all of you to dress and c-collect your properties."

There was another round of discontented murmurs. Mr. Heminges held up his hands for silence. "I would j-just like to add that the n-necessity of replacing the costumes p-puts rather a severe b-burden on the company's finances. As you've n-no doubt noticed, the s-size of the audience has been gr-gradually diminishing these l-last few weeks."

"Yes, I have noticed that," said Sam. "It's gotten so that they can scarcely see over the edge of the stage."

The jest drew a few halfhearted chuckles from the company at large, and a faint smile from Mr. Heminges. "Thank you, S-Sam, f-for that attempt to introduce a b-bit of levity into the proceedings. But I'm afraid there's n-nothing very amusing about the s-situation. Once we've m-met our expenses, gentlemen"—he lowered his voice a little—"including the p-percentage we g-give to the Cross Keys, there's b-barely enough left over to p-pay your wages. Now, as you m-may also be aware,

M-Mr. Henslowe has raised the pr-price of admission to the F-Fortune Theatre, by a p-penny."

Will Sly gave a low whistle. "That means it'll cost the groundlings twice as much to get in."

"V-very good, Will. We considered f-following his example, but we c-concluded that we would be in d-danger of pricing ourselves out of b-business. I suspect that a g-good half of our audience s-simply could not afford to hand over an extra p-penny just to see a p-play. They have b-better uses for the m-money—such as buying f-food, for example."

"How will we manage, then?" asked Sam.

Mr. Shakespeare answered. "We sharers have agreed to put some of our past profits back into the company, to keep it afloat until warmer weather, when, we trust, the playgoers will return to the Globe in great flocks, like so many swallows."

"An it will help," I said, "I'm willing to forgo me wages for a while."

Sam gave me a sharp poke in the ribs, and a look that said, *Have you gone mad?*

"Thank you, W-Widge," said Mr. Heminges, "but that won't be n-necessary." I thought I heard him add, under his breath, "I hope." I could not be certain, though, for the noise level in the room had escalated as the players began talking animatedly among themselves.

"You nupson!" Sam whispered. "Don't offer to give up money that way! They might ask us all to do the same!"

"I'm sorry. I only wanted to do me part." In truth, I would have given nearly anything—though heaven knew I had little enough to my name, and not even a proper name for that matter—to keep the Lord Chamberlain's Men from ruin. Julia had once said to me, soon after I joined the company, that she would gladly forgo her wages as long as she was allowed to perform. At the time I did not see how a person could want something so much. Now I understood. It was not just about performing; it was about belonging.

It had puzzled me, too, when Julia said that she and I were birds of a feather. I knew now what she meant: that neither of us had ever belonged anywhere before. Though she was not technically an orphan, she might as well have been, for her mother was dead and her father was a common thief with no interest in her beyond what money she could bring in.

Like me, she had found a family in the theatre. Unfortunately membership in that family was limited to men and boys, at least in England. I only hoped that, across the Channel in France, she had managed to make a more permanent place for herself.

Even as I was turning all this over in my mind, our all-male province was invaded by two fair and fashionably dressed young ladies. So finely turned out were they, in fact, that I almost failed to recognize them. But my heart did not; it leaped in my chest. "Judith!" I exclaimed softly.

Sam elbowed me again. "Come now, if you want her attention, you'll have to speak up." But even had I been brave enough to call out to her, I could not have done so, for my breath had deserted me. The company rose as one to greet the girls. "Who's the wench with her?" Sam whispered.

"Mary Mountjoy, the daughter of Mr. Shakespeare's landlord."

Sam pursed his lips appraisingly. "She's even better looking than Mistress Shakespeare."

I stared at him in disbelief. "You truly think so?"

He grinned. "No. I was just trying to get a rise out of you."

"I'm sorry," Judith was saying, "that we couldn't join you all for dinner. We were too busy buying things."

"What sort of things?" Mr. Shakespeare asked, apprehensively.

"Why, our dresses, Father!" Judith lifted the hem of her gown and turned in a slow circle so we might admire it, then gestured to Mistress Mountjoy, who giggled and made a cursory twirl. "And our shoes!" Judith gave us a glimpse of a pair of chopines with soles a good six inches high, designed to keep her skirts from dragging through the mud and slush. "And our billiments!" She patted the satin band, garnished with jewels, that adorned her hair.

Radiating disapproval as a stove does heat, Mr. Shakespeare led his daughter over near the window. But, though the rest of us did our best not to notice them, it was impossible. Over Mr. Armin's voice inviting Mistress Mountjoy to have some fruit and cheese, I could hear Mr. Shakespeare asking how much all their finery had cost, and Judith replying nonchalantly that she wasn't certain but it might have been seven or eight pounds. I nearly choked on my cheese; that was a full year's wages for a prentice.

Mr. Shakespeare sounded nearly as astonished as I was, and considerably more upset. "And how did you manage to pay for it?"

"I asked them to send the bill to you," she said, as though the answer should have been obvious. "They said they were happy to, and were certain you were good for it."

"Then they're far more certain than I am," growled Mr. Shakespeare.

"Oh, Father, you can't expect me to come to London and not buy a few new things for myself."

"I didn't expect you to come to London at all."

Mr. Armin, who had been patiently listening to Mary Mountjoy prattle on, saw that we were eavesdropping. "I'm sorry to cut short our delightful conversation, my dear, but it's time I took these wag-pasties upstairs and put them through their paces."

"Paces?"

Mr. Armin pretended to run her through with an invisible sword, eliciting a burst of giggles. "Sword practice, mademoiselle."

"Oh!" cried Judith from directly behind me. "May we watch, sir?"

I had seldom seen Mr. Armin taken off guard, either by sword or by speech. "Well, I—I—" He looked to Mr. Shakespeare for help. "What do you think, Will?"

Mr. Shakespeare took half a step back, as though he meant to stay out of it. "It's up to you, Rob."

Mr. Armin frowned. "I'm not certain it's such a—"

"We won't be any bother," Judith assured him. "Will we, Mary?"

"No! Not a bit!"

With obvious reluctance, Mr. Armin said, "All right—provided you're quiet and stay out of the way."

Since none of the chambers at the Cross Keys was spacious enough for swordplay, we held our practice sessions in the long gallery, before the stage. As we mounted the stairs, Judith called over her shoulder, "How is your play progressing, Widge?"

I groaned inwardly, knowing what was coming next. Sure enough, Sam spoke up. "His *play?* You're writing a play, Widge?"

I murmured something noncommittal, hoping they would let the subject drop. It was a vain hope. "Hasn't he told you?" Judith said.

"No, he hasn't." Sam gave me a reproachful look, as though hurt that I should tell Judith before him. "What's it about, then?"

"So far, it's about two pages."

"Pages? The sort that wait on nobles, you mean?"

"Nay, the sort you write on."

To my relief, Mr. Armin cut the conversation short by handing us our wooden singlesticks. "Sam, you and Sal square off. Widge, you'll work with me."

Judith and Mary were as good as their word, sitting far up in the two-penny seats, well out of reach of even the most wayward sword thrust. But perhaps it was too much to ask them to be silent as well. No sooner had we begun our practice than they began whispering and tittering behind their hands. I suspected, from their sidelong glances, that we were the source of their amusement.

We did not mean to be amusing. Under Mr. Armin's unforgiving eye, even Sam was on his best behavior—for a time, at least. We prentices had more or less mastered the basic cuts and thrusts—the *stoccata*, the *passata*, the *imbrocata*, the *stramazone*, the *dritta* and *riversa*—and had lately been working on a new move. The *montano* was an underhanded sweep of the sword, designed to catch the opponent's blade from beneath, where his wrist is weakest.

At first, I was painfully self-conscious, afraid of embarrassing myself before Judith. But serious swordplay requires such concentration, such precision, that after half a dozen blows I lost all awareness of being watched—until I heard the sounds of stifled laughter coming from the two-penny seats. I glanced toward the girls, and saw at once the reason for their merriment: Sam's last *montano* had not been quite according to

Caranza, as they say. It ended up not beneath his opponent's sword but between his opponent's legs. Sal Pavy was standing practically on tiptoe, with an extremely worried expression on his face. Sam was giving his singlestick little jerks upward and snarling, "Yield, varlet!"

Something struck my left shoulder painfully, making me cry out. "That is what happens," Mr. Armin said, lowering his weapon, "when you allow yourself to be distracted." He turned to the other two scrimers. "That's enough, Sam."

Sam hung his head. "I was only having a bit of fun."

"Oh? Well, I like a bit of fun myself. Why don't you and I have an amusing bout or two while Widge and Sal blade it out?"

Sam looked as though Mr. Armin had proposed a round of shin-kicking with hobnailed boots. Reluctantly he took my place and I took his.

The girls had gone back to merely whispering. I did my best to ignore them and concentrate on Sal Pavy. He wasted no time in striking the first blow. No doubt he was humiliated by Sam's horseplay and anxious to redeem himself, for he swung his stick much harder than he should have. My weapon went flying.

Angry, I snatched up the stick and delivered a blow that made Sal Pavy draw back. He replied with an edgeblow aimed at my knees. I knocked it aside and, without thinking, gave him a *stoccata* that would have knocked the wind out of him had he not dodged. Even so, it scraped his ribs. He cursed under his breath and swung at me again, harder than before. Without our really meaning it to, our friendly practice had degenerated into a hostile duel.

16

When Sal Pavy first joined the Chamberlain's Men, I had regarded him as a rival for the choicest roles and had naturally resented him. Though I had come to accept him as one of us, there were times when that old enmity welled up unexpectedly, like some intermittent fever that, just when you think you've rid yourself of it, makes you sweat again.

This was one of those times. Though I am not ordinarily a violent sort, I laid on as though I meant to disembowel him at the very least. In truth, I had no wish to harm him, only to show him up, to make him look bad and myself look good.

I was very much aware of the audience now. Judith and Mary called out words of encouragement, though which of us they were aimed at, I could not tell. Mr. Armin was shouting at us, too, and I suspected that his were not words of encouragement. We were too intent on each other to heed him.

Though I hated to admit it, Sal Pavy put up a good defense. Not only did he turn aside my every blow, he answered with several that nearly found their mark. For the first time, I began to wonder whether he might be the one to show me up.

But I knew his weakness. For all his skill at convincing folk that he was charming and a hard worker, when it came to scriming he was a poor deceiver. Each time he made a move, you could see it coming, in his eyes and in the way he set his body. I, on the other hand, was quite good at falsifying—feigning one sort of blow and delivering another.

I started what seemed to be a right edgeblow, deliberately leaving myself open. When Sal Pavy lunged at me, I stepped aside and swung a downright blow that would sorely have cracked his collarbone if it had connected. Luckily for both of us, it did not. It met Mr. Armin's singlestick instead, with a resounding clunk that numbed my forearm.

"If you two wish to kill each other," he said, "there are more efficient ways than with dull wooden swords."

"I'm sorry," I mumbled, rubbing my tingling arm. "I got carried away."

"So I noticed. And if that blow had landed, Sal might have been carried away as well."

I recalled La Voisin's prediction—that I would cause another's death—and a shudder went through me. "I'm sorry," I repeated, so earnestly that my voice cracked.

"I know. It was not entirely your fault."

"Well, it certainly wasn't mine!" put in Sal Pavy.

Mr. Armin gave him a look that said he'd be wise to put his tongue in his purse. Then he turned to Judith and Mary. "Ladies, I must ask you to leave."

Judith bit her lip and folded her hands demurely in her lap. "We'll behave, sir. I promise."

"The problem is not so much *your* behavior as the way you make these poor wights behave. Go on now, before I give you swords and set you to scriming."

"Oh, would you?" Judith exclaimed. "It looks like great fun!"

When they left, I was both disappointed and relieved. I apologized to Sal Pavy for attacking him so fiercely.

"Oh, were you?" he said. "I thought you were going easy on me, so I did the same." One thing about Sal Pavy; he was reliable. If I should ever forget exactly why I had once disliked him so, I could count on him to remind me.

After scriming practice, Sam did a bit more prying about the play. I dared not confess that the whole thing was a fabrication; however solemnly he might swear not to, he would surely let the secret slip out, and then Judith would know me for the liar I was. Besides, I might yet produce a play as promised, if only I could come up with a sensible story.

"So," Sam said, "what's this play of yours called, then?"

My original title, *The Mad Men of Gotham*, had begun to seem irredeemably stupid. I replaced it with the first thing that came to mind: "*Let the World Wag.*"

Sam nodded thoughtfully. "Not bad. A comedy, is it?"

"Aye. But not your usual comedy. It's got ghosts, and revenge, and star-crossed lovers."

"Ah," said Sam. "Sounds hilarious."

As the company stood behind the stage that evening, waiting to go on in *The Spanish Tragedy*, Will Sly said, "I hear you're writing a play."

Thanks to the hubbub from the audience, he probably did not hear the curse I uttered under my breath. "I'm trying," I said.

"I hope there's a part in it for me?"

"Of course." Knowing how fond he was of dashing, romantic roles, I added, "You get to play a leprous beggar."

To my surprise, he replied, "Excellent!" and rubbed his hands together gleefully. "Will I be horribly disfigured, with appendages falling off and such?"

"I was only jesting, Will. There's no leper." I did not bother to mention that neither were there any other characters of any description.

His face fell. "Oh. But you could put in a leper if you wanted, couldn't you? I mean, it's your play."

I sighed. This play was already getting out of hand, and I had yet to write a single word of it. "I'll do me best. I can't promise anything." I took out the small table-book I carried with me and jotted down a new title possibility: *The Leper's Revenge.* What audience could resist that? Well, in one way at least I had the advantage of Mr. Shakespeare—I had no shortage of compelling titles. Perhaps he and I should become collaborators; I could supply the titles, and he could write the scripts to go with them.

Though I was tempted to peek around the curtain to see whether or not Judith was in the audience, I talked myself out of it. I was better off not knowing. That way, I would have no call to be either disappointed or self-conscious.

As it turned out, I was wise to restrain myself. After the performance, Judith came clomping onto the stage in her chopines to congratulate us. She clasped one of my hands in hers; I would have expected them to be warm, but they were cold as a key. "You were very good, Widge. So convincing. If I hadn't known, I never would have suspected you were a boy."

Before I could compose a reply that did not sound half-witted, she had let go of me and latched onto Sal Pavy. "Master Pavy! You were . . . Oh, how shall I put it?"

"Superb?" he suggested.

She laughed. "I was about to say magnificent."

"That's even better." He swept off his wig as though it were a cap and made a small bow. "I thank you for your kind words, and will endeavor to be worthy of them."

"Oh, you are, I assure you! When you were lamenting Horatio's death, I nearly cried."

I could bear no more. I flung open the door and took the outside stairs two at a time, avoiding a broken neck only by grace of the fortune that protects fools, for the steps were coated with ice. I changed quickly and left without waiting for Sam; I had no desire to talk to anyone. Though I had forgotten my cloak, I was so hot with spite and shame that I scarcely noticed the cold.

By the time I reached Mr. Pope's, I had cooled down a bit. When Goody Willingson asked how my day had been, instead of shouting "Utterly miserable!" I replied in a relatively calm voice, "I've had worse." And it was true; I had had worse days—the day my mother died giving birth to me, for instance. The difference was, I couldn't remember that one.

Though I was hardly in a playful mood, I dutifully gave each of the younger boys a ride off to bed on my back, and consented to a game of One Penny Follow Me with the older ones. They seemed not to notice how distracted I was. But Tetty's dark eyes did not miss a thing. "What's wrong, Widge?" she asked as I tucked her in.

"What makes you think there's something wrong?"

"Your face."

"What about it?"

"You know how, when you've twisted your back, you hold it all stiff to keep it from hurting?"

"Aye?"

"That's the way your face looks."

"I'm tired. That's all." And, though it was not all that ailed me, I was indeed weary. But before I could give myself up to sleep, I had to make my nightly report to Mr. Pope.

Once again I skipped over certain selected portions of the day. I said nothing about the play that I was supposed to be writing but was not. Nor did I mention how Judith had been able to spare but a few bland morsels of praise for me, while Sal Pavy received a far more sweet and generous helping than he deserved. Though I was still secretly stewing over the incident, I did not wish to bring it up; it would only make Judith sound heartless and me sound foolish.

I did not expect Mr. Pope to let me off so easily, though, and I was right. When I finished, he said, with a trace of mischief in his voice, "So tell me, how is the fair Judith faring?"

I did my best to sound neutral. "Well enough, I suppose."

He gazed at me over the rim of his wine cup. "You certainly are taken with her, aren't you?"

"What makes you think so?"

"The expression on your face."

This conversation seemed familiar somehow. "What sort of expression?"

"Woeful, for want of a better word. Rather like a puppy who's been chastised for leaving a puddle on the floor."

"There's no call to make fun of me."

"I'm not, lad; I'm not. I'm only commiserating. I remember well enough what it's like to be lovestruck."

"You do?"

Mr. Pope laughed. "You sound as though you don't believe me."

"I didn't mean to. It's just . . . "

"I know. You find it hard to credit, a fat old fulmart like me, eh? But I was young once, and hot-blooded—and not bad to look at, either, if I say so myself."

I narrowed my eyes, trying to see him as he must have been. "You had a lady friend, then?"

"Oh, several. But one in particular. A stout, spirited girl with a smile that could stop your heart—or start it."

"What became of her?"

The wistful smile faded from his broad face. "She and her family disapproved of my profession. They gave me a choice: I could give up acting, or give up her." He sighed. "It was a difficult choice, and there are times when I ask myself whether I chose rightly. Especially now . . . now that I no longer have the company of the audience or of my fellow players to console me."

I had seldom seen him so melancholy. I searched for something to say that might lighten his mood. Before I found it, he drained his cup of clary and pushed his heavy frame from the chair. "Well, that's enough feeling sorry for myself. A fellow has to do a little of it now and again, just to keep from getting too complacent." He made a move to rumple my hair, as I had so often seen him do with the younger boys, but with my crown so closely cropped it did not rumple so much as bristle. "If you want my advice, Widge—and perhaps you do not—I'd advise you not to get too attached to the young lady; I have a feeling she'll be going back to Stratford soon."

I turned to look at him in dismay. "But—but she told her father that she despises it. She said there was no one and nothing there that held the slightest interest for her."

Mr. Pope smiled. "You know, Will once told me the very same thing. But I rather suspect that Judith is less her father's daughter than she is her mother's."

17

In my room, in the few minutes I had left before sleep claimed me, I tried to put my mind to work on the problem of the play, but it stubbornly insisted on bringing up again and again the same unanswered questions: Would Judith stay or go? Who was spying on the Chamberlain's Men, and who was stealing from us, and were they one and the same person? Would the queen recover, and if not, what would become of us?

I shook my head hard. What was the use in dwelling on such questions? They could not be answered, at least not by me. I could only wait and see. With the play, I had more control. I could make the story come out however I wished—provided I had a story—and could decide the fates of all the characters— provided I had characters.

Perhaps where I'd made my mistake was in attempting to write about highborn wights and ladies. Though I had imper- sonated them enough times upon the stage, what did I truly know about them or their problems? I might do better to people my play with the sort of folk I knew at first hand.

Let us say, for example, that the hero is an orphan, and that he's taken in by . . . by a band of players? No, not exciting enough. As Sam said, actors never actually *do* anything; they only pretend to. What, then? A band of lepers? No, too much of a good thing. A band of madmen? Or thieves? Yes, thieves were exciting. And then suppose he falls in love with . . . with someone. With the head thief's beautiful daughter, let us say. Only she's not interested in him, because she's in love with . . . with whom? A poet? No. A soldier? Yes! A soldier who has sworn to bring the band of thieves to justice. The hero knows, then, that he must kill the soldier, not only in order to save his friends, but also in order to get rid of his rival for the girl's affections.

Wait a moment. This was the *hero?* What sort of character would fall in with a lot of thieves in the first place, let alone wish to kill a wight just because he's jealous of him? He didn't sound much like a hero. He sounded, in fact, a good deal like me.

My previous master had been a thief, after all, and had made me into one as well. And I had more than once imagined various unpleasant fates befalling Sal Pavy, my rival for roles and now, it seemed, for Judith's attentions. Though I had never actually tried to kill him—at least not consciously—there was no denying that I was jealous of him.

Well, audiences did not come to the theatre to see the likes of me up there on the stage. I laid my pencil aside and once more fed my efforts to the candle flame. I lulled myself to sleep with promises that I would try again in the morning, when I was more alert.

• • •

But in the light of day—or rather the half-light before dawn—the notion of my writing anything worth reading seemed even more absurd than it had the night before. I made a few half-hearted attempts at ideas, only because I had promised myself I would and did not like to lie to myself. But I came up with nothing very useful, only a couple of new titles: *The Mad Monarch* and *Gamaliel Ratsey, the Masked Highwayman*—the latter inspired by one of the ballad sheets I was using for writing paper.

As I was up anyway, I thought I might as well get an early start at the theatre. After a quick breakfast, I set out for the Cross Keys alone. Sam would only have plagued me with questions I was in no mood to answer, such as how the play was going, or whether I had come into that fortune yet. Even worse, he might propose some harebrained scheme from his seemingly inexhaustible supply—an infallible method of winning the lottery, perhaps, or a plan for me to make Judith jealous by pretending to be in love with Mistress Mountjoy, or a method by which we might snare the costume thief.

It occurred to me then, for the first time, that Sam himself might conceivably be the culprit. No, surely not. Though he might be impudent and unreliable, he was no thief, I was certain of it. And yet . . . and yet, Madame La Voisin had said that he would turn traitor. Was this what she meant? Suppose he truly did have a scheme to win the lottery? Suppose he sold the stolen costumes and bought dozens of chances, meaning to pay the theatre back once he won the big prize?

I laughed aloud at my own folly. Such a story deserved to be burned, along with all the other implausible ones I had concocted. My suspicions had made me feel ashamed, and I quickened my pace, as though to leave them behind. I had another reason for making haste, of course: I had left my cloak at the Cross Keys, and though it was the second week of March, winter was stubbornly hanging on.

I meant to set to work on the property room, but I had forgotten the sharers' decision to keep it locked. I went looking for someone to let me in, and found Mr. Shakespeare in the office he shared with Mr. Heminges, hard at work on his script. Knowing now how much concentration the task required, I would have slipped away without disturbing him. But just then he put down his pen, sat back on his stool, and rubbed at his old injury.

"Shall I do some transcribing for you?" I asked.

He glanced up and, for a change, smiled; the play must be going well for him . . . the lucky wight. "God you good morning, Widge. Thank you for offering, but I'm not composing any lines just yet, only making some notes."

"Oh? I thought you were well into the play by now."

He laughed. "I may be quick, but I'm not *that* quick. I came up with the idea only last night."

"But . . . But two days ago you had half a dozen pages done."

"Oh, you mean the unnamed Roman play. I've given up on that. This is something new, and far more promising." He toyed with his earring reflectively. "But then they all seem that way at first blush, don't they?"

Ordinarily I was comfortable enough around Mr. Shakespeare, but the subject I wished to broach now made me shy as a suitor. "An I might interrupt you for a moment, sir," I said, my voice doing some of its octave shifting, "there's something I'd like to ask."

He gave me a rather suspicious glance. "Does it have anything to do with my daughter?"

"Nay! That is, not directly."

"Good. What is it?"

"Well, I was wondering . . . where do you get your ideas?"

His eyebrows lifted. "My ideas? For plays, you mean?"

"Aye."

He considered the question a moment, then leaned forward and said, in a low voice, "Well, you're not to tell this to anyone, but there's a certain stall at St. Paul's where you can buy them for half a crown—five shillings for really good ones."

I gaped at him. "Truly? Someone *sells* them?" Then I saw the hint of amusement hiding in his eyes, and my face went red. "Oh. You're tweaking me."

"Of course. Would that it were that simple. The truth is, I have no idea where they come from, or why. Sometimes they seem to rain down upon you from out of the ether. Other times, it's as though a drought has descended, and everything dries up, including your brain. When that happens . . . " He shrugged. "The only thing left to do is to steal from someone else."

I was taken aback for a moment, before I concluded that he was jesting again. "Nay, you'll not fool me again. I ken you don't mean that."

"But I do, Widge." He gestured at the pages of his abandoned script, which were crammed into a compartment at the back of the desk. "Take the story of Timon, for example. I found it in Plutarch's 'Life of Antony.' Come, now; you needn't look so dismayed. Don't you know that there are no new ideas in the world? Every story has been told—and lived—a hundred times before. The best we can hope for is to find some new way of telling them." He rubbed at his forearm again. "Now it's my turn to ask you something."

"All right."

"What do you care where I get my ideas?"

I had known from the moment I broached the subject that I would end up telling him about my own poor efforts at playwriting. But how could I, without sounding hopelessly naive and foolish? "I, um . . . that is . . . I'm attempting to, um . . . "

"To write a play?" he suggested.

"Aye. How did you ken?"

"It's no secret. You seem to have told everyone else in the company. I was wondering when you would get around to telling me."

"Actually, I told but one person."

He nodded knowingly. "Sam, I've no doubt."

"Nay. I told your daughter."

Mr. Shakespeare's expression changed from merely knowing to truly understanding. "Ah. I see. And now that you've told her, she insists upon reading it."

"Aye."

"Is there anything for her to read?"

I grimaced. "Oh, Lord, sir."

"Nothing at all?"

"Does a title count?"

"Well, it's a start. In fact, it's more than I ordinarily have to work with. What is it?"

"In truth," I said, "I've quite a number of them."

"Oh. Do you have a story or a premise of any sort in mind?"

"I've a number of those, too, all of them equally . . . what was the word you used? Putrid, that's it."

Mr. Shakespeare twisted his earring between his fingers. "Well, you know, Widge, if all you really need is something to show Judith, I have approximately two-fifths of a play I'd be happy to give you, just to be rid of it."

"You mean . . . the play wi'out a name?"

"Yes. The Roman play, that is. Not this one." He picked up the pages he'd been working on, and waved them. "This one has no name yet, either."

"You'd truly be willing to let me ha' what you've written?"

He shrugged. "I'm certain I'll never finish it. Perhaps you will, eh? Besides . . . " He leaned toward me again and said, sotto voce, "We men must stick together and help one another, else the ladies will always have the advantage of us." Mr. Shakespeare plucked the abandoned script from its compartment. "There you are. Do with it what you will." Before I could even thank him, he went on. "By the by, Ben Jonson informs me that he's finished censoring *Sejanus*, and will have it to us in a day or two. I'd like you to make a clean draft of it and write out the sides for the actors. I'm sure Sal and Sam can manage without your help for a few mornings."

"Aye, all right. That reminds me—I came to ask for the key to the property room so I might get started on 't."

Mr. Shakespeare looked uncomfortable. "I'm sorry, Widge. I'm afraid we'll have to wait until someone is here to oversee you. You mustn't think that I mistrust you. It's just that . . . "

I nodded. "I ken. It's the rule."

"Yes. Unfortunately." He took a ring of keys from his wallet. "I would like you to have a key to this room, though, so you have a place to work on Mr. Jonson's script." He gave me the key, and a conspiratorial smile. "And your own, of course. I wouldn't show it to Judith in its present form; she would recognize my abominable hand at once."

"Will she not recognize your words as well?"

"I doubt it. It's hardly my best writing. She'll probably just think you're imitating me."

18

All through the morning and the afternoon I was so occupied with the usual round of tasks that I had no chance to begin disguising Mr. Shakespeare's words as my own. It hardly mattered, though. Judith did not appear until dinner, and then she was too busy being the center of everyone's attention to say much to me, let alone inquire about my play.

Sam was one of the few members of the company who did not seem to care much what Judith had been up to all day. He was more interested in conversing with Mr. Garrett. I was concentrating on Judith and did not hear much of what Mr. Garrett was saying. Whatever it was, it held Sam spellbound. As we reluctantly followed Mr. Armin upstairs for scriming practice, I said, "What were you and Mr. Garrett going on about?"

"He was telling me more of his adventures in France, and Holland, and elsewhere."

"'A's certainly been a lot of places. Was 'a a soldier, do you wis?"

"No, I don't think so. He was just traveling about, having adventures, I guess." Sam caught me by the sleeve and whispered eagerly, "He says that perhaps one day, if he returns to the Continent, he'll take me with him."

I stared at him. "You'd truly be willing to give up the theatre?"

"Wouldn't you, if it meant a chance to see the world?"

I considered this for all of several seconds. "Nay," I said. "This is world enough for me."

Mr. Garrett continued to join us regularly for meals and card-playing. But, though he contributed much to the conversation, it was always information of a general sort; he seldom revealed anything of any consequence about himself. Aside from his own past, the one topic he carefully avoided was religion. When Ned Shakespeare asked his opinon on the question of whether Walter Ralegh, once the queen's favorite, was an atheist or merely a skeptic, Mr. Garrett replied, "My opinion, sir, is that gentlemen should not discuss matters of theology."

Though the man's tone was perfectly cordial, Ned reacted as though he'd been rebuked. "And it is *my* opinion, sir, that a gentleman should not be afraid to speak his mind on any matter, unless he has something to conceal."

Mr. Garrett seemed unperturbed. "Do you not suppose that everyone at this table—perhaps everyone everywhere—has some topic he would just as soon not touch upon?" He regarded Ned steadily with those unnerving coal-black eyes. "You, for example. Is there not some part of your life that you would prefer to keep to yourself?"

Ned could not meet the man's gaze. "That is not your business."

Mr. Garrett turned his palms upward as though to say he had proven his point. "You're quite right. As I believe your brother put it, a gentleman's business is his own."

Later, as the troupe was dispersing, each man to his own task, Judith approached me and Sam. "Master Pavy has graciously offered to show me the city this Sunday, after church services. I was hoping you two would come along. We could have a fine time, the four of us."

"It sounds good to me," said Sam.

It did not to me. It sounded like the worst idea I had ever heard. Though I wanted to protest that we could have a far finer time if there were but two of us, I kept sullenly silent.

"Widge?" said Judith. "You'll come with us, will you not?"

As an actor, I had learned that if you cannot play the leading role, the next best thing is to be a martyr—some character who faces his or her tragic fate with such dignity as to wring a tear from the audience's eye. "I'm sorry," I replied, in my most dignified voice, "I must work on my play, you know." The artist who suffers for his art—there was a role guaranteed to win her sympathy. I had even remembered to say "my" and "know," and thus avoided sounding quaint.

My speech did not have quite the effect I had intended. Judith pressed her petal-like lips together in a look of exasperation. "I might have known."

"What's wrong?"

"Oh, nothing. Nothing at all." She turned to Sam, suddenly smiling again. "We're meeting outside St. Olave's as soon as services are over."

As we headed upstairs, Sam said to me, "Don't think I don't know why you're not coming."

"I explained why."

"Much! That's not the reason. The reason is, you'd rather have her all to yourself. Am I right?"

"Nay! It's as I said—I need the time to work on me play."

"Well, even if that's true, I don't believe I'd have told her so."

"Why not?"

"Because, you noddy, I'll wager she's heard that very excuse from her father a hundred times, at least."

Though I longed to return to Judith's good graces, I knew I would never accomplish it by tramping about London with her in the company of Sam and Sal Pavy. I did not need Madame La Voisin to predict what would happen. I would be sulky and resentful, and then Sam would poke fun at me, and then I would grow angry. Though playing the martyr had not worked so well, it was better than playing the fool.

I made up my mind then that I would show them. I would make good on what had, until now, been no more than an empty boast: I would write a play, and it would be good, and it would be produced, and profitable, and praised, and then let them dare to make fun of me.

It should not be such a difficult task. After all, I had two-fifths of the script written already, and I hadn't even begun. As far as I knew, there were no ghosts or lepers in it, or even lovers, but it did have folk ranting about their money problems, and that surely was something everyone could relate to. So fierce was my resolve that if I could have, I would have set to work at once. But of course there was scriming practice, and then singing practice, and then a performance.

By the time I reached my room that night, after playing with the boys, tucking Tetty in, and reporting to Mr. Pope, my eagerness to work on the play had faded considerably. Nevertheless, I forced myself to the table and not the bed. I unrolled the script, set various objects upon it to keep it flat, and began to copy it in my own hand on a clean sheet of paper.

ACT I
Scene I: Rome. A Hall in Timon's House

Well, that was no good. Setting the play in Italy was like sending an engraved invitation to the queen's Privy Council, begging to be investigated. I crossed out *Rome* and, after a moment's thought, wrote in *Athens*. That was innocuous enough. The Greeks didn't even have a God, let alone a pope. I would have to find replacements for all those Roman-sounding names as well, but that could wait.

The first scene was a bit slow compared to *Hamlet*, which starts right out with a ghost. But there were several speeches that were worthy of Mr. Shakespeare, particularly those of Apemantus, a sarcastic, unpleasant wight who rather put me in mind of Sal Pavy. Well, I'd have to see to it that he was given the role. Buoyed by a wave of optimism, I transcribed the entire first scene. I changed almost nothing, aside from substituting *Athenian* wherever it said *Roman*.

When I reached Scene Two, however, my heart sank. I didn't know what acting company Mr. Shakespeare had in mind, but it must have been one considerably larger than the Lord Chamberlain's Men. There were at least eight Roman nobles—make that *Athenian* nobles—in the scene, each with several attendants. As though that wasn't impossible enough, an actor playing Cupid came on, accompanied by "a masque of Ladies as Amazons, with lutes in their hands, dancing and playing." Of course, we often met the demands of a large cast by playing several roles apiece—but generally not all at the same time.

I sighed wearily. Obviously I would have to do more with this scene than just copy it out. It would have to wait, however, until I could hold my eyes open.

In the morning, I set to work afresh and managed to dispense with about half the original cast before Sam called for me. "You look as though you've hardly slept a wink," he said. "I've heard that's a common plight among those tormented by love."

"It was the Muse that tormented me," I replied haughtily.

"Mews?" said Sam, feigning puzzlement. "Has Mr. Pope begun taking in orphaned cats as well?"

I gave him a disdainful look. "I would not expect you to understand. You have never experienced the throes of poetic creation."

"You're right. And if it turns a person into a total goosecap, I hope I never do." I pretended to ignore his unkind remark. After a while he said casually, "So, is there a good role for me in this play of yours?"

"Oh, aye. In fact, I've written a part especially for you."

"Really? What sort of part is it?"

"Cupid."

He stared at me incredulously. "*Cupid?*"

"Well, I thought it only fitting," I said, "as you seem to ken so much about love."

When we entered the courtyard of the Cross Keys, I caught sight of an unsavory-looking man in a dirty, seam-rent tunic standing outside the dark parlor with his face pressed to the window. Despite the cold, he wore no cloak, only a woolen scarf wrapped about his neck. All the talk I had heard of late about theft and spying had made me uneasy, and my hand went to the handle of my dagger. "Do you ken that wight?" I whispered to Sam.

"No. And I don't think I care to."

The stranger did not appear to be armed, which gave me the courage to call sternly to him, "You, there!"

He whirled about, a startled scowl upon his face. One hand reached inside his tunic, as though to retrieve a weapon. Then, apparently seeing no threat in us, he relaxed and his manner changed abruptly from menacing to ingratiating. "Good morning to you, young sirs. Might you by any chance be associated with the folk that put on the plays here?" His lower-class London accent was so thick that I understood only about half the words, but it was enough to catch his meaning.

"Ha' you some sort of business wi' them?"

"I do. Could you tell me where to find the gentleman in charge?"

Still wary, I replied, "I can carry a message to him, and ask whether or not 'a wishes to see you."

The man's friendly facade slipped a little. "Oh, he'll wish to, right enough. Tell him . . . " The stranger paused and, eyes narrowed, searched my face carefully. "Here, I know you. You're the lad that was so thick with Julia, ain't you?"

For a moment I was struck speechless by this unexpected reference to my old friend. "You—you ken Julia?"

He grinned, revealing a row of rotten teeth. "I should think I do," he said. "I'm her da."

19

Julia had mentioned her father a time or two, in rather contemptuous terms, but until now I had not set eyes upon the man. I saw no hint of a family resemblance. Though Julia had been gone more than a year, I could picture her perfectly. She was tall for a girl, with auburn hair, brown eyes, and the ruddy coloring common to folk of a sanguine humor. This fellow looked more like the choleric sort, with his sallow, yellowish skin and his blue eyes, so pale as to be nearly colorless. His hair and beard, had they been washed, might have proven to be a light brown. He was short of stature, and his frame was as slight as mine.

"Is she well, do you ken?" I asked. "I haven't heard from her in some time."

"Oh, she's healthy enough, if that's what you mean. But she's in a bit of a whipper just now."

"A *whipper?*" said Sam.

"You know, a plight. A tight spot. That's what I've come to see your masters about."

"What sort of plight?" I asked anxiously.

"Well, now, why don't you just take me to whoever's in charge here, eh? That way I won't have to say it all twice."

"Aye, all right. Sam, go ahead and start on the tiring-room."

"I want to hear about Julia's whipper," he protested.

"I'll gi' you all the details later." As I led Julia's father up the outer stairs, I said, "How is 't that you kenned who I was?"

"I seen you and her together. I never said nothing. She didn't fancy me coming 'round the theatre, or talking to any of her actor friends. She wouldn't want me coming here even now, I expect. She's always hated asking anybody for aught." He gave me that rotten grin again. "I don't know where she gets that. It's never bothered me."

"No, I suppose not." From what Julia had told me, he certainly did not hesitate to accept anything from anyone—usually without their knowledge or permission. Both Mr. Heminges and Mr. Shakespeare were in the office, one setting down columns of figures, the other lines of dialogue. "Excuse me, sir," I said softly to Mr. Heminges. "There's a wight here to see you."

"Oh? Wh-what sort of wight?"

"Julia's father, actually."

Mr. Heminges rose to greet the stranger. "I d-don't believe we've m-met, sir. John Heminges, the c-company manager."

Julia's father ignored the hand that Mr. Heminges offered. He pulled his scarf up under his chin, even though the room was warm, and looked about rather furtively; obviously he was not used to such surroundings, modest though they were. His manner was a curious mixture of sullen and obsequious, as though he recognized that he was not on the same social level as these men, but at the same time resented it.

"And your n-name, sir?" Mr. Heminges prompted him.

"It's Cogan. Tom Cogan."

"Of c-course. W-would you like to sit down?"

"No. This won't take much time. The long and short of it is, the girl's in trouble over there in France, and needs money to get home."

"Tr-trouble? N-nothing serious, I hope?"

Cogan drew a worn leather pouch from his grimy tunic and fished from it a sheet of paper folded into a small square. "Here's what she sent. I had a fellow read it to me, but I don't recollect it all." As he passed the paper to Mr. Heminges, he held the scarf in place with his other hand, as though afraid of catching a chill. "Read it for yourself."

"Aloud, if you will," said Mr. Shakespeare.

Mr. Heminges unfolded the paper and read its contents in the same way he spoke upon the stage—with no trace of a stutter. "She writes, 'Father. You will no doubt be astonished to hear anything of any sort from me, least of all a plea for help. However, I have no one else to turn to, and whatever our feelings toward each other, we are bound together by blood. For reasons I cannot go into here, I have had to leave Monsieur Lefèvre's acting company, and quit my lodgings as well.

" 'I have found a shabby sleeping room that costs only a few francs, and is worth far less, but I have been unable to find any sort of work that is respectable, and the little money I have saved is quickly disappearing.

" 'I know that it is unfair of me, after having nothing to do with you for so long, to ask you now for aid, but if there is any way you can send me three pounds to pay my passage home, I would be most grateful. If you cannot . . . Well, at the risk of sounding overly dramatic, I honestly do not know what will become of me.'" Mr. Heminges returned the paper to Cogan. "I assume th-that you intend to send her the m-money?"

"O' course I do! What do you take me for?"

"I m-meant no insult. Three p-pounds is a substantial sum, though. How m-much have you r-raised?"

"Not a gray groat," Cogan cheerfully admitted. "I'm out of work myself just now, you see. I was hoping you gentlemen might see your way clear to put up the money, considering she was a prentice here, and all."

Mr. Heminges exchanged glances with Mr. Shakespeare. "We will need to discuss this privately," said Mr. Shakespeare. "Widge, will you wait outside with Mr. Cogan, please?"

I wanted to ask them what there was to discuss. I wanted to point out that the amount neeeded to rescue Julia was less than half of what Judith had so casually spent on a gown and a pair of shoes. But I said nothing, only showed Tom Cogan into the hallway.

Once he was out of the room, all trace of obsequiousness vanished, and the sullenness took over. "You'd think they'd just hand it over. Three pounds is nothing for the likes of them."

I was inclined to agree. Though the company was having financial troubles of late, I was certain that most of the sharers were well-off, if not wealthy. Mr. Pope, with all the mouths he had to feed, was the exception.

After only a minute or so, Mr. Heminges called us in. "W-we would like to help J-Julia, of course," he said. "If she tr-truly is in trouble."

"What d'you mean *if?*" Cogan said. "You seen the letter!"

"But how can we be sure it's genuine?" said Mr. Shakespeare.

Cogan gave a derisive laugh. "D'you suppose I wrote it myself?"

"Of course not. But you might have had someone write it for you."

"For what purpose?"

"For the purpose of prying money out of us, perhaps."

Cogan stepped toward him, a threatening look on his face. "Here! Are you calling me a thief?"

"I don't believe I need to," Mr. Shakespeare said calmly. "*That* says it plainly enough." I followed his gaze. The scarf Cogan had kept wrapped so carefully around his neck had loosened, revealing a vivid patch of scar tissue in the shape of a *T*—the mark of a man who has been branded by the law.

Cogan pushed the scarf back into place. "That happened a long while ago. All I took was some bread, to feed my wife and my daughter."

"Really?" said Mr. Shakespeare. "I've never heard of a man being branded for stealing bread."

"Might I look at the letter?" I put in. "I've seen Julia's hand enough times to recognize it." Cogan held out the paper. "It's from her, right enough," I said.

"There, you see?" said Cogan triumphantly.

"All the same," said Mr. Shakespeare, "if we turned over three pounds to you, what reason do we have to believe that it would ever reach her?"

"She's my *daughter*, that's what reason!"

"You've n-never shown m-much concern for her welfare in the p-past," Mr. Heminges pointed out.

"So you'll not give me the money, is that it?" Neither man replied. Cogan stared at them fiercely for a moment, as though he were considering demanding the money at the point of a knife. Then he said disdainfully, "I might have known I'd get no help from you lot. It was you that brought this on her to begin with. If you'd let her stay on here, she'd never have had to go to France." He strode to the door and flung it open. "You know, if I'd been smart, I wouldn't have come here; I'd have met you in a dark alley somewhere. You'd have handed over the money then, I'll wager."

Dismayed, I watched him leave, then turned to Mr. Shakespeare. "You're not going to help Julia at all, then?"

"You know as well as I that if we handed the money over to her father, she would never see a penny of it."

No doubt he was right; Cogan was a thief, after all. But I couldn't help feeling that the sharers were more concerned about the fate of their money than about Julia's fate.

"P-perhaps we can f-find some other way of helping her," Mr. Heminges said. He tried to put a comforting hand on my shoulder, but I pulled away.

"How *can* we, when we don't even know where to find her?" I hurried out, hoping to catch up with Cogan and learn where Julia could be reached. I scrambled down the stairs, across the courtyard, and into the street. There was no sign of him in any direction. I started walking west at a rapid pace, thinking he might be headed for Alsatia, the foul and fearsome precinct that was claimed by the city's criminal class as a sort of sanctuary. I knew that Julia had once lived there; perhaps her father still did.

After a quarter of an hour I was forced to conclude that either he walked far faster than I or he had gone some other way. As I reluctantly headed back to the Cross Keys, I set myself to thinking about how I might help Julia.

It was clear that, for whatever reason, she had not wanted me or the company to know of her plight. Otherwise she would surely have written to us, not to her father. But now that we did know, we could not sit by and do nothing—or at least I could not. Though she was far off in France, I still considered her my nearest friend. If the sharers would not rescue her, then it was up to me.

The problem was, of course, that I hadn't three shillings, let alone three pounds. If only I had saved my wages all these months, instead of throwing so much away on things of no consequence. Some of my purchases, such as sweetmeats and stockings for Mr. Pope's orphan boys, I did not regret. But why had I wasted one penny after another having my future read while Julia's future hung in the balance?

There must be some way I could raise the money. I could not ask Mr. Pope for it, at least not all of it. The cost of running so large a household left him with little to spare, even in the best of times.

Sam would no doubt advise me to buy a chance in the lottery, but that was about as reliable as one of La Voisin's predictions. Though there was a slim possibility that I might win something eventually, there was no way of knowing how much, or when. I needed three pounds, and I needed it now.

There were always dishonest means, of course. According to Sam, one costume from the company's trunks might be worth several pounds. But the tiring-room was closely guarded these days. In any case, however angry I might be at the sharers, I could not have brought myself to steal from them.

I was certain that Tom Cogan had no such scruples. Why had he not simply gotten the money through his usual methods, then, instead of coming to us? Perhaps it was just too large a sum. No ordinary tradesman, and few gentlemen, carried about a purse that fat. Cogan would have had to hold up the lord mayor himself.

I would gladly have sold everything I owned to help Julia, but there was nothing among my paltry possessions that would fetch more than a farthing. Or was there?

A good play was a fairly valuable commodity. After all, I had been brought to London for the express purpose of stealing one. I wasn't certain just how much a playwright could expect for his work. Sam once told me that Mr. Shakespeare got twenty pounds per script, but then Sam was known to exaggerate.

In any case, no one in his right mind would pay twenty pounds for a script by an unknown apprentice player, no matter how good it was, unless . . . unless perhaps I put Mr. Shakespeare's name on it as coauthor. No, it would be unfair to trade on his reputation that way. But when he gave me the play, he clearly said that I might do with it as I wished. So I could in good conscience claim it as my own. With any luck, I might sell it for a couple of pounds—provided, of course, I could finish it.

As Hamlet would say, "Aye, there's the rub." I vowed that I would renew and redouble my efforts that evening, and make as quick work of it as I could. Then all that would remain was to find Cogan. Ah, well; compared to writing a decent play, venturing into a den of desperate criminals and convincing them to reveal the whereabouts of one of their own should be a lark. In the meantime, I was wanted at rehearsal.

To my relief, Judith did not attend. She had not been at our performance the night before, either. Whatever interest the theatre had held for her seemed to be fading.

Though I tried hard to give my full attention to my lines, Julia's plight weighed heavily on my mind, and I made nearly as many blunders as I had with Judith watching. The rehearsal seemed interminable.

When Mr. Heminges entered the room, I gave a silent sigh of relief, thinking that he had come to summon us to dinner. Then I saw that he was not alone. Four unfamiliar figures appeared at the top of the stairs. Three of them were guardsmen, clad in metal breastplates and helmets and armed with the combination of ax and spear that is called a halberd. The fourth was a tall, gaunt fellow who wore the garb of a gentleman. The man's eyes surveyed the room, searching the face of each player in turn, as though he was seeking someone in particular. Clearly, whoever he sought was not among us. He scowled and, turning abruptly, headed back down the stairs with the guards close behind him.

When they were gone, we gathered around Mr. Heminges, who looked uncharacteristically grim. "What did that lot want?" asked Sam.

"They were p-pursuivants," said Mr. Heminges.

"I beg your pardon?" said Sam.

"Pr-priest hunters."

Sam laughed. "And they expected to find one in a company of players?"

"Ap-parently so. It would s-seem that the man who calls himself G-Garrett is, in fact, F-Father Gerard—a J-Jesuit priest."

20

We were all of us momentarily struck dumb by this revelation. Though it had been clear all along that Garrett was hiding something, I doubt that anyone suspected what it was. Neither his appearance nor his behavior was the sort one expected from a priest. There was nothing remotely spiritual about him; on the contrary, he was clearly well versed in the ways of the world. And yet someone must have guessed his secret, in order to give it away.

Sam broke the stunned silence. "God precious potstick!" he breathed. "A priest!"

"Ha' the priest hunters looked downstairs?" I asked.

Mr. Heminges nodded. "G-Garrett—or sh-should I say Gerard?—has not t-turned up yet. He m-may be on his way, however."

"We must warn him!" said Sam.

"Why?" put in Sal Pavy. "Let them catch the mass-monger."

141

Sam cast him a venomous look. "Do you know what they *do* to priests?"

"I'll try to head him off," I said.

"G-good lad. You kn-know where he's staying?"

"Aye."

"Well, what are you waiting for?" exclaimed Sam. "Move your bones!"

I slipped down the outer stairs and hurried along Grace-church Street, toward the river. Mr. Shakespeare had said that Garrett—that is, Gerard—was lodging with Ben Jonson, and I knew that the playwright had lately taken up residence in the palatial house of his patron and fellow Papist, Sir Thomas Townshend, on the Strand.

I was nearly to Sir Thomas's house when I saw Gerard approaching along the Strand. I called to him and he raised a hand in greeting. Then he reached inside his cloak, produced a sheaf of papers bound with string, and waved it at me. "Jonson's play. He's laid up with a cough and a fever, and asked me to—"

"Never mind that! I've come to warn you! There's a band of priest hunters at the Cross Keys!"

He did not seem distressed by this, only resigned, as though he had expected it. "So you know my secret, then?"

"Aye."

Taking my arm, he led me across the street and down a nar-row alley. "We'd best stay out of sight. They may come here looking for me."

"No one will tell them where to find you."

"I wouldn't think so. But then I wouldn't have thought that anyone would betray me to the pursuivants in the first place."

"It could not ha' been one of the Chamberlain's Men, surely; none of us kenned you were a priest."

"Judith knew, and she may have let it slip. It's also possible that Ned Shakespeare knew."

"How could he?"

"For the past several years I've been traveling about the Midlands, saying Mass in secret for those of the old faith and ministering to the dying. One of those to whom I gave the last rites was John Shakespeare—Ned and Will's father."

"And Ned was still in Stratford then?"

Father Gerard nodded. "Well, there's little use in speculating about who's responsible. I knew I'd be found out sooner or later."

"Why did you come to London, then? Why did you not stay up north?"

"There are priest hunters there as well. Besides, my superiors felt I was needed here."

"To do what?"

"I have two missions. One is to convince young men to join the Society of Jesus." He gave me a sly look. "Interested?"

I laughed. "I mean to be a player, not a priest."

"Well, you can't fault me for trying. My other mission is to save the souls of prisoners."

"You actually go into *prisons?* Isn't that like sticking your costard i' the lion's mouth?"

"It is risky, yes. But I pose as a physician, and I pay the warders enough so they're willing to look the other way." He halted and placed a hand on my shoulder. "I want to thank you for coming to warn me. It was a brave thing."

"I couldn't let you be caught. You haven't done anything wrong." A bit uncertainly, I added, "Ha' you?"

"No." He smiled wryly. "Aside from being a traitor to the Crown, of course."

"Well, I should be getting back." I glanced about me. We had made several turns, and I was not entirely sure where the Cross Keys lay. "Assuming I can find me way, that is."

Gerard pointed to his left. "You'll want to head in that direction. But before you go, there's something I must tell you. I'm sorry for not bringing it up sooner, but I had to be certain I could trust you."

"Trust me?"

"As you will see, I couldn't very well reveal this without also revealing my profession." He paused, as though to collect his thoughts, then went on. "Several months ago, when I was holding services in Leicester, I was called to a tavern outside the town, to give the last rites to a thief who had been shot while trying to rob a wealthy merchant. Before he died, we had a chance to talk. When I mentioned that I was going to London soon, he asked if I would contact his son, who, he said, was a player . . . with Mr. Shakespeare's company." Gerard fixed his black eyes on me. "He seemed quite proud of the fact."

With the little breath I could muster, I said, "What . . . what was this fellow's name, then?"

I suspected what his reply would be, and I was right. "Jamie Redshaw," he said.

From time to time, some small-minded critic took Mr. Shakespeare to task because so many of his plays were neither strictly tragedy nor strictly comedy, but a mingle-mangle of the two. Mr. Shakespeare seemed unperturbed by such accusations. He was, he said, merely trying to reflect the nature of real life, which was invariably a mixture of the awful and the absurd— hilarity one moment, heartbreak the next, and sometimes both at once.

My situation proved his point. All my life I had longed to know who my parents were. Now that I had been given the final piece of the puzzle, I should have been overjoyed. But how could I be, when, at the very moment I learned at last who my father was, I also discovered that he was dead?

I was stricken not so much by grief as by a sad sense of regret. As the circumstances of his death showed, Jamie Redshaw had not been the most admirable of men. Yet he had possessed admirable qualities—among them courage and cleverness. Who could say what he might have become had Fortune dealt him a better hand? If he and my mother had not been kept apart by her parents, his life would no doubt have been quite different. And so, of course, would mine.

"I'm sorry," said Father Gerard, "that I was unable to save his life. The wound was too grave. But the fate of our earthly body matters little when compared to the fate of the soul. Be assured that he has gone to a better life."

"I hope so, for the one 'a had here was naught to boast of."

Gerard placed the script of *Sejanus* in my hands. "You should go. If they do find me, I don't want you implicated."

"You'll leave London now, surely?"

He shook his head. "Not for a while yet."

"But where will you stay?"

"I'll find a place. There are a number of the faithful here who are willing to put their lives in jeopardy by sheltering us. Go now."

When I returned to the Cross Keys, dinner was over, but the sharers were still sitting about the table with grim looks on their faces, talking in low, somber voices. They all seemed relieved to see me. "Widge!" said Mr. Armin. "Thank heaven you're all right. I was afraid the pursuivants might catch Gerard, and you with him."

"Nay. We saw no sign of 'em." I took a seat and scavenged what few morsels were left.

"G-good," said Mr. Heminges. "I wish the m-man no ill, even though he has c-caused us a good d-deal of trouble."

"Will they shut us down for harboring a priest, do you wis?"

"It's doubtful," said Mr. Shakespeare, "at least as long as we have the queen's protection." He sighed heavily and put his head in his hands. "I apologize to you all for my part in this. If I had known he was a priest, I would not have agreed to help him. Judith led me to believe that he was a recusant from Warwickshire who had refused to pay his fines and was forced to flee to avoid being imprisoned. She also said that he had been a friend to my father, at a time when my father had few others."

"Well, that much was true," I said. " 'A told me that when your father was ill, 'a tended him and gave him the last rites." I glanced about the room. "Where is Judith now?"

Mr. Shakespeare sighed again. "I'm not certain. We . . . we had words, and she ran off." He glanced down at the script of *Sejanus*, which lay on the bench next to me. "Where did that come from?"

"Father Gerard was on his way to deliver 't to us. Mr. Jonson is laid up wi' th' ague."

"You may as well set to work on it, then. For the moment, anyway, we're still in business."

I popped a boiled egg in my mouth and headed upstairs. When I entered the office, I found Judith sitting on the floor next to the windows, her legs drawn up, her face buried in the folds of her gown, weeping as though she had lost her only friend. I had experienced that sort of grief once, when Sander died, and feared that I might again, if I could not bring Julia home.

Judith had not actually lost a friend, of course; she was upset because Mr. Shakespeare had reprimanded her—rather harshly, no doubt, and in front of the entire company. I knew how that felt as well. Though I had little experience in comforting folk, I did my best. I knelt and laid a hand gently on her arm. "Please don't cry. It's not so bad, really."

She turned her tear-streaked face toward me; though her eyes were red and swollen from weeping, her fair skin mottled, she somehow contrived to look more appealing than ever. Mr. Pope had known a lady, he said, who could stop a man's heart with her smile. Here was one who could do it with her tears. "Yes, it is," she said, her words broken by sobs. "It *is* bad. I'm being sent home."

21

Stricken, I sank to the floor next to Judith. "Oh, gis! I suppose 'a has a right to be angry wi' you, but to send you home . . . Is there any chance 'a will change his mind, do you wis?"

Judith gave a trembling, bitter laugh. "You don't know my father very well. Once he's made up his mind to something, there's no changing it. He never wanted me here to begin with."

"I'm sure that's not so," I lied. "Anyway, surely 'a won't just pack you off on your own. 'A will ha' to find someone to travel wi' you." Had it not been for the unfinished business with Julia, I would have volunteered my services.

She wiped her eyes with the hem of her gown. "Yes, I suppose you're right. Perhaps it will be a while, then, before he can make the arrangements."

"Aye, it might be weeks—months, even." I did my best to sound confident and cheerful, though I felt quite the contrary. It was not enough that I must see to it that Julia got home; now I had to try to make certain that Judith did not.

I suddenly felt quite overwhelmed by it all. If love was difficult to play upon the stage, it was even harder to manage in earnest. I needed a respite from it; I needed to throw myself into some task that would make no demands on my mind or my emotions. "Listen. I really must get to work on this play."

"Oh. Well. If you'd rather do that than talk to me."

"It's not that, it's just—"

"I know, I know. I've heard it all before." She rose and straightened her gown. "You did promise to read some of it to me, though."

"Nay, it's not *that* play. It's Mr. Jonson's. Your father's asked me to copy it out."

"Well, then, of course you must do it. We must all do as Father says, mustn't we?" She examined her face in the small looking glass Mr. Shakespeare used for his makeup and rubbed at her cheeks with a kerchief. "You needn't feel too sorry for yourself, Widge, for never having had a father. They're a mixed blessing at best." As she went out the door, she whispered archly, "Have fun with your *play*." Her tone made it clear that she considered it just that—play, not work. Whatever it was, I was grateful to occupy myself with such an undemanding task.

According to rumor, one of the priest hunters' favorite methods of extracting a confession was a procedure known as *peine forte et dure*, in which a slab of stone is placed upon the chest of the reclining victim; the next day a second slab is added, then a third, and so on, until the subject either gives up the desired information or gives up the ghost.

Though I had so far been spared the slabs of stone, for the past week or so Fortune had been busy laying troubles upon me, one by one, until I felt at times as though I could not breathe. I had no notion, however, what I was expected to confess. All I could do was try to ignore the growing pressure by turning my mind to other things.

I had copied out no more than half a dozen pages of *Sejanus* before I was interrupted by a breathless, perspiring Sam, fresh from scriming practice. "Well?" he demanded.

I glanced up irritably. "Well, what?"

"Did you manage to warn Mr. Garrett in time?"

"Father Gerard, you mean."

"Yes, yes. Did you?"

"Aye."

Sam gave a relieved grin. "Thank heaven."

"You might wish to thank *me* as well."

"Thanks. He's not leaving London, is he?"

"Not for a while yet, 'a says. But 'a's not likely to come around here again."

"Oh, bones. I suppose not. Do you know where he's staying?"

"Nay. And I wouldn't go looking for him an I were you. Priests are dangerous company."

Sam scowled at me. "Will you stop it?"

"Stop what?"

"Playing the older brother." He rose and started from the room, then turned back to say, "Mr. Garrett's my friend, Widge; I'm not going to forget about him just because he happens to be a Papist."

That evening we performed *All's Well That Ends Well* again. I knew the play backward and forward and so was able to lose myself in it, as in a dream, and give no thought to anything. Julia had never acted in the play, so there was nothing in it to remind me of her, and since Judith did not turn up, I was even able to forget about her for moments at a time.

Ordinarily I looked forward to my time with Mr. Pope at the end of each day. But tonight I felt rather as though I were headed for a session of *peine forte et dure*, in which all the doubts and worries I had tried so hard to suppress would be squeezed out of me. Though it would have been a relief to unburden myself to someone, I dared not make Mr. Pope my confessor; we had been instructed not to bring up anything that might upset him.

When I reached the library, I found Mr. Pope asleep in his chair. I stole silently out again, grateful that I had neither to reveal nor to conceal the news that Father Gerard had given me concerning Jamie Redshaw. I needed to digest it myself first, to mull over what it might mean to me.

Though I knew now where I came from, did it really change anything? I had no notion whether any of Jamie Redshaw's relations—or my mother's—were still alive or, if they were, where to find them. And even if I did manage to uncover them, how likely was it that they would welcome some long-lost, illegitimate child who claimed to be their kin? And even if they did accept me, could I bear to leave London and the world of the theatre for some other world I knew nothing of?

Once again I was thankful to have something less confusing to turn my mind to, something more within my control. I retreated to my room, lit a candle, and sat down at my desk with Mr. Shakespeare's script—no, *my* script—before me. In a quarter hour or so, I had finished copying into my own hand all that Mr. Shakespeare had written, up until the end of the second act. After that, there were no complete scenes, only scraps of speeches, plus some notes he had made concerning the mechanics of the story.

Well, he had given me the bare bones; it was up to me to put flesh upon them. I took a deep breath and wrote on a fresh sheet of paper *Act III*. Then I sat staring into space for a very long time. I had only now begun to realize that being in control might prove to be more of a curse than a blessing. With perhaps ten thousand possible words at my disposal, how did I settle on just the right one, and then one to follow it, and so on?

And yet, was it really so impossible? After all, in real life we managed to speak to one another well enough without agonizing over every word. Well, then, perhaps what I must do was not write the lines but speak them, say whatever came into my head, as folk do in conversation. Sometimes, admittedly, the results were unfortunate. But I had the luxury of taking mine back.

Mr. Shakespeare had already established that Timon was in financial trouble. What I needed now was a scene in which he sends his servant, Flaminius, to ask one of the nobles—Lucullus, let us say—for a loan. So. *Scene I. A Room in Lucullus's House. Flaminius waiting. A servant enters* and says . . . says what? Well, I ought to know; I had played the part of a servant often enough. "I have told my lord you are here," I said aloud, under my breath. "He is coming down." Hardly inspired, but believable, at least, and certainly far better than a blank page. I wrote it down. And Flavius replies . . . "Tell him to hurry"? No, too cheeky. "I'll just sit down here"? No, that would require a chair. "Thank you"? Good enough. Now to bring Lucullus on. *Servant:* "Here's my lord." A bit obvious, but never mind. Lucullus is a greedy wight, so . . . *Lucullus (aside):* "One of Lord Timon's men? Bringing me another gift, no doubt."

As though I had broken through a barrier of some sort, the words began to flow from me, through my pencil, and onto the paper—only a trickle at first, but then such a steady stream that I was forced to switch from Italian script to my system of swift writing in order to keep up. I felt almost as if someone were dictating the lines to me—not Mr. Shakespeare, certainly; he would have dictated better ones.

Well, no matter that it was not deathless prose; I could always go back later and liven it up a bit. I made no attempt at meter. As with most of his plays, Mr. Shakespeare had begun writing this one in fairly regular iambic pentameter. But by the middle of Act II he was, for no apparent reason, putting in long passages of prose. If it was good enough for him, it was good enough for me.

For nearly two years, however, I had been spouting verse for several hours every day. It was bound to affect me. I found myself unconsciously composing ten-syllable lines, with the stress on the even-numbered syllables:

Has friendship such a faint and milky heart
It turns in less than two nights? Oh, you gods!

Sometimes the meter limped a little, but then Mr. Shake-speare's lines did not always glide as smoothly as swans, either.

Just when I grew used to the words pouring onto the page, without warning the source—whatever it was—dried up, and I was back to squeezing lines out of my brain, drop by drop. But even at its most frustrating, the task held a sort of perverse satisfaction. While everyone else in our household—and in other households all over the city—were in their beds, here was I at my desk, slaving away, creating a work of art. I felt noble, righteous, a martyr in the service of Melpomene, the muse of tragedy. Like those who slept, I was spinning out a sort of dream. But, whereas theirs would fade even before they awoke, mine would be written down and perhaps acted out, for others to hear and to see, again and again.

I did not feel nearly so righteous in the morning. I felt, in fact, less like a noble playwright than like a noddy who has slept half the night in a hard chair, with a pile of papers for a pillow, and who has wax in his hair from a melting candle. Well, I reminded myself, a martyr is expected to suffer for his cause, otherwise he would not be a martyr, only an ordinary wight doing an ordinary job that anyone might do as well. As I tried to get my stiff limbs in working order, I consoled myself with the knowledge that I was now nearly one act nearer to having a completed play and the money to rescue Julia.

Sam could not, of course, resist commenting upon my haggard appearance. "Don't tell me. The cats of creativity kept you up until all hours again with their infernal mewing."

"As a matter of fact, I was hard at work writing posies for the lottery." I had learned from Sam that when you bought a chance in the lottery, you gave the agent a slip of paper with some distinctive motto or verse upon it; when the winners were announced, their posies were read aloud.

"*You're* going to enter the lottery?"

I nodded soberly. "Not the royal one, though. This lottery is only for the Lord Chamberlain's Men, to determine which of us will get his wages this week."

Sam gaped at me. "Truly?"

"Nay. I was only jesting."

He swatted my arm. "That's nothing to jest about." As we entered the courtyard of the Cross Keys, he said, "I suppose you won't be favoring us with your company again today?"

"Nay. I'll be another two days, at least, copying Mr. Jonson's script—or should I say *deciphering* it. His hand is so poor, the whole thing looks as though it's in some sort of code that only remotely resembles th' alphabet."

"Perhaps it is!" Sam whispered dramatically. "Perhaps it's a secret means of communication known only to Catholics!" When I looked dubious, he said, "Well, it's possible. They have a whole mysterious language of their own, you know."

"Aye. It's called Latin. And it's not all that mysterious." I peered through the window of the office; there was no one inside. I dug from my purse the key Mr. Shakespeare had given me.

"It's mysterious if you've never studied it," Sam said.

"I ha', a bit."

"Have you? Say something in it, then."

"Umm . . . *Totus mundus agit histrionem.*"

"Ahh, I know that one already. It's on the front of the Globe. 'All the world's a stage.' Say something else."

I rolled my eyes long-sufferingly. "*Carpe diem, tempus fugit.*"

"What does that mean?"

"It means 'Get to work.'"

I was tempted to tell Sam the news about Jamie Redshaw. But if I told him, it would be the same as telling everyone, and I was not eager for Judith to know. As long as my heritage remained a mystery, there was always the possibility, however unlikely, that I was the son of some great lord, and not of a common brigand.

I found it harder than ever that morning to make sense of Mr. Jonson's scribbles—perhaps because my eyes were closed so much of the time. It was not only my lack of sleep that was to blame; no matter how well rested I was, Mr. Jonson's script would surely have sent me into a stupor.

How could such a coarse and colorful wight, I wondered, write such insipid stuff? Considered purely as poetry, there was nothing wrong with it. It was dignified, evocative, and eloquent. But as dialogue for the stage, it was, to use Mr. Shakespeare's term again, putrid—hopelessly stilted and unnatural. I wondered whether I should introduce Mr. Jonson to my method of speaking the lines aloud before I wrote them down. Probably not. If I did, he would no doubt speak aloud a few choice lines himself. They would not be suitable for use upon the stage, of course, but at least they would have some life in them.

Though copying the script was a struggle, it did teach me a valuable lesson. I still did not know much about how to write a play, but at least I knew a good deal about how *not* to write one. That night, I sat down at my own desk with a new determination. For the first time I actually believed that if I worked hard enough at it, I might write something worth reading, and worth acting—if not with this play then with the next one, or the next.

Perhaps, in the process, I might even manage to make something of myself—unlike my father. But, though Jamie Redshaw had done little enough for me, there was one thing I might thank him for: Like Mr. Jonson, he had instilled in me a fierce resolve not to follow in his footsteps.

22

To my surprise, I had no trouble staying awake to work on my play. It was as though, after so many hours of plodding along in a sort of daze, I had at last passed beyond the boundaries of weariness and into some other realm, where the body gives up trying to have its way, and the mind becomes master.

In the morning, of course, my body came to its senses again, and it was all I could do to drag myself to the theatre. But I had another half an act to show for it. I tucked several pages of the script into my wallet, meaning to read them to Judith if the opportunity presented itself.

It did not. In fact, Judith did not present herself, even at the midday meal. Though I longed to know where she was and how she was, I was not inclined to ask Mr. Shakespeare. I was still angry with him and with Mr. Heminges over their seeming lack of concern for Julia, and was doing my best to avoid them.

Sam, who never hesitated to ask anyone about anything, reported that Judith had been banished from the Cross Keys as punishment for putting the whole company in jeopardy. This only added to my resentment. If she could not come to the theatre, and I could not leave it, how would we ever meet?

There was, of course, tomorrow afternoon, when she had arranged for Sal Pavy and Sam to show her about the city after church. Though it would be hard to be content with one-third of her attention, perhaps it would be better than not seeing her at all. If Mr. Shakespeare made good his threat to send her home, there was no telling how many more chances I might have.

The weather had been so miserable of late that I feared it might spoil our plans. But for once Sunday lived up to its name, dawning bright and clear. By the time we set out for St. Saviour's, it was almost too warm for a cloak. Sam, who lodged with Mr. Phillips but a few streets away from us, ordinarily accompanied us to church, to the delight of Mr. Pope's orphan boys; they laughed at all his jests, however inane, and were awed by his simpleminded sleight-of-hand tricks, such as pulling pennies from their mouths.

When he failed to join us, the boys were sorely disappointed. As we filed into the church, I spotted Mr. Phillips; Sam was not with him, either. Before I could ask him what had become of the boy, Mr. Phillips asked me the same thing. I had no answer for him. I only hoped that Sam's absence would not be noted by the priest or the deacons.

It was possible, of course, that he was only late, and would show up at some point in the services. To my shame, I found myself wishing he would not; then I would have to share Judith only with Sal Pavy—who was, unfortunately, sitting in his usual spot at the end of our pew, alongside Mr. Armin.

The priest began by asking us all to join him in a prayer for the queen's health. Apparently there was some small hope that Her Majesty would yet recover. Though her body might be weak, her will was not; she was as stubborn and independent as ever. She had refused to take to her bed, for to do so would be to concede that she was near the end. Instead, she spent all her time sitting upright on cushions placed upon the floor.

After the services, I searched for Sam, but there was still no sign of him. I caught Sal Pavy coming out of the church and let him know that I intended to join him and Judith. To my surprise, he seemed agreeable, or at least as agreeable as Sal Pavy ever got. "What about Sam?" he asked.

"Whist!" I said softly. After making certain no one would overhear, I whispered, "'A never turned up."

"Oh. He won't be happy if we go without him."

"Then 'a should ha' been here. Besides, 'a would only ha' pestered us to cross over on th' ice."

"It would be a good deal quicker than going by way of the bridge."

"Aye, and perhaps a good deal wetter as well. Now that the weather's changed, th' ice may begin breaking up at any time."

Sal Pavy gave me a smirking smile. "You sound a bit white-livered to me."

"I'm not afeared, an that's what you mean. I'm cautious, that's all."

"Caution is but another name for fear."

"And daring is but another name for stupid."

"Well, I'll tell you what. You cross the bridge, and I'll cross the ice, and we'll see which of us gets to Judith first."

I searched his face for some sign that he was jesting, and failed to find any. "You mean it?"

"Of course."

He was clearly issuing a challenge, like the one I had issued several months earlier when I proposed an acting duel to determine who would play the part of Helena in *All's Well*. If I ignored his dare and took the bridge, he would most likely follow. But suppose he did not? Even if I ran all the way to St. Olave's, I might arrive to find him and Judith gone or, even worse, sharing a laugh over my foolish caution, which they would take for fear.

Whether he was truly serious or only bluffing, I had no choice but to take up the gauntlet he had thrown. "All right, then," I said, with a nonchalance that was badly damaged by my voice breaking. "Let's be stupid—I mean, daring."

"Good." Sal Pavy gestured toward the steps that led to the river. "After you."

"It was your idea," I reminded him.

He could not deny it. With his head held high, rather like a condemned man determined to make a good show on his way to the scaffold, he descended the stairs and, with a reluctance that was hardly visible, stepped onto the ice. He turned to me with a smug look, tinged with relief. "There, you see? It's perfectly safe."

I had no doubt it would be, this close to shore, where the water was still. It was the part farther out, where the current flowed fastest beneath its frozen shell, that worried me. As we shuffled toward the middle of the river, I took some heart in the fact that a dozen or so wights were out there already, fishing through holes they had cut in the ice. Of course, we had no notion how many more had made holes through it without meaning to, and were now down there with the fish.

"Sam will really be angry with us now, for going without him," said Sal Pavy.

"Assuming we survive, you mean."

When we had gone perhaps fifty yards, I began to notice dark patches here and there, where a pocket of air or a mass of floating debris had been trapped in the ice. Though I carefully detoured around these spots, Sal Pavy seemed to pay no attention to them—until he put his weight on one and the ice gave way like the trapdoor in our stage at the Globe, which could be used to send an evil villain plunging into the pit of hell.

Sal Pavy's cry of dismay was cut off as he dropped into the river and the water closed over his head. My instinct was to run headlong to his rescue; then my reason took over and told me that if I did, I might well join him instead. I flung myself onto my stomach and scuttled along like a crab until I reached the spot where he had fallen through. Sal Pavy had fought his way to the surface—within the circle of open water, luckily, and not beneath the ice—and was clinging with both hands to the crumbling edge of the hole, choking and coughing up water. Between spasms, he called out in a faint and trembling voice, "Widge! Help me!"

I crept several inches nearer. I could hear the ice creaking under my weight, and expected a new chunk to break loose at any moment. "I'm here! Take my hand!"

"I can't! I daren't let go!"

"All right," I said, as calmly as I could. "I'll take yours, then." I groped about until I located what I took to be one of his hands; it was hard to be sure, for it was as cold as the ice. I pushed myself forward another few inches and wrapped my fingers around his wrist. It was impossible to pull him to me, though, I could get no purchase on the slick ice. "You'll ha' to climb up me arm."

"I can't!" he gasped. "My cloak. Too heavy."

"Unfasten it wi' one hand, then. I'll keep hold of th' other."

"Don't let go!" he begged. For what seemed like a full minute or more I heard him thrashing about, trying to free himself from the waterlogged cloak. At last I felt his fingers clutch the sleeve of my shirt.

"Get a good grip," I said. "I'm going to let go of your other hand now."

"No!" he cried.

"I must, Sal. You'll need it to pull yourself out. The moment I let go, you grasp me arm. All right?"

"I'll try," he said weakly.

"Good." I released my hold on his wrist. He slumped down in the water, and for a moment I thought I'd lost him. Then his other hand slithered forward and seized the fabric of my sleeve. With painful slowness, using me as his ladder, he dragged himself from the river and onto the ice.

I let him lie there and recover a moment. Then I bent, draped one of his arms around my neck, and hoisted him to his feet. "Come along. We must get you indoors." As soon as he could support himself, I took off my cloak and fastened it around him. "That may help a little."

Through chattering teeth, he murmured something I could not quite make out, but I believe it may have been "Thank you." By the time we reached the stairs, he had warmed up a bit and was walking and speaking in a more or less normal fashion. He had also resumed his normal haughty attitude. "I can manage on my own from here," he said.

"Are you certain?"

He waved a shaky hand at me. "Yes, yes. Besides, you need to meet Judith. She'll be wondering what's become of us." He fumbled with the cords that tied the cloak together.

"You may keep that for now," I told him. "I'll be warm enough."

He gave me a slight, stiff smile. "That may depend," he said, "on what sort of mood she's in."

I soon discovered that the air was not as warm as I had imagined. There was a stiff breeze off the river. To make matters worse, my doublet and breeches were wet from lying on the ice. Even though I walked briskly—across the bridge, this time—I was cold as a cellar stone before I reached St. Olave's Church. The place was deserted—which was not surprising, considering how late I was.

Wrapping my arms about myself, I hurried on to Mr. Shakespeare's lodgings. I nearly wore the knocker out before anyone answered the door. To my disappointment, it was Mary Mountjoy. She regarded me quizzically, as though she felt she should know me but couldn't think from where. "Yes? What is it?"

So flustered was I at the prospect of seeing Judith, I could scarcely get the words out. "I—that is, we—that is, Mistress Shakespeare was to meet us. Me. At the church. But there's no one at the church. So. Is she here?"

"No, I'm afraid she's gone."

"Gone?" I echoed dumbly. "Gone where?"

"Why, to Stratford. She left half an hour ago."

23

In a week so full of distressing developments, I should not have been surprised, I suppose, to be struck by yet one more. I had known, after all, that Judith was likely to leave at some point. I just never imagined it would be this soon. So out of square was I that I thought perhaps I had not heard Mistress Mountjoy properly. "You mean . . . you mean *home?* To Warwickshire?"

"Yes," the girl replied, pouting a little. "And we were getting to be such good friends, too."

"But . . . but surely her father didn't pack her off all alone?"

"Of course not. An old acquaintance of his—a Mr. Quiney, I believe; or was it Quincy? Something with a *Q*, anyway—was going to Stratford on business, and let her travel with him. Mr. Shakespeare is accompanying them as far as Uxbridge."

"Can you tell me, did she leave any sort of . . . message, or anything?"

"For whom?"

"Well . . . for me."

She gave me that quizzical look again. "I'm sorry, which one are you?"

"Widge."

"Oh, yes."

"She *did?*" I said eagerly.

"No, I only meant, 'Oh, yes, now I remember you.' She left no message. In fact, she didn't say much of anything when she left, not even to me, she was that upset and angry. She did say she'd write back, though, if I wrote her. Is there anything you'd like me to pass on to her?"

"Nay. What's the use? As she told me herself, she's heard it all before, and from better wights than me, I wis."

"You look cold," she said. "Would you like to come in and warm up?"

I shook my head and turned away. If I was to be miserable, I might as well make a good job of it. It would not be difficult. A whole long afternoon and evening stretched ahead of me, and nothing better to do with it than to sit about feeling sorry for myself. I had neither money nor friends, and even if I had had both, I would have had no appetite for the frivolous pastimes with which we ordinarily occupied our Sundays.

I might as well go home and work on my play. I had reached the point in the script at which Timon, a destitute and friendless outcast, declares that he hates all mankind. It fit my mood and my circumstances exactly.

There is nothing like spite to motivate a person. Though my room was nearly as cold as the outdoors, I shrouded myself in blankets and sat scribbling away for the next several hours, giving voice to all the insulting and reproachful remarks that I could not say myself by putting them in Timon's mouth:

"Away, thou issue of a mangy dog!" "Would thou wert clean enough to spit upon." "I am sick of this false world, and will love naught."

But, as gratifying as this was, I knew that if I confined my hero to mere curses, he would not seem heroic, only hateful. I must provide him with some means of avenging himself. Besides, our audience loved revenge. According to Mr. Shakespeare's notes, he planned to have Timon raise an army and lay waste to Rome—now Athens. But that seemed unlikely. Soldiers don't fight unless you pay them, and Timon was so poor that he was reduced to living in a cave in the woods and eating roots.

Well, suppose he gets some money, somehow. Suppose he comes into a fortune, and suddenly all his former friends want to be his friends again, and he just laughs at them. Yes, that was good. But where would he get a fortune, living in a cave in the woods? Steal it? Inherit it? Write a successful play? Dig up gold nuggets while he's grubbing for roots to eat?

When this notion first struck me, I didn't take it seriously; it seemed rather silly, in fact. But the more I thought about it, the more the irony of it appealed to me. I knew it would delight the penny playgoers as well; if there was anything they loved more than guts and gore, it was gold. Certainly it would hold their attention better than watching Timon write a play, or read his uncle's will.

Though I had said little to Goody Willingson or Mr. Pope about the play, they seemed to sense my need for privacy and somehow kept the boys from pestering me for much of the afternoon. But boys, like spirited horses, may be kept in check only so long.

I was just bringing a band of thieves into the script when the boys burst into the room, surrounded me, and took me captive.

Though I showered them with curses only slightly less vile than Timon's, they merely laughed and vowed not to release me until I had played Banks's Horse with them—a favorite game they had invented in which I impersonated a celebrated gelding who could dance, do sums, and answer questions.

When I had had my fill of neighing and pawing the floor, they pressed me into a game of Barley Break that lasted until supper. As I was stuffing my mouth with mutton pie, anxious to return to my desk before the Muse grew tired of waiting for me, Goody Willingson said, "Is your writing going well, then, Widge?"

In trying to clear my mouth enough to answer, I nearly choked.

"Just paw the table," said a boy named Walter. "Once for yes, twice for no." This sent the others into fits of laughter. With a grin made lopsided by my mouthful of food, I gave the table a single swipe.

"Have you let Judith look at the script?" asked Mr. Pope.

My grin faded. "Nay. She's gone home."

"Oh. I'm sorry, lad. Though I'm certain you won't agree just now, I assure you it is for the best."

I wondered whether, if I had said I was struck soundly on the brain-pan and robbed, he would have told me that it was for the best. In truth, I believe I would have preferred to be beaten and robbed; it would surely have hurt less, and I would have lost nothing but my purse. I wiped my mouth and rose from the table. "An you'll excuse me, I'd like to get back to me play."

"Oh, good!" shouted Walter. "What shall we play this time?"

I worked uninterrupted until the bells at St. Bennet rang compline. I was in the midst of a scene in which the poet and painter come to ask Timon for some of his gold when I heard a faint knock at my door. I did my best to ignore it, but a moment later the door swung open a crack and a soft voice said, "Widge?"

I turned to see Tetty peering through the opening. "I'm sorry," I said. "I forgot to tuck you in."

"It's all right, you needn't. I only wished to bid you good night." When I held out my arms, she scurried barefoot across the cold floor and, standing on tiptoe, gave me a quick hug. "I'm sorry about Judith." After considering a moment, she added, "But not very."

"Oh? Why is that?"

"I told you, you must wait for me. I'm growing as quickly as I can."

I groaned as I lifted her onto my knee and wrapped my blanket about her bare legs. "You certainly are. You must weigh nine or ten stone, at least."

She snickered. "I'm not growing *that* quickly." She examined the papers spread before me. "Is this your play?"

"Aye."

"What's it called?"

"It doesn't have a proper name yet."

"Then it's like you, isn't it?"

"I suppose it is."

"Will you read it to me when it's done?"

"I don't ken whether you'd fancy it. It's not like *Romeo and Juliet;* it hasn't a dell of romance in it."

"Oh. Well, that's all right," she said. "I expect you've had enough of romance for a while."

I was reluctant to stop writing, not caring to be alone with my thoughts. But when the words ceased to make sense, I put my pencil down and crawled into bed, resigned to a night of fretting and tossing about. To my surprise, I fell swiftly to sleep and awoke feeling more rested and cheerful than I had for some time.

Sam, on the other hand, seemed unusually subdued and thoughtful as we walked to the theatre. Even when I recounted our near-fatal adventure upon the ice the previous day, he had little to say. "By the by," I said, "why were you not at church services yesterday?"

"I was," Sam replied.

"Nay, you never! I looked all over for you."

"I didn't say I was at St. Saviour's, did I?"

"Where, then?"

He gave me a haughty look. "As Father Gerard would say, a gentleman's business is his own."

"Tell that to the deacons when they fine you for missing church."

"A pox on the deacons," he said.

At the Cross Keys, as we were climbing the stairs to the second-floor balcony, the door to Mr. Shakespeare's office flew open with a crash that rattled the windows. A hefty, hairy wight who rather resembled a bear burst forth and came thundering down the steps, causing them to shudder and us to fling ourselves to one side, lest we be trampled. Though I had been too busy saving my skin to get a good look at him, I knew that I had seen that bearlike build before, and those bulging eyes, which made him look as though he were choking on something.

"Who was that unmannerly swad?" Sam asked loudly, before the fellow was quite out of earshot. The man cast us a glowering look.

When he had exited the courtyard, I said, "Mr. Henslowe, from th' Admiral's Men."

"Oh. That explains why he was trying so hard to wreck the place."

"I believe 'a was angry about something—the script of *Sejanus*, unless I miss me guess."

Mr. Heminges and Mr. Shakespeare confirmed my suspicions. Henslowe had come to demand Mr. Jonson's play. It was his by right, he reminded them, as he had paid the playwright ten pounds for it, in advance. "Then *I* r-reminded *him*," said Mr. Heminges, "that he had r-refused to perform it, on the gr-grounds that it was full of P-Papist propaganda. 'And so it was,' he replied. 'But I understand that Ben has succeeded in reforming it.'"

"Will 'a come back, do you wis?"

"I doubt it," said Mr. Shakespeare. "But if he does, he had best be armed."

I went at Mr. Jonson's script with a vengeance, determined to be done with it as quickly as possible, in case Mr. Henslowe did decide to return with reinforcements. I was well into the last act when the door to the hallway opened and Ned Shakespeare strolled in. I gave him a cursory nod, assuming he was seeking his brother—probably in order to ask for money.

"What's that you're copying?" he asked.

"*Sejanus.*"

He leaned over the desk. "It looks as though you're about done, eh?"

"Aye. I'll start on the sides tomorrow."

"Hmm. That's too bad."

"It is?"

"Of course." He slapped me playfully—and rather painfully—on the shoulder. "That means we'll have to perform it, doesn't it?"

"That's so. Perhaps I should write more slowly."

"Well, this will put it off a bit, at least: the sharers have called a meeting of the entire company upstairs."

"Oh? When is 't to be, then?"

"Now."

When Ned and I entered the long gallery, everyone else was there, with the exception of Sal Pavy. Mr. Heminges wasted no time in telling us the reason for the gathering. "The qu-queen has t-taken a turn for the worse. Ac-c-cording to her physician, she m-may have but a few more d-days. The Privy C-Council has asked that, out of r-respect for Her M-Majesty, all p-public performances be suspended for the t-time being."

"*Asked?*" said Ned. "Ordered, you mean."

"C-call it what you w-will; the r-result is the same."

"And what does 'for the time being' mean?"

"It means," said Mr. Shakespeare, "that we don't know. Her Majesty still has not named her successor, but I think we can assume it will be James. What *that* will mean, we can only guess."

"In the m-meantime," said Mr. Heminges, "we have d-decided to go on as always, re-rehearsing and l-learning lines, and so on, with one d-difference—you w-will all have your evenings free."

Though Sam was more subdued than usual, he was still Sam. "Speaking of free," he said, "will we still get our wages?"

Mr. Heminges smiled, a bit wanly. "F-for the time being."

When the meeting ended, I caught Mr. Armin and asked after Sal Pavy. "He's at home—his parents' home, I mean—

in bed. He's come down with a bad case of the coughs and sniffles—brought on by his swim in the river yesterday, no doubt."

"Oh, gis. Will 'a be all right, do you wis?"

"Most likely. He's being well cared for by his mother."

I shook my head. "I should never ha' let him cross on th' ice."

"Don't go feeling responsible now. After all, you were the one who saved him."

"Aye, I helped a bit. But 'a would not ha' needed saving had I not been so stupid as to accept his challenge i' the first place."

Mr. Armin shrugged. "You didn't wish to seem a coward; that's natural."

"Perhaps," I said. "And perhaps I would ha' shown more courage by refusing."

24

The prospect of the queen's death sobered us all. Though we went about our duties as usual, and even traded a bit of good-natured banter from time to time, we seemed less like comrades bound together by a common goal than like shipmates aboard a sinking vessel.

That evening, with several more hours than usual at my disposal, I brought my play to an end. I had performed in enough tragedies to know that the hero is expected to die. Mr. Shakespeare had jotted down three alternative fates for Timon: "Killed by thieves?" "Angry senators slay him?" and "Takes his own life?" As Timon was so disgusted with the world and everything in it, the last possibility seemed the most fitting. After giving him one last malediction to utter—"What is amiss, let plague and infection mend! Graves only be men's works, and death their gain!"—I had him hang himself from a tree—off the stage, of course. Though the audience would no doubt have perferred to actually see him dangling, I feared that the actor playing the part might object.

I had supposed that when I set down the final line, I would experience a great sense of satisfaction, of accomplishment. Instead I felt rather the way I did when awaking from a particularly vivid dream—a bit dismayed by the dreariness and the demands of the real world, and half longing to slip back into the world of my imagining.

I had another reason as well to regret having completed the script. Now I would have to show it to someone—at least if I hoped to make any money with it. Unless I wished to hire a hall and a troupe of players and present the play myself, I must submit it to one of the city's existing theatre companies. And the logical place to begin was with the Lord Chamberlain's Men. The notion should not have bothered me, I suppose. After all, I had grown accustomed to being criticized by them—for my acting, for my singing, for my dancing, for my scriming. But those were all external things, mere skills to be mastered. The play was personal, a product not of my muscles or my vocal cords but of my mind. If they found flaws in it, the flaws were mine; if they judged it foolish, I would be the fool.

Thoughts and events that seem plausible enough, or even profound, within the context of a dream often seem, upon waking, like so much nonsense. It was the same with my play. While I was caught up in composing it, the story had been sensible, the characters clear, the lines lyrical. But when I looked it over in the light of day, it seemed to have undergone a hideous transformation. The situations were now contrived, the characters shallow, the dialogue lame: "Now breathless wrong shall sit and pant in your great chairs of ease, and pursy insolence shall break his wind with fear, and horrid flight"? Had I really written such a hopeless line? I must have been not only dreaming, but delirious.

It was fortunate that I did not have a lighted candle at hand; I was so overcome with loathing for my creation that I would surely have sentenced it to the fiery death it deserved. Instead, I folded it haphazardly and crammed it into my wallet, to get it out of my sight. I must indeed have been dreaming or delirious to imagine that I, a paltry prentice player and offspring of an outlaw, might produce something remotely worth praising, or paying for.

As I was in no mood for conversation, I set out for the Cross Keys without waiting for Sam. The day was bright, almost balmy. Spring seemed to have remembered its cue at last. But I was in no mood for it, either. To my surprise, I found Ned Shakespeare, who ordinarily arrived half an hour later than everyone else, waiting outside the office. "What brings you here so early?" I asked.

"I wanted a word with you."

"Wi' me?" I dug out my key and turned it in the lock. "What about?"

He glanced this way and that, then pulled me abruptly inside the room. "Do you have the sides for *Sejanus* yet?"

Puzzled by his furtive behavior, I pulled my sleeve from his grasp. "Nay; as I told you, I'll get to them today."

"Oh, yes. Well, I was wondering whether you might copy out my part first."

"I suppose. But why?"

He looked uncomfortable. "I wouldn't want this to get out, but the truth is . . . I'm having difficulty remembering my lines."

"That's not exactly a secret."

"No, and I'm sure you all think it's because I put off learning them. But it isn't." He thumped his forehead with his knuckles. "I just seem to have trouble getting them to stick in my head, no matter how many times I go over them. I thought perhaps if I got started on them before anyone else, it might help."

"All right. I can ha' your side for you afore the morning rehearsal."

"Excellent. Thank you. I'll let you get to work, then." He slipped out the door and pulled it softly shut behind him.

As I wrote out Ned's speeches and the cues that led into them, it struck me again how lifeless the lines were. I began to wonder whether I had been too critical of my own efforts. I took the crumpled script from my wallet, smoothed it out on Mr. Shakespeare's desk, and tried my best to examine it with an objective, unbiased eye. It was impossible, like trying to see my own face the way others saw it, or to hear my own voice as it sounded to someone else.

As a person may be aware that his nose is too long or his chin too short, I was aware that there were awkward spots in the play. But it seemed to me there were also some passages that Mr. Shakespeare himself would not have been ashamed to admit to—though he might not wish to boast about them, either.

So absorbed was I in studying the script that I did not hear the inner door of the office open. It wasn't until Mr. Heminges cleared his throat loudly that I noticed him standing over me. "G-God you good morning, Widge. Hard at w-work already, I see."

"Aye," I said, feeling a bit guilty for being occupied with my own script and not Mr. Jonson's.

"Well, I'll tr-try not to disturb you. I m-must go over the b-books and see how long we m-may hope to survive w-with no income." He sat at his desk and opened the ledger in which he kept track of the company's finances. "Oh, b-by the by, has Will t-told you that we m-may have hit upon a way of helping J-Julia?"

"Nay! Truly?"

"Mountjoy, his landlord, is a f-former Frenchman who does a g-good deal of business with c-companies in Paris. He c-can arrange for one of them to loan Julia the m-money she needs for her p-passage. A b-bill of exchange, I believe it's c-called."

"Gog's nowns! That's good news! You ken where she may be reached, then?"

He turned to me with an anxious frown. "N-no. I th-thought *you* did."

"I ha' th' address of her old lodgings, but she's no longer there, remember?"

"Sh-shrew me! I hadn't th-thought of that. W-was there an address on the l-letter her f-father showed us?"

"I didn't notice."

"N-nor did I. There m-must have been, though, otherwise C-Cogan would have had n-no notion where to send the m-money—pr-presuming he m-meant to send it at all, wh-which I doubt. D-do you know where he m-may be found?"

"Somewhere in Alsatia, I expect. I've been meaning to seek him out. I thought that . . . I thought that you and Mr. Shakespeare were not willing to help Julia, so I planned to raise the money meself."

He gave me a look that was half reproachful, half astonished. "D-did you truly imagine that we w-would leave her stranded over there?"

"I . . . I didn't ken."

"Well, you sh-should have," he said sternly. Then, in a gentler tone, he added, "And how, m-may I ask, did you propose to c-come up with three p-pounds?"

I hung my head, embarrassed. "By selling me play," I murmured.

"What p-play is that?"

I patted the script. "This one."

"M-may I see it?" He scanned the first several pages. "This is the script W-Will gave up on, is it not?"

"Aye. 'A said I might do wi' it as I wished."

"And so you c-completed it?"

"Aye."

"Th-that's quite an accomplishment. Does it have a n-name?"

"Not yet. I've been thinking, though, that it should ha' something to do wi' revenge or retaliation—*An Eye for an Eye,* or *Like for Like,* or perhaps *Measure for Measure.*"

"*M-Measure for Measure,* eh? That has a r-ring to it. T-tell me, to whom d-did you expect to sell this?"

I shrugged. "Whoever was interested."

"Have you sh-shown it to Will?"

"Nay. I was afeared 'a would think it . . . well, putrid. Besides, I've been—" I broke off.

"You've b-been angry with him," Mr. Heminges finished.

"Aye."

"For s-sending Judith home, I expect."

"Aye."

"Well, it is a p-pity it had to c-come to that, but she br-brought it upon herself."

"I ken that. But 'a might ha' been kinder to her while she was here. 'A might ha' spent more time wi' her."

"That's so." Mr. Heminges leaned toward me and said softly, "B-but just between the t-two of us, I believe he was af-f-fraid to."

"Afeared? Why?"

"He t-told me that he never kn-knows what to say to her."

I laughed. "Sorry. It's just that it's hard to imagine the likes of Mr. Shakespeare being at a loss for words. I thought it was only me."

"N-no, I suspect that p-particular problem is a universal one. In f-fact, I'm convinced that m-men and women actually speak t-two separate languages, in which the w-words happen to s-sound alike but have t-totally different meanings."

"I never had any trouble talking to Julia."

"Ah, but you see, that was b-because she was pr-pretending to be a boy." He glanced at the script in his hand. "If you don't m-mind, I'll r-read through this, and then p-pass it on to the other sh-sharers."

"Including Mr. Shakespeare?" I asked apprehensively.

"Of c-course. He w-won't scoff at it, if that's what w-worries you. R-remember, he was once a n-novice playwright himself." Mr. Heminges leaned toward me confidentially again. "Well, you've d-done *Two Gentlemen*, so you kn-know well enough that his w-words are not always g-golden, and his structure s-sometimes creaks a bit, eh?"

I sighed. "Aye, all right, show it to him, then."

"G-good lad. And d-don't worry about Julia, either. We'll tr-track her father down somehow."

25

Despite Mr. Heminges's assurances, I could not help fretting about Julia's fate. In her letter, she had said that her funds were fading fast; by now she might well be wandering the streets of Paris, starving. Nor could I help wondering how my first faltering efforts at playwriting would be received by men who had been performing plays half their lives.

With these matters occupying my mind, I had little to spare for Mr. Jonson's script. I did manage to copy all of Ned Shakespeare's lines before rehearsal, as I had promised, but not much else. As we assembled downstairs for dinner, I spotted my script changing hands, from Mr. Armin's to Mr. Shakespeare's. I cornered Mr. Heminges and asked anxiously, "Has Mr. Armin read it, do you wis?"

"Ap-p-parently so," said Mr. Heminges.

"And you? You've read it as well?"

He smiled at my expectant, insistent manner. "I have."

"Well?" I prompted him. "What did you think?"

"I th-think that you show a g-good deal of promise. We'll t-talk about it this evening, after the others have had a ch-chance to look at it, eh?"

I nodded without enthusiasm. I didn't like the sound of that word, *promise*. It was the very term that had been applied to me by various members of the company, back when I first began acting with them in insignificant roles. Now that I was more experienced, I realized that it had been a euphemism, a kind way of saying that I was hopelessly incompetent, but might have a faint hope of someday becoming adequate.

Though I had never considered myself a glutton for punishment, I went begging for it that afternoon at scriming practice by asking Mr. Armin his opinion of my play. He clapped a hand on my shoulder, as he sometimes did after I had shown unusual skill with the sword. "Very promising," he said.

As I had given such short shrift to *Sejanus* that morning, I did my penance by returning to the office to copy another side or two before I headed home. The door that opened into the office from the hallway was locked. I drew my purse from within my doublet and dug into it. My fingers encountered nothing but the few coins—mostly pennies and farthings—that made up my enire fortune.

Puzzled, I turned the purse upside down, shook its contents into my hand, and examined them incredulously. Perhaps someone had replaced my purse with one of those trick purses used by sleight-of-hand artists, for the key had unaccountably disappeared. I searched my wallet and found only my table-book, my plumbago pencil, and a petrified sweetmeat that Mr. Pope's boys had somehow missed.

I extended the search to my brain. When had I last seen the

key? Earlier that morning, I was sure, when I let myself and Ned in through the outer door. Ned had distracted me by asking for his side; perhaps without thinking I had tossed the key onto the desk. Or had I left it in the lock? Surely I had not been that much of a harecop.

Well, there was but one way to find out. I descended to the dark parlor, meaning to go into the courtyard and up the outside steps to the balcony. As I headed for the door, I heard my name called. I turned to see four of the company's sharers sharing a booth and a round of ale.

Mr. Armin beckoned to me. "We were wondering what had become of you."

"I was about to copy some more of *Sejanus*." I carefully avoided any mention of the missing key.

"Well, come and sit with us a moment, first." While I pulled a chair up to the end of the table, Mr. Armin summoned the tapster and ordered an ale for me.

"We've j-just been discussing *M-Measure for Measure*," said Mr. Heminges.

I stared at him, momentarily baffled. "What's that, then?"

"Your play?"

"Oh? Oh, aye! I've considered so many titles, I'd forgotten that one."

"It's a good title," said Mr. Phillips.

"Yes," said Mr. Shakespeare. "I wish I'd thought of it."

"Well, you may ha' 't, an you like. I can easily call mine something else. I've no shortage of titles."

"Thank you," he said.

"It's naught." I glanced nervously about at the four of them in turn. "So . . . is that all you liked about it, then? The title?"

"No, no," said Mr. Shakespeare. "In fact, it has quite a number of good qualities."

I waited for him to go on, to cite some of its good qualities. When he did not, I swallowed hard and said, "But it's not good enough, is it?"

Mr. Shakespeare cast a beseeching glance at Mr. Heminges, as though asking for help from a more tactful quarter. "N-not as it stands," said Mr. Heminges gently. "P-perhaps if you were to w-work on it a b-bit more, and then sh-show it to us again."

Unaccountably, I found myself fighting back tears. I felt nearly as forlorn as I had when Judith left, or when I learned that my father had died. Though none of the sharers had said, or even suggested, that my work was worthless, it was what I heard—or at least what that part of me that was governed by emotion heard. Yet, at the same time, some more reasonable part acknowledged that they were right, of course, that I could not possibly expect to turn out a well-made play on the first try, any more than a scrimer could expect to defeat the first opponent he ever faced. It was just that I had worked so hard on it, and hoped for so much from it.

"You mustn't be discouraged, Widge," said Mr. Shakespeare. "We're all agreed, I think, that the play shows—"

"Aye, I ken. It shows *promise*."

"I was about to say that it shows considerable skill, and a good ear for dialogue. There were several speeches in there that I would have sworn I wrote myself."

"You d-did," Mr. Heminges reminded him.

Mr. Shakespeare laughed. "I meant in the parts that Widge composed." He turned to me. "You know, if you intend to be a playwright, you may wish to take a *nom de plume*, one that will look a bit more distinguished on a playbill."

"And with your talent for titles," said Mr. Phillips, "you should have no trouble coining a good name for yourself."

It struck me, then, that none of them knew yet about Jamie Redshaw. I had not meant to keep it from them, only from Judith, and now that she was gone, what did it matter? "Actually," I said, "I do ha' a name—or the nether end of one, at least."

Half my audience seemed astonished by my news; the other half were not. Mr. Phillips and Mr. Armin confessed that they had never really believed Jamie Redshaw's story. Mr. Shakespeare and Mr. Heminges said that though they had not completely trusted the man, they had never doubted that he was my father.

"Will you take his name, then?" asked Mr. Armin.

I stared thoughtfully into my pot of ale. "I've not made up me mind."

"Redshaw never indicated what your Christian name might be?" said Mr. Phillips.

"Nay. 'A was not around when I was born, and me mother didn't live long enough to name me. I do recall Mistress MacGregor saying once that the priest who baptized me gave me his own name, for want of any other. No one has ever called me by it, though."

"Do you know what it was?"

"William, I believe."

"That's an excellent name," said Mr. Shakespeare.

Mr. Heminges nodded approvingly. "W-William Redshaw. That would not l-look amiss on a playbill."

I gave a skeptical sniff. "Assuming I ever manage to write a decent play."

"Oh, you w-will." He turned to Mr. Shakespeare. "Will he n-not, Will?"

Mr. Shakespeare shrugged and gave me a rather sly smile. "If he has the will, he will."

I refused to be coaxed out of my sour mood by their banter. "Well, i' the meanwhile, will you gi' me back the putrid one?"

Though I wanted nothing less than to look at another play just then, I forced myself to return to the office, this time by way of the outside stairs. Even if I did not work on *Sejanus*, I must at least determine what I had done with the key. The sky was nearly dark now, and even before I reached the second-floor balcony, I noticed a faint glow of light issuing from the small window of the office.

Someone must be working within. But who? All the sharers had either gone home or were gathered in the dark parlor. Curious and a little alarmed, I crept along the balcony, crouched down next to the window, and peered inside.

A single lighted candle sat atop Mr. Shakespeare's desk. Bent over it, one large hand cupped about the flame as though to keep its light contained, was a hulking figure that I did not recognize at once. Only when the man's face moved from the shadows and into the candle's light, revealing thick, unruly eyebrows set above bulging eyes, did I realize who the intruder was—Henslowe, from the Admiral's Men. It was easy enough to guess why he was here; he wanted the script of *Sejanus*.

26

If I had had a dell of sense, I would have run and fetched the sharers. What prevented me was the thought that had I not left the key in the lock, the man could not have gotten into the room. If I handled this myself, perhaps no one need know of my blunder.

I was not foolish enough to try to subdue Henslowe; he was roughly twice my size. I would do better to trust my wits. I took a deep breath, stood, and flung open the door. Henslowe spun about with a quickness surprising in such a bulky wight. In one hand he clutched the script of *Sejanus*. "I wouldn't take that an I were you," I said. Despite my efforts to keep my voice calm and confident, it cracked a little.

Henslowe looked me up and down, as though assessing how much of a threat I might pose. He seemed to conclude that it was very little. "And why is that?"

"Because. That's th' old script, the one wi' all the Papist propaganda. The new version is locked in a trunk i' the property room."

Scowling, he glanced at the script, then back at me. "No. It can't be." But it was clear that if my lie had not convinced him, it had at least given him pause. With a look that warned me to keep my distance, he turned and held the script to the light. "You're lying. This is not in Jonson's hand; someone has copied it. Who would bother to copy out a script they couldn't use?" He stuffed the papers into his wallet and headed for the door.

I blocked his way with my body. "I won't let you—" I managed to say before his fist knocked all the breath out of me. I doubled over and fell to my knees. Henslowe shoved me out of the doorway and was gone.

Gasping, I struggled to my feet and stumbled after him. When I reached the top of the stairs, I halted, taken aback by the scene below me. Henslowe lay sprawled upon the steps, with the point of Mr. Armin's rapier at his throat. Mr. Shakespeare was bent over Henslowe, digging through the man's wallet.

Mr. Armin glanced up at me. "We've caught the culprit. Are you all right?"

"Aye," I groaned. "More or less." I slowly descended the stairs, holding the railing with one hand and my aching gut with the other. "Shall I fetch a constable?"

"No," said Mr. Shakespeare. "We may as well let him go; we have what we want." In one hand he brandished the purloined pages; in the other, the key to the office.

Mr. Armin lowered his blade and Henslowe got to his feet, straightening his doublet. "It's I who should call the constables," he growled. "I was only taking what already belonged to me."

"Well, you may as well bring on the catchpolls," said Mr. Armin. "Heaven knows you've tried everything else to shut us down."

To my surprise, there was very little real rancor in either man's voice. In truth, they sounded less like enemies than like members of opposing teams engaged in some rough-and-tumble sport, a sort of grown-up version of King of the Hill that would decide once and for all which was the premier theatre company in London.

"I've no idea what you mean," replied Henslowe.

"Why, Henslowe," said Mr. Armin. "I do believe you've missed your calling. You feign innocence and indignation so well, you should have been a player."

"And you two should have been thieves." Henslowe scowled at his empty wallet, then at the bundle of pages in Mr. Shakespeare's hand. "You have a paper there that's not part of the script. I'll have it back."

Mr. Shakespeare held up a sheet that had been folded several times. "Is this what you mean?"

"Yes." Henslowe reached for it.

Mr. Shakespeare drew it back. "No, I believe we'll keep this for now. If you want it so badly, there must be some reason."

Henslowe glared at him a moment, then shrugged. "Well, it doesn't matter; you won't be able to read it, anyway." He turned to me. "How can you bear to be part of this band of thieves?"

"At least they don't go about walloping folk i' the gut," I said.

Henslowe gave a short laugh. "I like your spirit, lad. If you ever decide you'd prefer to work for a reputable company, come and see me." Pushing roughly past the sharers, he stalked off into the night.

"I tried me best to stop him," I said.

"Well, it looks as though you stopped his fist, at least," said Mr. Armin. "Come, let's lock up and go home. You've done enough work for one day."

As we climbed the stairs, Mr. Shakespeare said, "What I wonder is, how did Henslowe come by this key?"

"Um . . . I can answer that," I said reluctantly. "I left it i' the lock this morning, I wis."

Though Mr. Shakespeare did not exactly look happy, he did not chide me. "Well, there's no harm done, I suppose, except perhaps to your stomach—assuming that the play is all here, that is." He held the crumpled pages up to the light and examined them.

I peered over his shoulder. "That looks like all of it."

He unfolded the sheet that Henslowe had said was not a part of the script. "Well, he was right. I can't begin to read this." Mr. Shakespeare handed the paper to me. It was smaller than the script pages, and contained neither Mr. Jonson's handwriting nor mine, but several rows of curious symbols that might have been some foreign alphabet:

"It's some of your scribble hand, is it not?" said Mr. Armin.

I shook my head emphatically. "Nay. A few of the characters are similar to ones I use, and a couple of them look like numerals, but most I've never set eyes on afore. It's obviously a message of some sort, though."

"Obviously. The question is, from whom?"

Mr. Shakespeare was looking at me in an odd fashion, not unlike the way Henslowe had looked when I told him he had the wrong script. He took the paper from me, refolded it, and tucked it into his wallet. "I have no doubt," he said, "that it's from our spy."

Mr. Armin looked thoughtful. "You know, perhaps we should give Henslowe a dose of his own poison—hire someone in *his* company to be *our* informant."

"Do you have anyone in mind?" asked Mr. Shakespeare.

"No," admitted Mr. Armin. "I'm sure Henslowe has convinced them all that we're Satan's minions." He held up a hand. "Ah, I have it! One of us will cleverly disguise himself and convince the Admiral's Men to hire him!"

Mr. Shakespeare laughed. "That's the worst idea I ever heard."

"Oh, I don't know," said Mr. Armin. "It always seems to work in your plays."

Neither of the men had paid Mr. Pope a visit for some time, and they decided to make up for it now. In fact, as Mr. Armin revealed, that was the very reason they happened to meet Henslowe on the stairs—they had been on their way to fetch me and accompany me home.

Mr. Pope greeted them with such enthusiasm that I feared his health might suffer. "This calls for a round of brandy!"

"I'll fetch it," I said, not wishing him to overtax himself.

"Thank you, Widge."

Mr. Armin held up an admonishing hand. "Tut, tut, Thomas. You must address the boy properly. From now on it's to be William Redshaw, Esquire."

Mr. Pope gave me a baffled look. "Redshaw?"

"Aye. 'A was me father after all, it seems."

"How long have you known?"

"A few days, is all."

"Why did you not tell me sooner?"

"I—I don't ken. I suppose I was waiting for the right moment."

"I'm sorry, Widge," said Mr. Armin. "I assumed he knew."

"You called me Widge," I said.

"I'm sorry. William, then."

"Nay. I'll not be William, either. That was no more a real name than Widge was, only a sort of expedient. If I'm to have another name, I'll choose it meself." I turned and left the library. I had nearly forgotten about La Voisin's predictions, but one of them came back to me now: *You will make a name for yourself.*

When I returned with the brandy, the three sharers were huddled together like conspirators, talking in low tones. "Thank you, Wi—" Mr. Pope broke off. "Well, whoever you may be. Why don't you find Goody Willingson and ask her for something to eat? The three of us have business matters to discuss."

The manner in which he dismissed me seemed brusque and impersonal, not like Mr. Pope at all. I supposed that he was cross with me, for not telling him about Jamie Redshaw. I felt almost as though I had been cast out, like Timon. But instead of retreating to the woods, I went only as far as the kitchen, where, as I had no roots at hand, I cut a slice of bread and buttered it, then sat nibbling halfheartedly at it while I mulled over what my name should be.

• • •

I could not work on the sides for *Sejanus* the next morning; Mr. Shakespeare had kept both the script and the key to his office, as though he no longer trusted me with them. Instead, I helped Sam in the property room. As there had been no performance the night before, there was little for us to do. Nevertheless, in the time-honored tradition of prentices everywhere, we managed to make it look as though we were hard at work.

"It's a pity Sal Pavy isn't here," said Sam. "He's so good at pretending to be busy. He could give us a few pointers."

"Ha' you looked in on him?"

Sam reacted as though I'd asked whether he had looked in on the inmates of Bedlam, the asylum for the insane. "Don't you know that the grippe may be passed on, like the plague?"

"That may be. But it's not quite as likely to kill you."

"I prefer not to take the chance. Besides, he'd only tell us how they never had the grippe at Blackfriars."

The prentices and hired men gathered for rehearsal, just as though we had every expectation of performing again soon. We were attempting to revive Mr. Shakespeare's *Much Ado About Nothing*, which had lain buried in the book-keeper's trunk for at least a year. It was not responding.

As we were making much ado ourselves about who should read Hero's part in Sal Pavy's absence, Mr. Shakespeare and Mr. Armin appeared and asked to speak to me privately. "Can't it wait?" asked Mr. Lowin, who was conducting the rehearsal.

"I'm afraid not," said Mr. Armin.

They took me aside, scarcely out of earshot of the other players. Mr. Shakespeare drew two sheets of paper from his wallet and held them up, side by side. "This is the coded message we took from Henslowe. This is a page from *All's Well*, written in your charactery. We've compared them, and find a number of similarities—too many, in our opinion, to be the result of coincidence."

I stared at him incredulously. "What are you saying? That *I* wrote this? That I'm in league wi' Henslowe?"

"Soft," said Mr. Armin, "unless you wish the others to hear."

"Let them! I've nothing to hide!"

"We believe you do. How could Henslowe have gotten the key, unless you gave it to him?"

"It's as I told you—I left it i' the lock!"

"Deliberately, perhaps."

"Nay! What would I ha' to gain from Henslowe stealing the script?"

"Money?" suggested Mr. Shakespeare.

"Money?" I fairly shouted. "For what?"

"For Julia, perhaps. You said yourself that you didn't think we would help her."

The rest of the company had given up any pretense of minding their own business and were gaping at the scene unfolding before them, which must have been as compelling as any play ever acted. Tears had sprung to my eyes, and I made no effort to stay them. "I would never do such a thing, so help me God and halidom!" My voice broke like thin ice.

"Not even to save Julia?" said Mr. Shakespeare.

I could not deny that the idea had occurred to me. Though I had not acted upon it, I could hardly blame them for believing that I had, especially in view of my past record as a thief and a liar—and, of course, the even worse record of my father. Still, I was innocent, and I must not let myself appear otherwise. With all the dignity I could muster, I looked Mr. Shakespeare in the eye and said, "An you and the other sharers truly believe that I would betray you, then I can no longer consider meself a part of this company."

"Under the circumstances," said Mr. Shakespeare, "I think that would be best. But you needn't give up acting altogether; remember, Henslowe has promised to take you in."

27

So it was that the thing I had feared the most—more than the death of the queen, more than the plague itself—had come to pass.

We prentices had been taught always to exit the stage as swiftly as possible so as not to draw the audience's attention away from the next scene. Accordingly, I made my exit from the Cross Keys a quick one, not wishing to be a part of the scene that I knew would follow. I could not bear to face my fellow players and their questions, their disbelief, their doubts, perhaps their derision. I should have known that no matter how nimble I was, I could not escape Sam.

Just as I left the courtyard I heard him calling behind me, "Widge! Wait!" Though I hurried on, heedless, this did not discourage him in the least. He came trotting up alongside me to ask breathlessly, "Where are you going?"

"To see whether the Admiral's Men ha' room for another prentice."

"You can't!"

"What do you suggest, then? I'm too old for the Chapel Children, and too young to be a hired man wi' one of the small companies."

"Come back to the Cross Keys. The sharers will change their minds. The rest of us will stand up for you. No one believes that you're a traitor. I *know* you're not."

Another of La Voisin's forgotten predictions came bobbing to the surface of my mind. *You will turn traitor*, she had told Sam. "What makes you so certain?"

"Because. I know you."

"So do the sharers. They ken that I tried to steal a script from them once before. They also ken that me father was a thief—and, as they say, the seedling bears the same fruit as the tree."

"But perhaps they were just uncertain; perhaps they were testing you, making accusations to see whether you would confess."

"The way the pursuivants do wi' the Jesuit priests, you mean? An the sharers would stoop to that, I don't care to be part of their company."

Sam scowled. "All right, then. If you're set on leaving, I'm going, too. Without you there to hold me back, I'm certain to strangle Sal Pavy within a week."

"Nay, you won't. Wi'out me there, you two will ha' to become friends. Besides, Henslowe would never hire you. 'A would suspect you of being a spy for the Chamberlain's Men."

"And what makes you think he won't suspect you?"

"Why would 'a, when the Chamberlain's Men ha' given me the chuck?"

"How will he know that?"

"The real spy will tell him."

"If you can get Henslowe to trust you, perhaps he'll reveal who it is."

"Oh, aye. And perhaps 'a will gi' all of Mr. Alleyn's roles to me as well."

This notion was so ludicrous that it drew a halfhearted laugh from Sam. Next to our own Mr. Burbage, Edward Alleyn was the most celebrated player in London. We walked on in silence for a while. Finally Sam said, "How will you break this to Mr. Pope?"

I groaned. "Oh, gis. I dare not tell him at all. It would upset him too much. You're not to say a word about it, either. Promise me."

"All right. But he's sure to find out sooner or later."

"Let it be later, then."

Though Sam seemed to have given up on bringing me back, he went on walking with me, all the way across the city and through the wall to the parish of St. Giles Cripplegate, where Henslowe's theatre lay.

Unlike the Globe, which was eight-sided, the Fortune playhouse had been built in the shape of a square. Each side was eighty or ninety feet in length. On the side that faced Golding Street was an elaborate carving of Dame Fortune, wearing a cloth over her eyes to show that she was blind. She held one hand poised next to a wheel, as though about to give it a spin.

Four small figures rode upon the wheel, like prentices riding the roundabout at Bartholomew Fair, except that not all these fellows looked happy with their lot. The one who sat at the top of the wheel was clearly pleased with himself, and the one who appeared to be on his way up looked hopeful. But the upside-down face of the man on his way down was a mask of dread and dismay—and small wonder, for the figure below him, at the lowest spot on the wheel, was roasting over carved wooden flames. His mouth was wide open in a soundless scream.

"You see that wight at the bottom?" I said. "I ken how 'a feels."

Adjacent to the playhouse was a tavern, also owned by Henslowe and also called the Fortune, where the Lord Admiral's Men played during the coldest months. Now that the weather was becoming more springlike with each day that passed, their company and ours would soon be performing upon our outdoor stages—provided, of course, that we were permitted to perform at all. Once we were deprived of the queen's influence, we might all find ourselves cast out and falling to the foot of Fortune's wheel.

Sam surveyed the alehouse, then the playhouse. "Which Fortune will you choose?"

"Neither," I said. "But as I've come this far, I may as well go inside." Sam turned slowly to face me, a look of astonishment, or perhaps revelation, upon his face.

"What is it?" I asked.

"You will come into a fortune," he said.

"What?"

"Madame La Voisin's prediction: You will come into a *fortune*." He gestured at the buildings before us.

I made a scoffing sound. "She said *a* fortune, not *the* Fortune."

"Well, there's more than one, isn't there?"

"Oh, gis," I said. Could she truly have been referring to a tavern or a theatre, and not to a treasure, as I had imagined? Of course she could. She had also predicted that I would make a name for myself, and I had foolishly supposed she was talking about my reputation, when in fact she was using the phrase in a very literal sense.

"You're certain I can't come with you?" said Sam.

"I'm certain."

He looked down at his feet. "Well, then, I suppose I should get back to the Cross Keys. No doubt I'll have to pay a fine to Mr. Armin as it is."

"Aye, go on. You needn't worry about me."

Sam shook his head. "I don't see how you can just accept all this so calmly."

"What choice do I ha' ? It's Fate." I held out a hand and he grasped it. "We will still see each other, in church and elsewhere."

"Well," he said, "perhaps not in church."

"What do you mean?"

He seemed about to reply, then apparently thought better of it. "Nothing." He raised a hand in farewell and started off down Golding Lane. But he was not the sort to leave without an exit line, so I waited for it. Sure enough, he turned back and called to me, "Break a limb—preferably one of Henslowe's."

I tried the dark parlor of the Fortune tavern first, but saw no one there I recognized. Aside from my painful introduction to Henslowe the night before, I had not met any of the Admiral's Men in person, but I had seen them all act more than once. The Lord Chamberlain's Men sometimes sent us prentices here to spy upon the performances of their rivals, particularly when the play they were doing was one of ours, or purported to be. Several of Mr. Shakespeare's works had been published in the form of playbooks, and any company was free to perform these. But Henslowe had also been known to present his own slipshod versions of our more popular plays, or to falsely advertise Mr. Shakespeare as the author of some script composed by one of Henslowe's own hacks.

Unless you counted *Sejanus*, our sharers did not steal Henslowe's plays. That would have been like stealing jewelry made of paste or glass when you already owned genuine diamonds and pearls. They were not above copying a good bit of stage business, though, or borrowing an idea and improving upon it. Some said that the story of *Hamlet* was based upon a far inferior script that the Admiral's Men had presented many years before.

According to the tapster, the company had just finished moving all their properties and costumes from the tavern to the playhouse. I went next door and, finding the main entrance to the theatre open, stepped inside. The interior looked much like the Globe's, with three covered galleries for those playgoers who could afford them, and an open yard for those who could not.

Their stage was nearly identical to ours—perhaps forty feet square and three feet off the ground. At the moment it was occupied by only one actor, who was performing an odd sort of jig, skipping sideways across the boards, then forward, then back. But it was not one of their clowns rehearsing his dance steps; it was none other than the famous Edward Alleyn, a tall, broad-shouldered wight with rugged features framed by a curly black beard.

When he spotted me, he broke off his curious dance in midstep and came forward to the brink of the stage. "I was testing the boards," he explained a bit sheepishly, "to see whether any are rotten. So far the only thing I've discovered that's rotten is my dancing."

Despite my gloomy mood, I had to laugh. "I must admit, your acting is considerably better."

"You've seen me upon the stage, then—other than just now, I mean?" Mr. Alleyn sat on the edge of the platform; his long limbs almost reached the ground.

"Aye. Several times. You're nearly as good as Mr. Burbage." I had meant it to be a compliment, but it sounded more as though I were calling him second-rate. "That is—"

"No, no, don't apologize. I value an honest opinion. So, I take it you've seen the Chamberlain's Men perform as well?"

"I'm a—I *was* a prentice wi' them . . . until today."

"What happened today?"

"They gave me the chuck."

"Oh. I'm sorry." There was genuine sympathy in his voice. Clearly he understood what a dismal fate it was for a player to lose his position. After years of hearing our company speak badly of the Admiral's Men, I had expected to find them a rather loathsome lot. But Mr. Alleyn seemed quite amiable. In that respect, at least, he had the advantage of Mr. Burbage, who was aloof and conceited.

"They suspected me of being a spy for you and Mr. Henslowe," I said.

"Really? You're not, are you?"

"Nay!"

"Sorry. Philip doesn't keep me very well informed about his various schemes. I knew he was getting inside information from the Globe, but I had no idea who his source was. So, now that your old company has—what was it? Given you the chuck?—you've come to see whether we'll take you on, is that it?"

"Aye."

"Can you act?"

"Ha' you seen any of our—*their* plays?"

"Recently? Only *Hamlet*."

"I played Ophelia i' that."

"That was *you?* Well, that answers my question; you can act, all right." He held out a hand to me. "Jump up here, and we'll go talk to Philip about you." As we headed for the rooms behind the stage, he said, "You haven't told me your name."

Out of old habit, I nearly said, "Widge," but I stopped myself. I had made up my mind to choose a new name, and what better time could there be than now, when I was entering upon a new stage, quite literally, of my career?

I had never really considered taking Jamie Redshaw's family name, for I didn't care to be identified with him. Yet there was no escaping the fact that he was my father. Though he himself had done his best to deny it, in the last moments of his life he had acknowledged it and made certain that I would know. It was his attempt, I supposed, to ensure that someone in this world would remember him when he was gone. Though I did not feel that I owed him much, I could at least see that some small part of him survived, even if no one realized it but me.

"James," I said. "It's James."

28

The area behind the stage was very like that at the Globe, too—so much so that I would not have been surprised had Sam or Mr. Armin emerged from the tiring-room or the property room and greeted me. The Fortune was a good deal newer than our theatre, though, and less worn and weathered. I felt almost as though I had been transported back in time, to the Globe as it was when I first joined the company—before Julia left, before Sander died, before I knew Judith or Jamie Redshaw, before I was so burdened by ambitions and responsibilities, when I was still just Widge.

The sudden sense of loss that swept over me was so powerful that it staggered me, like an attack of vertigo, and I had to stop and steady myself. "Is anything wrong?" asked Mr. Alleyn.

"Nay," I murmured. "Just gi' me a moment."

"You're feeling a bit homesick for your old company, I expect."

I nodded. "Aye."

"Perhaps they'd take you back if Philip were to go to them and plead your case, tell them that you're not his informant."

"They'd never believe him. They'd only think 'a was trying to get me back i' their good graces so I could resume me spying."

He placed a hand on my shoulder, much the way Mr. Heminges was accustomed to do, or Mr. Pope. I wished it had been them. "Well, I think you'll find our company as cordial as the Chamberlain's Men, once you get to know us."

"I've not been accepted into it yet."

"You will be, though, if I have my way." He smiled a bit smugly. "And I usually do."

We found Henslowe in his office, writing in a bound journal. When he saw me, his bulging eyes fairly started out of his head. "Well, well! When I invited you to come and see me, I never imagined it would be so soon. How's your belly?" Before I could reply, he addressed Mr. Alleyn. "The lad tried valiantly to keep me from snatching *Sejanus*, and I was forced to resort to violence."

"You have the script, then?" asked Mr. Alleyn.

Henslowe scowled. "Regrettably, no. I ran into Armin and Shakespeare, who took it from me at the point of a sword, like the pirates that they are." He glanced at me. "I see you're not bothering to defend them. Have you some grudge against them, too?"

"Aye. They've cast me out."

"Why, the ungrateful wretches! After you practically risked your life trying to save their precious play?"

"They think I'm i' league wi' you—that I told you where to find the script, and gave you the key."

Henslowe shook his head. "They're even bigger fools than I

thought. You're better off without them. I suppose you've come to ask me for a position."

"You did offer me one."

"Now, I didn't promise anything. I merely said to come and see me. In any case, I didn't expect you to take me up on it right away. We've been shut down, the same as every other company, and without money coming in, we can barely meet the expenses we already have."

Mr. Alleyn laughed. "Oh, don't go playing the pauper, Philip. With all your various enterprises, you have more money than you can count. The boy's a fine actor; I've seen him. He'd be an asset to the company."

"That may be. But we don't need another actor, no matter how good he is, if they won't let him act."

"The theatres will open again eventually."

"Then let him come back eventually."

"And what do you expect him to do in the meanwhile? Starve?"

For all his skill as a player, Mr. Alleyn was playing this scene all wrong. I knew that Henslowe cared no more about whether or not I starved than he did about whether or not I could act. He was a man of business and was likely to be swayed only by the promise of a profit.

Luckily I had kept a trump card in reserve that I might play if the game was not going my way. "Oh, I don't expect I'll starve," I said calmly. "I have more to offer to a company than just me acting ability."

"Oh?" said Henslowe. "And what might that be?"

"Two things, actually. One is me skill at swift writing." I opened my wallet, drew out a sheaf of papers, and laid it on the desk before him. "This is the other."

"A script?" He picked up the first page, read it over rapidly, and gave me an incredulous look. "Unless I miss my guess, this is Shakespeare's work."

I did not reply, only sat there with what I hoped was a mysterious smile on my face.

Henslowe handed the page to Mr. Alleyn, who, after perusing it but a moment, said, "If it's not his, then it's a very good imitation. Where did you get this?"

"Mr. Shakespeare gave it to me." Even though this was perfectly true, I had a notion that it would not sound that way to Henslowe.

I was right. He smiled skeptically. "*Gave* it to you, eh?"

"Aye. 'A said I might do wi' it as I wished."

At this, Henslowe laughed outright. "Did he, indeed?" He shook his head. "I suspect that you're a better thief than you are a player, lad. I don't believe your story for a moment." He examined several more pages of the script. "So, I'm supposed to want this enough to hire you as a prentice, is that it?"

"Nay. You're supposed to want it enough to hire me *and* to pay me eight pounds for the script."

Henslowe's bulging eyes went wide. "Eight pounds? Are you mad? What's to prevent me from simply tossing you out on your ear and keeping the script?"

"Well, for one thing, you wouldn't be able to read it."

"And why is that?"

"See for yourself."

He shuffled through the pages until he came upon the scenes that I had written in charactery. "What's this?"

"The swift writing I mentioned."

"You transcribed this for Shakespeare, then?" He scowled at the strings of symbols. "You know, this looks very much like the . . . " He trailed off.

"Like the code you and your spy use to communicate," I finished.

"Yes. But it's not, is it?"

"Nay."

Henslowe leaned back in his chair and regarded me with a mixture of amusement and respect. "You're a clever lad. I believe you're right, Edward. He would be an asset to the company." He drummed his fingers together thoughtfully. "I will pay you," he said finally, "six pounds for the play—three pounds now and three more when you've put it into a form we can read."

"And you'll take me on as a prentice?"

"Yes."

"Done," I said. And, like two merchants concluding a business transaction, we shook hands on it.

My first task as a member of the Admiral's Men was agreeable enough: to adjourn to the tavern for dinner. I'd had little to eat that morning and was growing light-headed from hunger, yet I was not at all eager to join the others. In fact, I felt as apprehensive as I did just before a performance.

Though playgoers might be raucous and hard to please, seldom were they downright hostile, as these wights were sure to be, considering I had come to them from the company that was their fiercest rival. Still, I could not refuse to appear before them, any more than I could refuse to make my entrance in a play.

To my surprise they welcomed me, as members of a congregation might welcome into their church a convert from some other, less enlightened faith. A few of the faces around the table regarded me with disapproval or suspicion, but those sorts were to be found everywhere, even within the Chamberlain's Men. For the most part they were, as Mr. Alleyn had promised, a cordial and companionable lot—except when the conversation turned to the Chamberlain's Men.

The Admiral's Men held as low an opinion of my old company as the Chamberlain's Men did of them. Their ill will was founded upon more than mere jealousy, though. They voiced several complaints that, even had I been in a position to defend my comrades, I would have been hard-pressed to answer satisfactorily.

They seemed to resent most the fact that Mr. Shakespeare was so closefisted with his plays. Most playwrights, they said, sold their works to a printer after a dozen or so performances so that other companies might have a chance at them. Only a handful of Mr. Shakespeare's plays were in print, and those were pirated versions, scribbled down during a peformance, or recited, usually inaccurately, by some cast member in exchange for a few shillings.

They were also out of square over their rivals' refusal to raise the price of admission. Mr. Henslowe was more than just out of square; he was fairly furious. "The amount we pay for costumes has nearly doubled in the past several years, as has the amount we pay for properties and scripts, and for hired men and musicians, and for meals, and for coal, and for renting rooms. How can we hope to survive, let alone make a profit, if we do not increase our prices as well?"

• • •

After dinner, he and Mr. Alleyn escorted me back to the office, where I was to begin writing out in a normal hand the indecipherable passages of my script. "If I were you," Mr. Alleyn said to me in a stage whisper, "I would not set down a word of it until I'd seen the color of his money."

Mr. Henslowe shook a huge fist at him. "I've given the boy my word; that should be good enough."

"Not quite as good as gold, however," I said.

The big man cast me a dark look, but he also cast three sovereigns upon the table, which I promptly put into my purse. "It's just as I said," he growled. "I have to pay twice as much for scripts as they're worth. What's this one called, by the by?"

I had been giving so much thought to my own name lately that I had neglected to christen the play. "*Timon of Athens*," I said blithely, as though that had been in my mind all along.

"Hmm. Not much of a title. But at least Shakespeare had the sense not to set it in a Papist country. Although, once the queen is gone, who knows what will be acceptable and what will not? In six months it may be the Catholics who are taking us to task for sounding too Puritan."

They went to deal with other matters, leaving me alone in the office. I copied out one page of the play as rapidly as I could. Then, after taking a quick look out the door to make certain no one was about, I began a systematic search through the various papers and ledgers on the shelf above the desk. Before I could discover anything of use, I heard footsteps approaching. I thrust the journal I was examining back into place and bent over the script.

One of the company's clowns stuck his head into the room. Seeing how absorbed I appeared to be in my task, he murmured, "Pardon me," and moved on. It went that way the rest of the afternoon. Each time I tried to resume my search, one of the players passed by, forcing me to scramble back to the script.

In spite of myself, I had nearly all the play in a readable form by the end of the day. I did not reveal this to Mr. Henslowe, however. Instead, I complained that with all the interruptions, I was having trouble concentrating. I suggested that I might make better progress early in the morning, when the place was quieter.

"You'll be here early, right enough," he said. "We expect all our prentices to be in the theatre by prime. No doubt you were accustomed to sleeping late when you were with the Chamber Pot's Men, but we run this company like a business, not a midsummer fair."

29

That evening, after supper and a round of shove-penny with the orphan boys, I was summoned to the library to give my daily report. "So, how is Fortune treating you?" asked Mr. Pope.

I smiled in appreciation of his wordplay. "Well enough." I pulled out my purse and jingled it. "They gave me three pounds for the play, wi' three more to come."

Mr. Pope gave a low whistle. "Not bad, for a novice playwright."

"Well, they assumed it was all Mr. Shakespeare's work, of course, and though I didn't actually say it was, neither did I say that it wasn't. Unfortunately, I wasn't able to find the key to their code. I'll try again tomorrow."

"They weren't suspicious of you, then?"

"Not that I could tell. They considered the Chamberlain's Men a bunch of blackguards already, so when I told them I'd been sacked unjustly, it only served to confirm their opinion.

What about our company? Did anyone suspect that it was all a sham, do you wis?"

"Not according to Will. He says you played your part very convincingly."

"It wasn't difficult. I just imagined how I would feel an I were truly given the chuck. It's not as bad as I feared, though, being a member of the Admiral's Men. They actually treated me quite kindly, except for Mr. Henslowe—and even 'a was not altogether a swad. I' truth, I feel a bit guilty for deceiving them."

"They've never had any such qualms, you may be sure."

"Perhaps not. All the same, it's a pity the two companies can't be on better terms. They're not blackguards, either. They're just players, like us." I got wearily to my feet. "Me throat's parched. I'm going to ha' a drink of ale. Shall I fetch some for you?"

"No, thank you. I'm off to bed."

"You don't look as well as you might. I wish Mr. Armin and Mr. Shakespeare had not made you a part of their scheme. The doctor said you were not to be upset."

He shrugged. "They didn't want to send you off behind enemy lines, as it were, without my approval. Besides, I'm not upset, only tired. It's something that happens when you get old, you know."

I yawned. "Then I must be getting old."

Goody Willingson was in the kitchen, wiping clean the supper dishes. As I drew a mug of ale from the keg, she sidled up to me and said softly, "You know, if you're looking for a new name, you could do worse than take Mr. Pope's. He's been far more of a father to you than that Redshaw fellow ever was or ever would have been."

"That's so. I'm not certain 'a would care to ha' the son of an outlaw using his name, though."

"Do you really suppose that matters to him? You once said yourself, it's not your heritage that matters, it's what you do with it."

"Aye, well, so far I haven't done much of anything, have I?"

I woke well before dawn the next morning but still had to hasten, for the walk to St. Giles was a long one and I could not abbreviate it by taking a wherry boat across the Thames. Though the ice in the middle of the river had broken up, there was still a wide border of it along the banks, too rotten to set foot upon.

By the time I neared St. Olave's, its bells were already ringing prime. Yet even though I was late, and even though it meant going out of my way to do so, I could not resist passing by the church and pausing a moment to gaze at the steps where Judith was to have met me several days before. It was as though I hoped to find some trace of her still there—some small item that she might heedlessly have dropped, perhaps, or the faint scent of cloves lingering in the air. But of course there was nothing, not even the memory of a fond parting to console me. I hurried on.

I need not have worried about my tardiness. For all Mr. Henslowe's talk of running the Fortune like a business, neither he nor any of the other players had arrived yet, only the tiring-man, who, fortunately, had been instructed to let me into Mr. Henslowe's office.

Certain that I would not have the place to myself for long, I set to work at once—not on the script of *Timon*, but on the assortment of books and papers that lay upon the shelf. After a few minutes of frantic searching, I found what I was looking for, at the back of the journal in which Mr. Henslowe had been writing the previous afternoon. So much the methodical man of business was he that he had labeled the page in a clerk's precise hand so there could be no doubt about what it contained: *Cypher Key*. Beneath this heading he had set down in neat rows, as though he were doing accounts, the following:

I considered copying the symbols, but it would take so long that I risked being discovered. Instead I drew my dagger and ran the point of it down the left margin of the page; then I tore the cypher key from the book, tucked it inside my doublet, and returned the journal to its place.

Within half an hour I had finished translating *Timon*'s passages of charactery into the queen's English. After straightening up the pages and stacking them neatly on the desk, I dipped Mr. Henslowe's pen into the inkwell and wrote carefully at the top of the first page:

Timon of Athens: A Lamentable Tragedie. By James . . .

I hesitated only a moment before setting down the latter half of the rightful author's name: *Pope*.

I was halfway back to the Cross Keys before the irony of what I had written occurred to me. Mr. Henslowe was so fearful of performing anything that smacked of Catholic sympathies. Imagine how distressed he would be, then, to discover that he had paid good money for a play composed by a Pope.

At least he could console himself with the fact that it had cost him only three pounds instead of the six we had agreed upon. No doubt I could have collected the other three if I had gone on pretending that the work was Mr. Shakespeare's. But that would have been unfair, both to Mr. Henslowe and to Mr. Shakespeare. I had no qualms about keeping the three sovereigns I already had, however. Surely, even with all its faults, my play was worth that much.

The courtyard of the Cross Keys was the scene of more frenzied action than a French farce. The company's two-wheeled carts sat in the yard, piled high with trunks full of costumes and properties. Ned Shakespeare stood in the bed of one of the carts, shifting the trunks a few inches this way or that, with an intent look upon his face, as though he were performing some essential task. When he spied me, his expression changed to one of astonishment. "What the devil are *you* doing here? I thought they'd given you the sack."

"And so they did. But I've some unfinished business. Ha' you any notion where I might find your brother?"

He jerked his head toward the second-floor balcony. "Up there—fetching all the stuff that doesn't weigh much, I'll wager."

Mr. Shakespeare was, in fact, stuggling to drag his desk across the floor of the office. When I entered he gave a sigh of relief. "Ah, Widge; it seems you have the one quality essential to a player."

"What's that?"

"Good timing. Give me a hand with this infernal furniture, will you?"

"We're moving back to the Globe, I take it?"

"Very perceptive. Take hold." As we manuevered the desk out of the door and onto the balcony, he said softly, between grunts of effort, "Any success?"

"Aye. I've got the code."

"Excellent." He stood erect and rubbed at his old injury. "Let's leave this for someone larger to wrestle with, shall we? Come." We went down to the dark parlor, where Mr. Shakespeare, after ordering ale for both of us, drew from his wallet the coded message he had found on Mr. Henslowe. I, in turn, produced the cypher key and placed it before him. "Where did you find this?" he asked.

"I' Mr. Henslowe's journal."

"He actually left you alone with it?"

"Aye. 'A seemed to trust me. So did most of the Admiral's Men. I feel a bit as though I've betrayed them."

"Yes. I can see how you would. You also have that other quality that makes a good player—the ability to identify with others, to see things through their eyes. Unfortunately, you can't very well be loyal both to them and to us."

"I ken that. But why does being loyal to this company mean that I ha' to hate th' Admiral's Men? Why must we be rivals, and not simply fellow players?"

"All the theatre companies in London want the same thing—as large an audience as possible. That means we're in competition."

"Isn't there enough audience to go around? Besides, an all the theatres close down, *none* of us will have an audience.

Would it not be better an we all formed an alliance or something, to try and prevent that? Even oxen ha' sense enough to pull together, instead of always trying to outdo one another."

Mr. Shakespeare was regarding me with a rather startled look. Prentices did not ordinarily speak their minds quite so forcefully. "I'm sorry," I murmured. "It's just . . . well, it puts me i' mind o' the way the Catholics and Anglicans are at each other's throats, while the Puritans despise them both. How can they be such deadly enemies, when they all serve the same god? It seems to me that it's the same wi' us theatre folk: we all serve the same god. Do we not?"

Mr. Shakespeare was twisting his earring between thumb and finger, and staring thoughtfully—but no longer at me. His gaze seemed fixed on something far off, as though he were trying to see all the way to St. Giles and into the hearts of the Admiral's Men. There was a long stretch of silence, during which the tapster brought our ale and I began to regret that I had been so outspoken. Finally, Mr. Shakespeare said, "You're very persuasive with words, Widge. Perhaps you'll make a playwright after all."

"I hope to try. But not under the name of Widge."

"William, then?"

"Nay. James."

"Oh? Very well. I still favor William, myself, but James is a perfectly respectable name—especially as there's likely to be one on the throne. I hope you didn't choose it for that reason."

I laughed. "Hardly. It's after me father."

"You're taking his surname, too, I suppose?"

"Nay. I've decided—" I broke off. I had not yet told Mr. Pope of my decision, and he should certainly be the first to know.

"I understand," said Mr. Shakespeare, even though I had not attempted to explain. "Now. Let us see if we can determine who our spy is, shall we?"

Because Mr. Henslowe's code provided more than one symbol for each letter of the alphabet, it took some effort to decipher the message. As I completed each group of words, Mr. Shakespeare read it aloud. "Script of *Sejanus* finished . . . Company gone by vespers . . . I enclose key to . . . "

As the last few words emerged, letter by letter, Mr. Shakespeare trailed off, unable to speak them. I went back over the symbols, thinking perhaps I had translated them wrong. But there was no mistake. The final sentence read, "I enclose key to my brother's office."

30

Mr. Shakespeare sat motionless for a long while, staring at the words as though waiting for me to translate them yet again, into some form that he could comprehend. At last he said, so softly that I could scarcely hear, "Ned. I should have known."

"So should I, after 'a cornered me i' th' office that morning so early, wi' so flimsy a reason. I *did* leave the key i' the lock, then, and Ned made off wi' it."

Mr. Shakespeare nodded grimly. "I have no doubt that it was he who betrayed Father Gerard, as well."

"But why would 'a do such a thing?"

"For the same reason he served as Henslowe's spy, and the same reason he stole costumes from the company. He needed the money—to pay off gambling debts, and bribe his way out of trouble with the law, and God knows what else." He buried his face in his hands and sighed heavily. "*Money*," he said, in the tone one uses for uttering a curse. "Would that it had never been invented."

"Folk would only ha' found something else to covet. Salted herrings, perhaps, or fern seeds."

Despite his melancholy mood, there was a hint of amusement in the glance Mr. Shakespeare gave me. "Fern seeds?"

"Aye. Up Yorkshire way folk say that an you eat enough of them, they make you invisible. The problem is, they also make you puke."

"I know the feeling." He took several long swallows of his ale. "Would you be so kind as to send Ned in here? I may as well have done with it; it's not likely to get any easier."

Ned was still pretending to rearrange the load on one of the carts. When I told him that Mr. Shakespeare wanted to see him, he scowled. "What about?"

"Something about fern seeds, I believe."

He gave me an incredulous look. "Fern seeds?"

I grinned. "That's exactly what Mr. Shakespeare said."

Ned stalked off, shaking his head, and nearly collided with Sam, who was hurrying across the courtyard toward me. "Widge! Gog's blood! What brings you back here?"

"Shank's mare," I said, meaning my feet. "I've done meself out of a Fortune, you see."

"You've quit already? Are you going to rejoin us, then?"

"I never actually left. It was all a sham, designed to get me into the Admiral's Men so I might do a bit of spying."

He aimed a blow at me, which I dodged. "You sot! You let me believe you'd been sacked!"

"I had to. We dared not let the truth be known lest Henslowe get wind of it, by way of his informant." I did not let on, of course, that I had half suspected Sam of being that informant.

"Did you find the culprit out, then?"

I hesitated, unwilling to be the one to break the news, and then merely nodded.

"It's Sal Pavy, isn't it?"

"I can't say. You'll learn soon enough, I expect."

"It's him, though, isn't it?" Sam insisted, but I would not be moved.

I surveyed the courtyard. "Where *is* Sal Pavy, by the by?"

"Still home in bed, being waited on hand and foot, and enjoying every moment of it, no doubt, while the rest of us are here working our arses off."

"You don't appear to be working very hard just now," I observed.

"I'm trying to pry an answer out of you. I call that hard. Come now, you may tell me; it's Sal Pavy, right?"

When we gathered for dinner, Mr. Shakespeare announced that Ned had quit the company. Though he did not specify the reason, it was clear that everyone knew, and that no one was surprised—except Sam, who shook his head and muttered, "I would have sworn it was Sal Pavy."

"I would appreciate it," said Mr. Shakespeare, "if the circumstances of Ned's departure were kept among ourselves. I don't wish to harm his chances of finding a position with another company."

"I w-wonder whether there's any th-theatre left in London that hasn't already had a t-taste of him," said Mr. Heminges.

"Probably not," Mr. Shakespeare admitted. "He may have to go farther afield."

"I ken a company i' Leicester that may be able to use him," I said. This drew a laugh from the others. They knew well enough what company I meant—the very one that had sent me here to steal the script of *Hamlet*, and the one that had caused us so many problems the previous summer, when we toured the northern shires.

Thinking of *Hamlet* had brought Julia, who had once been our Ophelia, to the forefront of my mind again. As we went back to loading the carts, I caught Mr. Heminges and asked whether he had tried to locate Tom Cogan. "R-Rob has," he said. "I'll let him t-tell you about it."

Mr. Armin had been to Alsatia, Cogan's home ground, to make inquiries. "Which," he said, "was rather like climbing into a pit of snakes to inquire about one viper in particular. I got a lot of hisses and venomous looks and very little information. Eventually, though, I found a beggar who was willing to talk to me—for a price. According to him, Tom Cogan was placed under arrest several days ago, for stealing a gold bracelet from the queen's treasury."

"The queen's treasury?"

"Well, that part may have been only a rumor. He seemed certain, though, that Cogan had been arrested for *something*, which means we may have to look for him in prison."

"Oh, gis. Which one, do you suppose?"

"There's no telling. I've sent word to Father Gerard asking him to keep an eye out for our man when he's ministering to his Papist prisoners."

I felt inside my doublet for my purse, to reassure myself that I still had the three pounds Julia would need for her passage home. The money was there, right enough. What good was it, though, if I had no way of getting it to her?

"Oh, before I forget," said Mr. Armin, "Sal has asked that you come by to see him."

"Me?" I hardly considered myself a close friend of his. But perhaps I was the closest thing to it. "How is he?"

Mr. Armin shook his head soberly. "Not good. The grippe has infected his lungs."

By the time we carted all our possessions across the bridge to the Globe and unloaded them, it was all but dark, and I was all but dead. I would have put off visiting Sal Pavy until another day had it not been for the guilt that was still lodged inside me, like a sliver, reminding me that I had been responsible, at least in part, for his near drowning.

Sal Pavy's mother, a small, grim-looking woman, showed me to her son's room. "You mustn't stay long, and you mustn't let him do much talking. He's very weak."

"Ha' you brought in a physician?"

She nodded. "He says the boy should recover in time, if he's kept quiet."

In truth, Sal Pavy did not appear to be very near to death's door. Perhaps it was only an effect of the fever, but his face was flushed and his eyes were bright. Propped up in his bed by a multitude of down pillows, he looked rather smug and pampered. Then I glimpsed the kerchief that lay crumpled between his hands. It was covered with rust-colored stains.

"We've missed you," I said, which was not altogether a lie. Sal Pavy was like one of those obnoxious secondary characters that playwrights so often create—Parolles, for example, or Polonius, or Apemantus. Though their main function seems to be to irk the other characters, the play would be poorer without them. He seemed about to reply, but was seized by a fit of coughing that imprinted the kerchief with a fresh stain. "Perhaps . . . perhaps I should come back another time, when you're stronger."

He shook his head and motioned for me to sit on the end of the bed. After struggling for several moments to find enough breath, he got out a few words. "Mr. Armin . . . says that . . . you blame yourself . . . for what happened to me."

"Aye. I should ha' had more sense. You never would ha' gone out on the ice had I refused to."

He shook his head again. "You're wrong. I would have . . . done it anyway. Only you . . . would not have . . . been there . . . to pull me out."

I gazed at him curiously. "Why are you telling me this?"

"Because. You've always tried . . . to be . . . a friend. When I die . . . I don't want you . . . feeling responsible."

I forced a feeble laugh. "What makes you think you're going to die?"

"What makes you . . . think I'm not?"

"The doctor. He says you'll be good as new in a week or so."

He pressed the kerchief to his lips and stifled a cough. "Well . . . if I do die . . . I won't mind so much . . . really. This way, you see . . . I'll be remembered as a . . . talented youth . . . full of promise. If I'd lived . . . to be sixty . . . I'd have been . . . just another old actor."

I arrived home so weary and downcast that even the boys noticed. They let me forgo the usual games and settled for hearing a story instead. Though it was a rousing one, replete with ghosts and magic and bloody deeds, it was far less taxing than being Banks's horse.

Mr. Pope suggested that my daily report could wait until morning, but I had one matter to discuss that would not wait. "I was wondering," I said hesitantly, "whether you would mind me taking your last name as me own?"

He stared at me for a moment, as though I'd asked his permission to sprout wings and fly. Then he laughed and, seizing both my arms, shook them so hard that my teeth rattled. "Mind? I'd be honored, Widge!"

"Umm . . . I've decided on a new first name as well. I'd like to be called James."

"James it is, then!" He tested the words on his tongue. "James Pope. James Pope. I like it! We must christen you, like a ship, with a bottle of brandy!" He called for Goody Willingson and sent her to the cellar to fetch the spirits.

When she returned, she announced, "That same gentleman is here as was here a week ago, and is asking for you, Widge—or James, should I say?" She shook her head. "That will take some getting used to."

"Show him in," said Mr. Pope. "I'll take myself off to bed."

"There's no need," I told him. "Perhaps it's time I began letting you in on things, instead of keeping them from you."

Father Gerard had altered his appearance yet again. He wore the sort of linen robe favored by physicians, and he had dyed his beard a shade of red that matched his wig.

"Can I offer you a nip of brandy?" said Mr. Pope.

"No, thank you. I mustn't linger. I have a message for Widge. From Tom Cogan."

"You've found him, then?" I said.

Gerard nodded grimly. "He's in Newgate."

"Gog's blood! That's where they take wights that are to be hanged!"

"Yes. He's been convicted of theft, and it's his second offense. I was told to ask Cogan for a letter of some sort—something to do with his daughter?"

"Aye. Did 'a give it to you?"

"No. He'd scarcely even talk to me. He said he didn't trust me. When I told him I was a priest, he said that was all the more reason to distrust me. The only person he will speak to is you, Widge. He says you were his daughter's friend."

"All right. Should I go now?"

"No. Meet me outside the prison tomorrow at nones. The warder on duty then is a good Catholic—and an even better one since I slipped him a sovereign. We can tell him you're Cogan's son. That'll get you in."

The moment Gerard was gone, Mr. Pope began unexpectedly to chuckle.

"What is 't?" I asked.

"Sorry. I know this is serious business. It's just that up until a week ago, you had no father at all. Now, suddenly, you've got three of 'em—Redshaw, Cogan, and me." He poured an inch or so of brandy into a glass and handed it to me. "Now. Tell me about Julia."

Ordinarily I did my best to avoid Newgate. No doubt it had once been an attractive edifice, especially the stone gatehouse. But over the course of nearly two centuries, the soot from the city's chimneys had given the walls a dark and forbidding aspect that hinted at what lay inside them.

Mr. Henslowe would no doubt have found the prison admirable, for it was run like a business. Those prisoners who could afford it were put in well-lighted, airy quarters, with reasonably comfortable furnishings, and given decent food and drink. Those who could not were thrown together in dark, damp cells that reeked of human waste. They slept on straw—if they were lucky—and dined on gruel and water. The only consolation for these poor wretches was the thought that they might cheat the hangman by dying of jail fever before their execution day arrived.

Tom Cogan was, of course, one of the unfortunate ones, as he had been all his life. Unlike his fellow prisoners, who lounged about playing at cards or dice, or simply sat hunched hoplessly in a corner of the cell, Cogan was pacing restlessly back and forth, back and forth, like a caged lion I had once seen on display at the Tower. Like that beast, he seemed oblivious to everything around him, including the curses of one of the dice players, who threatened to break his kneecaps if he didn't stop his infernal pacing.

When the warder let us into the cell, Cogan descended upon me like a lion upon its prey. "Good lad! I knew I could count on you!"

"You could have trusted Father Gerard."

Cogan gave the priest a dismissive glance. "Ahh, all he's interested in is saving my soul, which ain't worth the trouble. It's my neck I'm worried about." He sank his fingers painfully into my arm and drew me to the far end of the cell. "And you," he whispered, "are going to help me save it."

31

"Me?" I said. "What can *I* do?"

"Julia never told me nothing much about her actor friends, but she did say once that you was prenticed to a physician."

"Aye. But what—?"

Cogan's fingernails sank more deeply into my arm. "This wight I once met—a bid-stand, he was"—this, I had learned, was the London term for a highwayman—"told me that he'd got himself out of prison by taking some stuff that put him into a sort of trance, so they mistook him for dead. As they were hauling him off to the graveyard, he came to and made his escape. Now, have you ever heard of a root or a plant or the like that would do such as that?"

I pried his fingers from my arm. "As a matter of fact, I ha'. But not as a physician's prentice; as a player. When I'm acting the part of Juliet, Friar Laurence gives me a vial of distilled liquor. An I drink it, 'a says, it will bring on a cold and drowsy humor that has the appearance of death: 'No warmth, no breath, shall testify thou livest.'"

"That's but a play!" Cogan scoffed. "Anything may happen in a play!"

"I ken that. But I asked Mr. Shakespeare what was supposed to be i' the vial, and 'a said the juice of mandrake root. According to him, it truly works. 'A learned about it from an apothecary."

Cogan considered this a moment, then leaned in to me and whispered, "I want you to get me some of it."

"Mandrake?"

"Whist! Keep your voice down!"

"Sorry. But how would I manage to get it past the warder? 'A searched us on the way in."

"Tell him I'm sick, and you're bringing me medicine."

"You don't look very sick."

He grinned, disclosing his rotten teeth. "You're not the only wight that can act, you know."

His scheme sounded doubtful at best and, at worst, risky. But if we did nothing, there was no doubt about what the outcome would be: he would hang. I must at least try—if not for him, then for Julia. "All right. I'll do 't. But you must do something for me first."

"What's that?"

"Gi' me the letter wi' Julia's address so I may send her money to get home."

He gave me another unpleasant grin and shook his head. "No, no. First you bring me the mandrake." He clapped a hand on my shoulder. "It's not that I don't trust you, lad. It's just that I've learned a wight is more likely to do what you want if you've got something *he* wants."

• • •

As we passed from the gloomy, stinking interior of Newgate into sunlight and fresh air again, I told the warder, "I'll be back in a little while. Me da's feeling poorly, and I'm to fetch him some wormwood, to settle his stomach."

The man nodded sympathetically. "I expect I'd feel poorly, too, if I was to be hanged in a few days."

When we were well away from the prison, Father Gerard asked, "Is Cogan really ill?"

I shook my head. "'A wants me to bring him mandrake, not wormwood."

Gerard stared at me. "Does he mean to take his own life?"

"Nay, only to feign death, in order to escape."

"He may do more than just feign it; mandrake is a deadly poison."

The apothecary we called upon agreed that in a large enough quantity, mandrake would surely prove fatal. "However, a drop or two of the diluted juice is often used to deaden pain."

"What about half a dozen drops, then?" I asked.

"I'm not certain. It might cause temporary paralysis and unconsciousness."

Father Gerard did his best to convince me that Cogan's plan was foolish, and that I must not be party to it. "Suppose you give him too large a dose? Do you wish to be responsible for a man's death?"

His words brought another of La Voisin's predictions back into my mind, where it rang like a death knell: *Because of you, someone will die. Someone will die.* "But suppose I do naught, and they hang him? Will I not still be responsible? Besides, 'a refuses to tell me Julia's whereabouts unless I do as 'a says."

"There are other ways of escaping. I gained my freedom from the Tower of London by sliding down a rope."

"Truly? I've heard folk say that no one has ever escaped from the Tower."

"Well, they're wrong. Some six or seven years ago, during my first assignment to London, the pursuivant's men brought me in for *questioning*, as they called it—which meant stringing me up by the arms and beating me, in an effort to make me tell them who my superiors were and where they could be found. That's how I came by these." He touched the several scars on his face. "When I refused to cooperate, they locked me in the Salt Tower. No doubt they would have executed me eventually, as they did so many of my fellow priests, had my friends not managed to smuggle a rope in to me."

"But how did you get out of your cell?"

"I wasn't confined to a cell. I was free to walk about on the battlements."

"Is Tom Cogan permitted out of his cell?"

"Probably not," Gerard admitted.

"Then a rope would not do him much good, would it?"

When we came within sight of Newgate, the priest halted. "I'm sorry, Widge. Go on, if you must, but I'll have no part of it. It's my duty to save souls, not to damn them." He turned and walked away.

I called after him, "Would his soul be saved, then, an he met his end on the scaffold?" He did not reply.

The warder took me to the condemned cell at once. "Your da's gotten worse since you left," he said. "I think he's going to need something stronger than wormwood."

Cogan was no longer pacing back and forth. He was curled up in a corner of the cell, twitching and groaning pitifully. A communal water keg sat against one wall, with a metal cup next to it. I dipped out a cup of water and knelt next to him. He gave a cry so startling that I nearly dropped the cup. "Don't you think you're overdoing it just a bit?" I whispered.

He opened one eye and peered at me. "I'm supposed to be dying, ain't I?"

"Most folk don't make such a fuss about it." I took out the apothecary's vial and eyed the dark liquid within. "Perhaps this is not such a good idea. What an I gi' you too much? Th' apothecary says that a large dose is fatal."

Cogan shrugged. "In any case, I'll be no worse off than I would have been at the end of a rope, will I?"

"I suppose not." Feeling that it was better to err on the side of caution, I put only four drops into the water and stirred it with my finger. I was about to hand the cup to him when I remembered his end of the bargain. "Where's the letter?"

His mask of make-believe agony slipped a little, and a look of genuine discomfort showed through. "Ah," he said. "The letter."

"Aye, from Julia. You ha' it, do you not?"

"Actually . . . no. The constables who nabbed me took it, along with the bracelet."

"Oh, gis! So you've no idea, either, where to find Julia?"

"Well, I wouldn't say no idea at all. I mind that the name of the woman who runs the lodging house was Hardy. I remembered it particularly because it don't sound French."

I sighed. "That's all very well, but I can scarcely send a package i' care of Madame Hardy, Paris, France, can I?"

"I could take it there."

"Then we'd need another three pounds for *your* passage. In any case, you can't go anywhere until we get you out of here." I handed him the cup.

He raised it to his lips, then lowered it. "If I take this, there's a chance I won't wake up again?"

I nodded glumly.

"It ain't that I'm afeared, you understand. It's just that . . . well, I've a confession to make first."

"You should ha' spoken to Father Gerard, then."

"It ain't that sort of confession. It has to do with Julia. I know I can trust you to pass it on to her, in case I should hop the twig."

"Hop the twig?"

"Knock off. You know—die."

I pointed out that he was supposed to be dying even now, or at least should appear to be. He ignored me, and launched into a long and complicated narrative that was every bit as astounding and unlikely as any I had concocted in my fevered attempts to compose a play. Yet he related it all in such a matter-of-fact manner and provided so many convincing details that I did not doubt for a moment that it was true.

32

When it came to lengthy parting speeches, Cogan managed to outdo even Hamlet—who, after saying, "I am dead, Horatio," goes on for another twenty lines or so. Cogan spoke without pause for a good quarter of an hour. When his tale finally reached its end, it left me as stunned as I had been at the conclusion of the first play I ever saw performed. It took me several moments to collect myself enough to speak. "Does—does Julia ken any o' this?"

Cogan shook his head. "Not a bit."

"Why did you never tell her?"

With one hand he gestured at the dismal prison cell that surrounded us. "You see where knowing it has gotten me." He lifted the cup and stirred the contents with his finger. "Well, one way or another, I won't be here much longer." He threw back his head and downed the mandrake potion in two great gulps, then gave a shudder. "Aggh! That's nasty stuff. I only hope it does its job." He waved a dismissive hand at me. "You go on now. I can die well enough by myself."

"Aye, but can you come back to life by yourself? An you stay unconscious for long, they may bury you."

He scratched his beard thoughtfully. "Good point. Then it's up to you to get my corpse off the meat wagon—the cart that takes away the dead prisoners. It comes around every day, just after dark. Revive me if you can. If not . . . " He shrugged. "Well, give me a decent burial, will you? It's more than I'd have got if they'd strung me up."

I considered returning to the Globe and enlisting Mr. Armin's help. After all, someone might well object to my carrying off a body. And even if no one did, I wasn't certain I could carry Cogan by myself.

An hour or two of daylight remained. I could probably make it to the theatre and back before the meat wagon arrived. But what if I did not? When Cogan came to, he might find himself locked inside a charnel house, in the middle of a pile of stiff, staring corpses—or, worse yet, under the ground.

I had chosen, against Father's Gerard's advice, to be an accomplice in Cogan's cock-brained scheme; it was up to me to see it through. I concealed myself in the shadows at the mouth of a narrow alleyway and waited.

When at last a one-horse cart bearing a few bodies rumbled up Newgate Street and stopped before the prison, I sorely regretted not having gone for reinforcements. Instead of the single, shambling carter I had expected, the meat wagon was escorted by two guards in breastplates and helmets, with rapiers at their sides.

"Gog's nowns!" I breathed. If I had had a sword of my own—which I did not—I might conceivably have overcome a single guard, provided he was not too good a swordsman; against two of them, I stood no chance at all.

Something tapped me lightly upon the shoulder. With a gasp, I spun about. A tall robed figure loomed over me, indistinct in the shadows. "Soft!" said a familiar voice. "They'll hear you!"

"Father Gerard?" I whispered. "Why are you here?"

"To help."

"But—you said you wanted no part of our plan."

"I said I would not be a party to poisoning a man. I have no objection to resurrecting him."

"Ha' you a weapon?" I asked hopefully.

"I'm no more willing to stab or to shoot a man than I am to poison him."

"Then how i' the name of halidom will we deal wi' those wights?"

"Well," said the priest, "we might try trickery."

Tom Cogan, as I soon learned, had no monopoly on cock-brained schemes. But any action we might take, however ill-conceived, would be better than none at all. For the next several minutes, all I did was hide there in the alleyway, watching as the warder and his helper carried three bodies, one at a time, from the prison and tossed them onto the cart. From where I stood, it was impossible to tell whether or not one of the corpses was Cogan's.

"That's the lot," the warder told the guards. The moment he and his helper went inside, I dashed out of the alleyway and up the street toward the wagon, calling in the same pitiful voice

I used for playing Lavinia—before her tongue is cut out, of course—"Help me, sirs! Please help me!"

"What is it, lad?" asked the smaller of the guards.

"It's me da! 'A's being robbed and beaten!" I pointed to the alley. "I' there! Hurry!" I seized the man's sleeve and began dragging him along. When his companion hesitated and glanced toward the meat wagon, I cried, "There's three of 'em! Come quickly, afore they murder him!"

Newgate Street was not entirely dark; every twenty or thirty yards, a lanthorn on the front of a house cast a feeble glow. But once we were within the narrow confines of the alley, the sole source of light was the thin strip of stars overhead.

"Where's your da, then?" demanded the larger guard. "I don't see nothing."

"At th' end of th' alley! Come!" Though they were clearly reluctant to advance into the unknown, I might have lured them a little farther along. But at that moment the horse that hauled the meat wagon let out a startled whinny. The guards headed back toward the mouth of the alley, drawing their swords as they ran.

I scrambled after them. "Wait! What about me poor da?"

They ignored me, for they had caught sight of the tall figure pulling at the horse's harness in an attempt to calm the rearing, neighing animal. "You there!" shouted one of the guards. "What are you up to?"

I expected Gerard to run. Instead he snatched the horsewhip from its socket on the side of the cart and turned to confront the two armed men. Though the whip was not a long one—perhaps six feet from handle to tip—it was longer than a rapier blade, and Gerard used this fact to his advantage. By snapping the whip this way and that, he kept the guards at a distance—

for a few moments, anyway. Unfortunately they had enough sense to separate and come at him from opposite directions. Gerard could not face them both. If I did not come to his aid, one of the guards would find an opening soon, and skewer him.

Since joining the Chamberlain's Men, I had spent a good deal of time honing my sword-fighting skills. But I had not forgotten altogether the skills I had learned in the orphanage, defending myself against boys who were considerably larger than I.

Apparently my mock distress had been so convincing that the guards still did not suspect me of being in league with Gerard, so I played the part for all it was worth. I descended upon the smaller guard, wringing my hands and sobbing, "Oh, please, sir! You must save me da! Please, sir!"

"Get away, lad!" the man growled, never taking his eyes off the madman with the whip.

I let out a wail of distress and tugged frantically at the back of his breastplate, pulling him off balance. "You can't let him die!"

The man's patience broke, and he swung the hilt of his rapier about, meaning to club me with it. I ducked under the blow and flung myself at the backs of his legs, which folded under my weight. The guard pitched forward; his sword flew from his grasp and clattered across the cobbles.

I dived headlong for it. The instant my hand closed around the hilt, I rolled onto my back—but too late. The guard was already upon me, with his dagger drawn. He thrust the tip of it against my throat-bole. "Don't move, boy!" Keeping the dagger painfully in place, he turned his head to check on his comrade. From the corner of my eye, I could see that Father Gerard had disarmed his adversary and was advancing toward mine, swinging the whip before him.

"Stay where you are," called the guard, "or the lad will have a new breathing hole!" The priest halted uncertainly.

"Get Cogan!" I managed to shout, before the guard's dagger cut off my words and very nearly my windpipe as well.

"Drop the whip!" the man ordered. After a moment's hesitation, Gerard obeyed. "Jack?" said the guard. "Are you all right?"

"I believe my arm's broken," came the reply.

"Well, see if you can manage to tie up that fellow while I take care of this—" He was interrupted by the sound of spectral moaning somewhere nearby. "What the devil was that?"

"It's—it's coming from . . . in *there*," said Jack in a voice that trembled.

Something moved within the wagon, making the horse snort and shuffle about nervously. Then a groping hand emerged from between the wooden slats. "God's bloody bones!" gasped the guard who stood over me. "They're coming to life!"

"It's sorcery!" cried Jack. He stumbled backward a few steps, then turned and fled, clutching his broken limb. His comrade, unwilling to face the undead alone, followed as fast as his feet could carry him.

I got unsteadily to my feet, holding the spot where the dagger had pricked my neck, and regarded the hand that projected from the cart, fluttering feebly. "I trust that belongs to Cogan," I said hoarsely.

Gerard peered over the side of the cart. "I think so. Help me get these other bodies off him."

We lifted the two dead prisoners from the top of the pile and laid them gently on the cobblestones. "I hope these wights did not die o' the plague."

"Plague victims are taken out separately," said Gerard, "and not by armed guards. No one wants to steal their bodies."

"You mean someone *would* want these poor wretches?"

"Medical students—for studying anatomy."

The corpse that showed signs of life was, to my relief, Tom Cogan's. His head bobbed about as though he had St. Vitus's dance, and he was making guttural, half-intelligible noises—the sort that Sander used to make in his sleep when he was dreaming something unpleasant.

Though I had bought a vial of smelling salts from the apothecary to revive Cogan, this did not seem the proper time to use it. It was more important just now to get him well away from Newgate. Gerard hoisted the man's twitching form almost effortlessly and draped it across his shoulders. "Let's find a tavern," he said. "A fellow who's staggering and babbling incoherently will not seem out of place there."

Keeping to the backstreets and snickleways, we got safely to the Warwick Inn, where we installed ourselves in a private chamber. Even with the help of the smelling salts, it took Cogan some time to come around. "It's fortunate that I gave him such a small dose," I said. "'A came back to life at just the right moment." I paused and gave a short, ironic laugh. "La Voisin was right yet again."

"La Voisin?"

"A cunning woman. She said that someone would return to life because of me." Though one-half of her prediction had come to pass, the other half still troubled me. "She also said that . . . that I would be the cause of someone's death."

"Well, Cogan was mistaken for dead; perhaps that was what she saw."

"Perhaps." After all, none of the other things she predicted had come true in the way I imagined; there was no reason to believe that this one would, either.

"Did you get the letter you were after?" asked Gerard.

I shook my head despondently. "It was taken from him. All 'a remembers is the name of the woman Julia is lodging wi'—Madame Hardy."

"That may be enough information to let you find the place."

"It might be—provided I was i' Paris."

"Well," said Gerard, "it may be that I can find it for you."

Gerard's superiors, he said, had ordered all Jesuit priests to return to the seminaries in France. The queen's death now seemed certain and imminent, and if history was any indication, it would be followed by a period of dismay and disorder. Elizabeth had been beloved, even revered, by most of her subjects; the bitter truth—that she was but a frail mortal—would not go down easily with them. They would look for a scapegoat, and their blame would fall on those same groups that they had always suspected—sometimes rightly—of conspiring against Her Majesty: the Jews, the atheists, and the Papists.

Most Catholics, it seemed, believed that if James took the throne he would usher in a new and better era for the faith; his mother had been a Catholic, after all, and so was Anne, his queen. But in the meantime, Papists were likely to be more persecuted and reviled than ever. Gerard planned to leave England soon, taking with him the small contingent of future priests he had recruited. "I don't suppose," he said, "that Sam has told you yet."

I stared at him, uncomprehending. "Told me what?"

"That he is one of my recruits."

"'A means to be a *priest*?"

Gerard nodded. "He's spent a good deal of time with me lately, learning about the faith."

"Shrew me," I murmured. "'A's turned traitor after all."

He gave me a startled glance. "You consider Catholics to be traitors?"

"Nay, not I. It's another of La Voisin's predictions." Though I suspected that Sam's interest in religion was not nearly so strong as his admiration for Gerard, I did not say so. I did not need to. The priest seemed to have read my mind.

"I am not so naive," he said, "as to think that it was my lectures on the Trinity and original sin that won Sam over. More likely it was my accounts of exotic places and hairbreadth escapes. But the Church is not particular about our reasons for joining." He gave a wry smile. "If it were, I would be a gentleman farmer now, managing my father's lands, trying to save sick sheep and not souls. Like Sam, I was attracted more by the prospect of travel and adventure than by the faith itself. That came later."

"Aye, well, don't expect too much of Sam. 'A's not a bad sort, but a bit of a scamp." I drew my purse from inside my doublet and shook the three sovereigns from it. "An you find Julia, will you give her these, to pay her passage home?"

The priest closed one hand around the money and the other around my arm. "I'll find her," he said.

With the aid of the smelling salts and a bit of brandy, we brought Tom Cogan fully back to life at last. But, as Gerard pointed out, that life would be worth very little if he remained in London, for he would surely be apprehended again.

"I don't know where else I'd go," Cogan said sullenly.

"I can take you to France with me," Gerard offered. "Of course," he added, "you'd have to agree to join the Society of Jesus."

Cogan snorted. "I'd as soon join the Society of Satan." He poured himself another drink of brandy and downed it. "No, gentlemen, I'll take my chances here in London. If I keep to Alsatia, the authorities can't touch me. Where I made my mistake was in stepping outside it, and mixing with well-bred folk." He shook his head and gave a bitter laugh. "It's funny, though, isn't it? If I'd just gone ahead and stole the money to send to Julia, instead of humbly asking folk for it, none of this would have happened." He fingered the T-shaped scar on his neck. "I guess it's best just to be what's expected of you."

His words sounded familiar, but it took me a moment to recall where I had heard them before: Julia had said something almost identical, when she was forced to quit the company because she was a girl.

In the morning, I woke to the sound of church bells. They were not the gentle treble bells, though, that rang prime each dawn; these were deep-voiced bells with melancholy tones, and they were tolling slowly, rhythmically, without ceasing.

I sat up and peered through my window. Across the river, in the vicinity of St. Paul's, a shifting tower of gray smoke was climbing into the sky. To the east, somewhere near the Cross Keys, rose another. I sighted a third far to the northeast, where Finsbury Fields lay, and a fourth in the northwest—at St. Bartholomew's, no doubt.

My first muddleheaded thought was that we were being invaded by some foreign army—from Spain, perhaps, or France—and that its soldiers were setting fire to the city. But it was not an alarm that the bells were ringing, either; it was a death knell. Once I realized that, it was easy enough to guess what the source of the smoke was: It came from the bonfires that, by tradition, were lighted to signal the passing of the Crown from one monarch to another.

33

The queen's was not the only death we mourned that day. When I reached the Globe I learned that Sal Pavy had passed away during the night. So La Voisin's last unfulfilled prophecy had come true: someone had died because of me—because I had not had sense enough, or courage enough, to ignore a foolish dare.

I had hoped to say farewell to Sam. But soon after the news of Her Majesty's death spread through the city, Father Gerard and his recruits boarded a ship bound for France. I knew that the priest would do his best to locate Julia and send her home, as he had promised; what I did not know was whether his best would be good enough. I could only wait and see.

The fate of the Chamberlain's Men was equally uncertain. In her final hours, Elizabeth had indicated at last, through the use of signs—for her voice had deserted her entirely—that her successor would be James, the current King of Scotland. We had all expected that, of course. But we had no idea what else to expect of him; no one seemed even to know when he might arrive in London, let alone what he might do once he got there.

Nearly a week passed without news from any quarter, aside from a rumor that the Admiral's Men had hired Ned Shakespeare as a player, not merely an informant. It seemed that, like us, they had determined to go on as though the future of the London theatre were assured.

We could not truly go on the same as always, though. With Ned and Sam and Sal Pavy all gone, the company was as sparse as it had been on tour the previous summer. There were not enough actors left to cast any of our usual plays, and yet we could ill afford to take on new prentices or hired men until we knew where we stood.

The weather had grown so warm that on the afternoons when it did not rain, we held our rehearsals upon the stage. The long winter had been hard on the boards; many were warped and a few were rotten, so that treading on them was nearly as risky as walking on the river ice had been. We were willing to put up with it, though; we all longed to play to an audience again, and when we were on the stage we could at least have the illusion of performing.

Occasionally some tradesman or truant prentice passed by and, hearing our voices declaiming and our swords clashing, peered in through the entrance and perhaps lingered for a while to watch. No one attempted to chase off these interlopers. Any audience was better than none.

As the weather improved, so did Mr. Pope's health. Several days a week he joined us for dinner at the Globe, or sat in on a rehearsal and read all the unfilled parts. He had already grown accustomed to calling me James. The rest of the company was just as quick to adjust. It was nothing new to them, after all, having to address a fellow player by a different name; every one of us changed his identity, sometimes even his age and gender, from performance to performance.

On the days when Mr. Pope did not visit, I made my nightly report to him as usual. One evening as we sat talking over mugs of ale, Goody Willingson entered the library with a curious look on her broad face—half eager, half guarded, as though she had received some delicious bit of news but had been forbidden to tell it. "There's a young gentleman here to see you," she said solemnly.

"What sort of young gentleman?" asked Mr. Pope.

Goody Willingson lowered her voice almost to a whisper. "A rather scruffy-looking one, sir, to tell the truth."

"Did he say what he wanted?"

"No, sir."

Mr. Pope sighed. "Well, I suppose you may as well send him in." When the housekeeper departed, he turned to me. "Collecting for some charity, no doubt." A few moments later the boy appeared in the doorway—a slight lad, dressed in a shabby tunic and trousers, with a woolen prentice's cap pulled low over his ears. His face was liberally smudged with coal dust.

"Begging your pardon, sirs." He had the same thick, working-class accent as Tom Cogan. "I was wondering whether your acting company might have room for another prentice."

"They may, in a few weeks." Mr. Pope looked the lad over. "Can you act?"

"Apparently so," said the boy. Laughing, he yanked off the cap, revealing a wealth of auburn hair.

"Gog's blood!" I cried. "Julia!"

Mr. Pope was even more astonished than I. Clutching his chest, he staggered backward and slumped into his chair.

"Oh, gis! The shock was too much for his heart, I wis!"

Julia ran to the old man's side and seized one of his limp hands in hers. "I'm sorry, Mr. Pope! I'm sorry! Are you all right?"

His lolling head suddenly popped upright and he beamed at her triumphantly. "Apparently so!"

She flung down his hand. "You were *pretending?*"

"No, my dear, I was *acting.*"

"Whatever you call it, it was cruel. I thought you were dying."

"And I thought you were a lad, so we're even."

Julia could not suppress a smile. "I suppose we are, at that." She turned to me with a mischievous look. "I had you fooled as well, didn't I?"

"Only for a moment," I said indignantly. "It was the dirt on your face that did it. It hid your features."

She wiped one cheek with the sleeve of her tunic. "That's the idea. I thought I'd be safer among all those sailors if they didn't suspect I was a girl."

"Gerard gave you the money I sent, then?"

"Gerard?"

"The priest."

She shook her head. "I talked to no priest."

"Then how did you pay for your passage?" asked Mr. Pope.

"Well, after a week or so I despaired of ever hearing from my da, so I did the only thing I could think of: I sold my clothing."

"Your *clothing?*"

"Two very elegant gowns, given to me by—" She paused, clearly embarrassed. "Well, at any rate, they fetched a good price, enough so that I could pay the rent I owed and purchase these rags—" She plucked distastefully at the worn tunic and trousers. "—and still have enough left over to buy my passage."

"You needn't ha' done that," I said. I went on to recount the whole story of how Tom Cogan had come to us, and everything that ensued—or nearly everything. I made no mention of the things Cogan had confessed to me prior to taking the mandrake potion. He had asked me to reveal them to Julia if he died. But since he had survived, he could do it himself, if he chose.

"There," said Mr. Pope. "James has told you what went on here; now we'd like to hear your side of the tale."

Julia gave me a puzzled glance. "*James?*"

"It's me new name. I'll explain later—after you've told us why you had to leave France."

Julia lowered her gaze. "I'm afraid it's not a pretty story."

"Well, you needn't tell us if you'd rather not," said Mr. Pope. "But you're among friends now, my dear."

She smiled faintly. "I know. And I'm grateful to be. I've missed you all, very much." She wiped at her face again, this time leaving damp, pale streaks in the coal dust. Then, in a voice so soft at first that I could scarcely hear, she gave us a brief account of all that had befallen her during her fifteen months in Paris.

I knew many of the details already, from her letters. She had had the good luck to arrive in France at a time when the notion of women acting upon the stage was just beginning to gain acceptance. Because there were so few experienced actresses, Julia had found a position at once with one of the most successful companies in Paris.

What she had never revealed in her letters was that most of the public still regarded female players as degraded and immoral, little better than women of the streets, and treated them as such. And, as the companies themselves did not consider actresses the equal of actors, they were paid a pittance. In an attempt to improve their social and financial status, most of the women players found a patron, some wealthy lord who would offer them protection, money, and a measure of respectability in return for their favors.

Julia flatly declared that she would be no man's mistress. For a time she managed well enough, lodging with the company manager and his wife and discouraging the amorous advances of male players and playgoers with the help of a concealed dagger.

As her popularity and the number of roles she played increased, she caught the eye of the Comte de Belin, who was well known for his many affairs. At first he expressed his admiration only with gifts—including the two gowns she had later sold for passage money. But with each month that passed his attentions grew more and more ardent, and the more she resisted them the more insistent he became, until at last he declared that if she would not come to him willingly, he would take her against her will. That same day, she quit the company and found a room in a seedy section of the city where the count could not find her.

When she had finished her story, she bowed her head, as if in contrition. "You've nothing to be ashamed of, my dear," said Mr. Pope. "You behaved courageously and virtuously."

"Oh, yes, I know," she replied. "I was not very shrewd, though, was I? In being so courageous and so virtuous, I lost my one remaining chance to be a player."

34

Though Julia could never have brought herself to ask for charity of any sort, when Mr. Pope insisted that she stay with us for the time being, she was clearly relieved. For the next several nights, she and I sat up long past the time when the rest of the household had retired. Mostly, we talked; it had been an eventful year for both of us, and there was much to tell. But sometimes we sat silent for long stretches, lost in our own thoughts yet always aware of each other—not separated by the silence so much as sharing it, the way folk may share a warm and satisfying meal.

During one of these times, I caught Julia gazing at me in a peculiar fashion, as though I had done something amusing or unexpected—let go a belch, perhaps, or torn a hole in my hose. "What?" I said.

"You've changed."

I ran a hand self-consciously over my close-cropped head.

"It's me hair, no doubt, or the lack of it. No more pudding basin."

"I noticed. But that's not it."

"I'm an inch or two taller than when you saw me last."

"I noticed that as well. But it's not that, either. I think it's your manner."

"Me manners?" I thought perhaps I had belched after all, or passed wind without knowing it.

She laughed. "Your *manner*. The way you speak and act."

"Well, me acting's got a bit better, but me speech has stayed the same. Folk still make fun of 't."

"You sot. That's not what I meant, and you know it."

"Aye," I admitted. "I suppose I have changed. I could hardly help it, given all that's happened in the past year—or even the past few weeks. I lost one father and gained another, wrote a play, did a bit of spying and a bit of fighting, fell in—" I broke off. Like Tom Cogan concealing the brand upon his neck, I had no wish to reveal how badly I had been burned.

"Yes?" Julia prompted me. "Fell in what? A well? The space beneath the stage?"

"No," I said sullenly.

"In love?" she suggested, in that same bantering tone. Though I made no reply, I was certain that my face answered for me. "Oh. I'm sorry, Widge. I didn't mean to make light of it."

I shrugged. "It doesn't matter. I'm over it now."

"Yes, I can see that." There was another silence, more awkward this time, and then she said softly, "You're fortunate, you know."

"Fortunate? Like those wights who survive the pox or the plague, you mean, and carry the scars all their lives?"

"Yes. The only love I've ever felt is for the theatre, and it was not returned."

"Nor was mine."

She smiled and laid a hand on my arm. "Perhaps not. But there will be others."

In the second week of April, the Privy Council announced that the king had begun his progress south from Scotland at last. There seemed to be some doubt over whether or not His Majesty would actually come to London, for with the return of warm weather the plague had begun to make its presence felt again in the city.

In the past, when the death toll from the contagion rose, the queen and her retinue had taken refuge at Hampton Court or Windsor, both of which lay far upriver, where the air was less corrupted. James would undoubtedly do the same.

We ordinary wights did not have the luxury of moving to healthier surroundings, unless we wished to emulate those townfolk who followed in the queen's wake, bearing bundles of straw with which they constructed makeshift shelters on the riverbank. The only measure we could take, aside from wearing pomanders filled with marjoram and rosemary, was to keep the household as free as possible of vermin—lice, fleas, bedbugs, rats, and the like.

Julia had always been a willing worker, and she lent her efforts to the cause. She also cooked meals and cared for the younger orphans, who found her nearly as entertaining as they had Sam. Though I urged her almost daily to pay a visit to the Globe, she refused. It would be, she said, like my paying a visit to Judith; she did not wish to be reminded of what she could not have. She showed little inclination to visit Tom Cogan, either. "I don't need him," she said shortly. "The one time when I did, he failed me."

"'A tried to raise the money," I said.

"Yes, the same way he always does—dishonestly."

I had told her how he was arrested and imprisoned for stealing a bracelet; I had not, however, revealed the whole truth—that he was not, in fact, guilty. I did not see how I could, without also revealing a good deal more. Tom Cogan should be the one to do that. But how could he, if they never spoke? "Julia. 'A never stole that bracelet. It was planted on him."

"Planted? By whom?"

"I can't tell you."

"Why not?"

"I can't tell you that, either. Just go and see him, will you?"

After several days of delaying, she set off at last to seek out Cogan. When dusk came and she had not returned, I began to regret that I had talked her into going. Alsatia was a dangerous place, and even though Julia had grown up there, she might not be immune from its dangers.

I resolved finally that if she did not turn up by compline, I would fetch Mr. Armin and try to find her, even though it would mean breaking the curfew. Ordinarily a wight could do so with relative impunity, but since the queen's death the mayor had doubled or trebled the number of night watchmen in an attempt to quell the riots that had been flaring up, in protest of one thing or another.

Many of the demonstrators were denouncing the new king, even though they had no notion of what he looked like, let alone how he would rule the country. They claimed that this latest outbreak of the plague was an omen, a clear sign from God that James was not meant to wear the Crown. Who *was* meant to wear it was apparently not so clear.

As I was putting Tetty to bed, she said, "I've decided that you may marry Julia, if you like."

"Oh? You said before that I was to wait for you."

"I know. But perhaps you won't want to wait that long, and I wouldn't really mind very much your choosing someone else, if it was Julia."

A few weeks earlier, such a notion would have seemed to me quite odd, even ludicrous. I had always thought of Julia as a close friend, like Sander or Sam, nothing more. In truth, I believe I still had not quite gotten over thinking of her as a boy. But in the weeks since she had joined our household, I had begun to see her with new eyes—the eyes of James Pope, I suppose, and not Widge—and to feel toward her something more than mere friendship. I could not have given a name to it; I did not seem to be experiencing any of the startling symptoms that Judith Shakespeare had inspired in me. When Julia and I were together, I was comfortable and contented, not dumb and desperate. When we were apart, my thoughts of her were pleasant, not painful—except for now, when I was anxiously wondering what had become of her.

I was just about to ask Mr. Pope's permission to go after her when the front door opened and Julia hurried in, wide-eyed and breathless. I was so overcome with relief that I came very near to throwing my arms about her.

"I'm sorry, James," she said, for she had finally broken the habit of calling me Widge. "I know you must have been worried."

"Oh, I wasn't worried," I said.

"You weren't?"

"Nay. *Frantic* would be a better word, I wis."

She stared at me. "Truly?"

"Of course. I was afeared you'd been . . . Well, I don't ken what, exactly, but something dreadful."

She took hold of my hand. "I'm glad."

"*Glad?* That I was half out of me wits?"

"No. That you should care so much what happens to me."

"Did you doubt it?"

She smiled. "I suppose not. Come, let's sit. I'm exhausted from outrunning the night watchmen." I led her to the library, where Mr. Pope, in his delight at seeing her safe and sound, actually did embrace her. "I have a good reason for being so late, I assure you," Julia said. She paused and lowered her eyes. "Well, I should not say a *good* reason. In fact, it was rather a tragic reason. I was attending my father's funeral—such as it was. His body, and perhaps a dozen others, were all dumped into a single grave."

"Oh, dear," said Mr. Pope. "The contagion claimed him."

She nodded. "It's even worse in Alsatia than in the rest of the city." With a weary sigh, she sank into a chair. "It's odd. The thing that distresses me most about his death, I think, is how little sorrow I seem to feel."

"That's natural, my dear. It hasn't quite struck you yet, that's all."

"I don't know. As heartless as it may sound, I'm not certain that I'll ever mourn him very much. The truth is, I never felt as though . . . " She trailed off.

"As though 'a was truly your father," I said.

Julia turned her sad gaze upon me. "Is that how you felt? When Jamie Redshaw died?"

"Aye, more or less. But you ha' more reason than I to feel that way."

"What do you mean?"

"What I mean is . . . " I paused, drew a deep breath, and began again. "What I mean is that Tom Cogan was not your father."

35

Thanks to my actor's memory, I had no trouble recalling every detail of the confession Cogan had made to me in his prison cell. The difficult part was bringing myself to reveal it to Julia. I feared that once I had, nothing would ever be quite the same between us. Yet neither could I bring myself to keep it from her.

The story was so intricate that I could not tell but one piece of it, any more than I could have recounted a single scene from *Hamlet* or *Comedy of Errors* and expected my audience to make any sense of it. I had to begin, as a play does, at the beginning.

Several years before Julia was born, Tom Cogan married a childless widow named Alice—not so much for love, he admitted, as for the wages she made as a charwoman at Whitehall. Like every other female who worked or lived in the palace, Alice was smitten with the queen's dashing young master of the horse, Robert Devereux, Earl of Essex. Not content with being the queen's favorite, Essex seemed bent on seducing, one by one, all of Her Majesty's ladies-in-waiting. Each time the jealous queen got wind of such an affair she was furious, and sent the unfortunate girl home in disgrace.

One of Essex's conquests was Frances Vavasour, the daughter of an impoverished nobleman. When Frances learned that she was carrying Essex's child, she became frantic. Unable to trust the other ladies, who were envious of her, she confided in a friendly servant—Alice Cogan. They managed to hide her condition until the queen departed on her annual progress from one great lord's house to another. While Her Majesty was gone, Frances gave birth to the baby, attended only by Alice. Her motherly instincts proved less powerful than her fear of the queen's wrath. She offered to pay Alice a small sum yearly if she would raise the baby as her own, and the childless charwoman readily agreed.

Alice died of a fever three years later, leaving her husband to raise the child—and, of course, collect the stipend—on his own. By this time, Her Majesty had arranged a very favorable match for Frances; she was to wed Thomas Shirley, the son of the royal treasurer. Now she had even more reason to want her affair with Essex kept a secret. When Essex tried to stir up a rebellion and was beheaded, it became downright dangerous to admit any association with him.

For nearly thirteen years, Tom Cogan's only contact with Frances Shirley was through a servant, who brought him the annual payment that ensured his silence. But the time came at last when he needed a far larger sum, in order to pay Julia's passage home from France. After Mr. Shakespeare and Mr. Heminges turned him down, he went to call on Madame Shirley, confident that though she might not claim Julia as her daughter, she would not let the girl starve.

When she refused to give him the money, he foolishly threatened to speak to her husband. She seemed to change her mind, then, and offered him a gold bracelet that would, she said, easily fetch three pounds from a moneylender. He had not gone half a dozen blocks before the constables caught him and charged him with stealing the bracelet.

I had supposed that Julia's reaction to these revelations would be much the same as mine. But I saw no sign of astonishment on her face, only skepticism. "My da told you all this?"

"Aye. Well, not your *real* da. Tom Cogan."

"And you believed him?"

"What reason would 'a ha' to lie?"

"I don't know. To make you believe that he wasn't a thief, perhaps. Besides, he didn't need a reason to lie; it was a habit. Right now, I'll wager, he's trying to convince the Devil that it's all a mistake, that he merely got on the wrong coach."

I shook my head emphatically. "'A told me those things only because 'a thought 'a might not survive the mandrake potion. Folk don't tell lies when they're about to die."

"You don't know my da. What do you think the last thing was that anyone heard him say before the plague took him? He said that . . . that he loved me." She gave a bitter laugh that was very like a sob. "What a lie *that* was."

"Well, perhaps he did, though," put in Mr. Pope. "After all, he raised you as though you were his own daughter."

"His own daughter? Don't tell me *you* believe his story as well?"

"I believe that when a man is looking death in the face, he tends to tell the truth about things."

She stared at him incredulously. "You don't really suppose that I'm the illegitimate child of the Earl of Essex?"

Mr. Pope smiled. "You would not be the only one, my dear, I assure you. It's well known that he had a son by another of the queen's ladies-in-waiting. The boy was raised by Essex's mother." He studied Julia's face. "Besides, I met Essex a number of times, and I can see the resemblance. You have the same hair, the same eyes . . . and the same impetuous nature."

Julia considered this for a long moment. "Well," she said finally, "there is one way of settling the matter for certain."

"What's that?" I said.

"I'll pay a visit to Madame Shirley, my supposed mother."

"Nay!" I cried. "You can't! An she's as desperate to hide the truth as Cogan says, she may ha' you tossed i' prison as well!"

"Or she might simply laugh in my face. In any case, she's not likely to throw her arms about me and invite me in, is she?" Julia got to her feet. "Well, thank you for such an entertaining tale, James. I wish I could believe it." She started from the room, then turned back to us with a faint, melancholy smile. "You know, when I was a young girl, I used to console myself by imagining that my da was not truly my da, that I'd been abducted as an infant from some respectable family. But then . . . " She shrugged. "Then I grew up."

When she was gone, I moved over next to Mr. Pope and said softly, "I'm certain that Tom Cogan was telling the truth. Why does she doubt it?"

Mr. Pope scratched thoughtfully at the bald spot atop his head. "I expect that the idea frightens her a bit. She grew up among thieves and beggars, after all. The notion that she has noble blood in her veins will take some getting used to."

"Why should it? She's played fine gentlemen and ladies a hundred times on the stage."

"That's so. But playing at something is not the same as *being* it. You've feigned death a hundred times; it's a good deal different, actually being dead. Or so I would imagine."

"In truth," I said, "I almost hope that she goes on doubting it."

"Why is that?"

"Because. An she begins to think of herself as one of the . . . the *better sort*, as they say, perhaps she'll no longer ha' any use for us."

Though Julia gradually accepted the possibility that she was the daughter of a lord, it did not seem to affect her much. She went on as always, helping with the chores and with the children. She behaved no differently toward me, either, except perhaps that she was a bit more quiet and somber than usual.

When I asked whether I might tell my fellow players the news, she made no objection. The company reacted much the way they had when I told them of my true father. Half of them were astounded; the other half declared that her likeness to Essex was so unmistakable that they should have seen it before.

I returned from the theatre late that afternoon to find Julia gone and Goody Willingson growing anxious. "She said she'd be back in time to help with supper. I don't mind that she's not; I'm just wondering what's become of her."

"Did she say where she was going?"

"To see a friend. Someone named . . . Frances, I believe."

"Oh, gis!" Without pausing to explain, I dashed out of the house and down to the river, where I paid a wherryman sixpence to make the quickest crossing he could.

I knew well enough where Sir Thomas Shirley's mansion lay. It was one of the grandest in a string of grand houses that stretched out along the north bank of the river, their red tile roofs glowing like great gems in the light of the sinking sun. The moment the boat touched shore, I leaped from it and scrambled up the stairs. When I reached Thames Street, I hurried down it, scanning both sides of the thoroughfare, praying that I might see Julia heading home, safe and sound.

Instead I found her sitting on a low stone wall across the street from Shirley House, gazing at the imposing structure. "What are you *doing?*" I demanded breathlessly.

She gave me a startled look. "I might well ask the same of you."

I sank down next to her. "Trying to keep you from doing something foolish."

"You needn't have bothered. I wasn't planning to burst in and declare myself the rightful heir, or anything."

"You told Goody Willingson you were going to see Frances."

"And so I did. She came out not a quarter of an hour ago. She crossed the street and passed by me, so near that I might have reached out and touched her."

"But you didn't."

"No. Nor did I speak to her. I only wanted to have a look at her, to see . . . "

"To see whether you resembled her. I ken. I did the same wi' Jamie Redshaw. And do you?"

She gave a small, self-conscious laugh. "No. She's very beautiful."

I shrugged. "Oh, well, wi' enough face paint and a costly gown and the right wig, anyone can look beautiful—even me. Besides, I think you're quite comely."

"Do you?"

"Aye."

"Well. Thank you."

"You're welcome. Can we go now, or do you want to have a look at Sir Thomas as well?"

"No. I'm done." As we headed toward the river, she said, "That's one of the things I miss most about acting—getting to wear those elegant gowns." She sighed. "I suppose it's caps and aprons for me from now on."

"There may yet be hope. I've heard that the new queen enjoys performing in plays and masques and such. Perhaps she'll talk her husband into letting women appear upon the stage."

Julia laughed humorlessly. "He'd have to get rid of all the Puritans first."

"That's not a bad idea," I said. "He could send them all off to colonize the New World."

36

Though Julia and I had by now discussed in great detail nearly all that had befallen us in the year we were apart, there were two subjects I had carefully avoided. One was my infatuation with Judith; the other was my pitiful attempt to compose a play. I had been foolish to imagine that either was within my limited reach. The most I hoped for now was that I might manage to forget about them both.

Unexpectedly, Judith proved easier to get out of my head than did the notion of writing a play. Ideas and characters and titles came to me unbidden at the most inconvenient times—often in the dead of night—and I found that the only way to stop them plaguing me was to write them down. Once I had done that, I refused to have anything more to do with them. They could sit at the back of my desk until they moldered into dust for all I cared.

One of my titles, however, had found a place for itself. Mr. Shakespeare was calling his latest play *Measure for Measure*.

Without the demands of a nightly performance to occupy his time, he had finished the script in record time, and even though it was still uncertain whether or not we would ever perform again, he instructed me to begin copying out the players' sides.

By the time the new king arrived at last in London, the plague was claiming nearly a thousand lives each week. His Majesty remained in the city scarcely long enough for the Crown to settle on his royal costard, and then he retreated to Hampton Court, some ten or fifteen miles upriver.

Our sharers had concluded that if we hoped to win the king over to our cause, we must get to him before the Puritans did. To my surprise, they also concluded that it would be far wiser if, instead of each company pleading its case alone, we combined our forces. What was even more surprising was that Mr. Henslowe agreed. The less renowned companies were only too eager to join this unlikely, uneasy alliance.

So it was that, toward the end of June, a delegation made up of members of all the London companies, from the largest to the smallest, set out for Hampton Court, determined to convince the new monarch that the theatre was not an evil influence upon his subjects, as the Square Toes claimed, but an innocent source of entertainment and enlightenment.

The half dozen of us who remained were given the day off. It was just as well; we were all so distracted with worry over the company's fate that it would have been useless to try to rehearse. I was unaccustomed to being idle, though. By midday I had grown so restless that I decided I would be better off at the theatre, copying out sides.

"I'll go with you," said Julia.

I stared at her. "Truly? But you said—"

"I know what I said. I've decided I was being silly. After all, I can't very well refuse ever to enter a theatre again, can I?"

"I suppose not. None of the company will be there, though, except for me."

"Good. This will be hard enough without having to face them as well."

As we neared the Globe, Julia halted and stood gazing at it, in the same wistful way she had regarded Shirley House—as though she would have liked to feel she belonged there, but knew that she never could. When we entered the area behind the stage, her face took on an expression of such longing that I had to look away. "Perhaps you were right to begin wi'," I said. "Perhaps you should not ha' come."

"No, it's all right." Though her voice was a bit unsteady, it was calm and determined. "You go on and do your work. I'll just . . . have a look about."

By now I had done so much transcribing for the company that I scarcely needed to give any thought to what I was copying; my hand seemed almost to have a mind of its own. But ever since I began struggling to write a play, I had been paying closer attention to Mr. Shakespeare's verse. In truth, I believe I was looking for flaws in it. As petty and mean-spirited as it may seem, I found it curiously comforting to be reminded that even the most accomplished and highly regarded of playwrights sets down his share of putrid passages.

I had, in fact, just copied one: "Go to your bosom; knock there and ask your heart what it doth know." Had I composed such a line myself, I would have burned it. Though I gloated each time the script struck a sour note, the truth was that they were few and far between. For every awkward speech, there were a score of others so graceful and well made that I found myself speaking them under my breath, just to savor the sound of them.

As I was finishing up Isabella's part, which I thought of as mine, I heard a clamor of voices outside and rose from the desk to investigate. Before I reached the rear door of the theatre, it burst open, revealing Mr. Heminges and Mr. Shakespeare. They were clearly in good spirits—and, from the looks of them, they had gotten some of those spirits in an alehouse along the way. It took them a while to actually come inside, for each of them was loudly insisting that the other enter first. "Age before beauty, " said Mr. Shakespeare.

"N-no," protested Mr. Heminges. "William the C-Conqueror always goes before K-King John." He spotted me, then, and, pushing Mr. Shakespeare aside, sprang through the doorway, lost his balance, and used me to steady himself. "James! W-we succeeded! Your n-namesake has proclaimed that all the th-theatres in London are to resume b-business as usual!"

"Gog's blood! How soon?"

"Well," said Mr. Shakespeare, "we can't actually reopen the Globe until the plague deaths decline a bit. In the meantime we'll be presenting our performances at the court." He shifted his gaze to something behind me, and I turned to see Julia coming through one of the curtained entrances that led to the stage.

She curtsied slightly to the sharers. "God you good day, gentlemen." Her manner was a bit guilty, as though she'd been caught trespassing. "I was just seeing whether anything had changed."

"Well, I'm glad you're here," said Mr. Shakespeare. "We've some good news for you."

"Yes, I heard." Though she wore a smile, it seemed a bit forced. "I'm happy for you all."

"Thank you. But that's not the news I meant. This concerns you directly."

"Oh?"

Mr. Heminges wiped his brow. "Let's sit d-down to discuss it, shall we? I'm f-feeling rather light-headed, and there's a s-sort of humming in my ears."

"I believe it's the hum in your belly that's the problem," said Mr. Shakespeare. *Hum* was the London term for a mixture of ale and spirits. Mr. Shakespeare stepped into the alcove at the rear of the stage and dragged forth the two chairs that served as our royal thrones. He helped Mr. Heminges into one and seated himself in the other. "If we're to be the King's Men we should begin behaving accordingly."

I gaped at him. "The *King's* Men? His Majesty himself is to be our patron?"

Mr. Heminges nodded enthusiastically; his head appeared a bit wobbly. "It seems he's quite f-fond of the theatre after all. His son, Pr-Prince Henry, is to be H-Henslowe's new patron, and Worcester's c-company are henceforth the Queen's M-Men. And speaking of the creen— the queem—" He turned unsteadily to Mr. Shakespeare. "P-perhaps you'd best tell it, Will. My t-tongue has t-turned trader. Traitor."

Mr. Shakespeare gestured at the book-keeper's bench. "You two may as well sit; this will take some explanation. You see, after our audience with the king, Queen Anne summoned me to her chambers, to discuss the possibility of my writing a masque for her court to perform."

"And did you agree to?" I asked. I knew how contemptuous he was of those stilted, stylized spectacles, which, he said, were no more like a real play than a plate of marchpane is like a meal.

"Not exactly. I told Her Majesty that a good masque—if indeed there is such a thing—required a lighter touch than mine, and I recommended Ben Jonson as the best man for the job. But the point is, during this discussion, Julia, your name came up. As a woman with acting ambitions of her own, I thought Her Majesty would appreciate your plight. I also took the liberty of mentioning that you were Essex's daughter. Well, it was as though I had told her you were the daughter of Zeus. It seems that Essex visited the Scottish court several times—no doubt plotting with James to seize the English throne—and, like most women, Anne found him irresistible. She insisted that you come to court at once, to join her retinue of young ladies."

Julia gave an astonished laugh. "*Me!* I know nothing about waiting upon a queen!"

"I don't believe it's your waiting ability she's interested in; it's your acting ability. She wants you to perform in her plays and masques."

For a day or two, I fooled myself into believing that Julia would not accept the queen's offer—which in truth sounded less like an offer than like a command. Though she would not have admitted it, Julia was clearly intimidated by the prospect of mingling with royalty. But she had never before let a little fear prevent her from getting what she wanted. The main thing that seemed to be holding her back was a reluctance to leave Mr. Pope and Goody Willingson and the children—and, perhaps not least of all, me.

Had the lot of us implored her to stay, I suspect she would have done so. I also suspect that she would have been miserable. However strong her wish to remain with us might be, I knew that her desire to be a player was stronger. Of course, if she left, then I would be the miserable one. But given the choice between her happiness and mine, I preferred hers. Perhaps that is the true measure of love.

37

If the country's Catholics had imagined that a new monarch would mean a new era of religious tolerance, they were sorely disappointed. Those who converted to the Old Faith, or preached it, were still considered traitors, and those who failed to attend Anglican services on the Sabbath still risked paying a substantial fine. I was content enough to spend my Sunday mornings in church; at least it was something to do. Now that Julia was at court, playing the part of a maid of honor, I no longer had any companions my own age, and the one afternoon I had to myself seemed empty and endless, more of a burden than a boon.

For all the grief the contagion had caused, it had one benefit: the streets of the city and its public places were practically deserted. I had never grown quite used to the hurly-burly here, and though I would have welcomed the company of a friend or two, I rather relished not having to rub shoulders with a thousand strangers.

Even the churchyard of St. Paul's, which was ordinarily as crowded as a cheap coffin, had no more than twenty or thirty folk wandering about like lost souls. Most were purchasing herbs and infusions that were guaranteed to guard against the plague. Should the herbs fail, of course, the buyer was seldom in a position to demand his money back.

I had little faith in such nostrums. I was drawn, instead, to the rows of sixpenny playbooks displayed at the printers' stalls. As I was leafing idly through them—looking, I suppose, for putrid passages at which I might scoff—a particular title caught my eye. I picked it up and stared at the cover. *Timon of Athens*, it read. *A Lamentable Tragedie. By Wm. Shakspear.* I waved it at the printer. "Who sold you this script?"

"Mr. Henslowe, from the Lord Admiral's Men."

"Do you mind telling me how much you paid for 't? I'm a beginning playwright meself, you see, and I was wondering how much a good play might fetch."

"I gave him ten pounds for it—but only because it's Shakespeare's work. If it had been anyone else, I wouldn't have paid more than six."

So I need not have bothered feeling guilty because I had taken three pounds for the play under false pretenses. I might have known Henslowe would manage somehow to turn a profit on it. "Is it a good play, then?" I asked nonchalantly.

He shrugged. "I read no more than half an act—just to be sure it sounded like Shakespeare."

"Oh." I tried to put myself in the role of someone who had never encountered the script before, to see how it would strike me. I opened the playbook at random and silently scanned the first passage that met my eye:

O, the fierce wretchedness that glory brings us!
Who would not wish to be from wealth exempt
Since riches point to misery and contempt?

Not bad, really. I turned the page and sampled another speech:

The sun's a thief, and with his great attraction
Robs the vast sea; the moon's an arrant thief,
And her pale fire she snatches from the sun.

If I had not recalled writing those lines myself, I might have taken them for Mr. Shakespeare's. Perhaps I was not so poor a playwright as I had imagined. I could string words together well enough, if only I could find a thread strong enough to support them. I recalled Mr. Shakespeare's reply when I asked how he came up with the stories for his plays. "You wouldn't happen to have any ideas for sale, would you?"

The man looked at me blankly. "Ideas?"

"Never mind." I tossed the playbook aside and turned away. What was the use in dredging up that foolish ambition again? It was no more likely to succeed than anything else I had attempted lately. If the experiences of these last few months had taught me anything, it was that the efforts we mortals make to determine our own fates are as feeble and fruitless as trying to change the course of the wind by blowing against it.

Nothing I had put my hand to had turned out as I planned. I had hoped I might win Judith's affections; instead, she had gone home. I had dreamed of becoming a great playwright and discovered that I was merely promising. I had dragged Sal Pavy from the cold clutches of the Thames, only to have him succumb to the grippe. Fate had mocked me yet again by letting me rescue Tom Cogan from the hangman's rope and then striking him down with the plague. All my scheming to save Julia had come to naught; she had ended up saving herself.

I had been walking west, with no particular destination in mind, and now found myself at the wall. If I went on through Ludgate I would wind up in Salisbury Court—hardly the best neighborhood to explore on one's own. But I had been here before and come to no harm. Besides, what was the use in being cautious? If Fate had it in for me, I was not safe anywhere, and if I was in her good graces, then I had nothing to fear.

If only a person could know in advance what Fate had planned for him, he might save himself a good deal of trouble and worry. Had I known that Tom Cogan would die anyway, I need not have put myself and Father Gerard in danger. Had Julia foreseen that she would end up performing at the royal court, she could have forgone her ill-fated trip to France.

The ability to anticipate Fate would let a wight prepare a bit, too. Julia could have been practicing her maid-of-honor skills. The Chamberlain's Men could have hired half a dozen new players. Had I been forewarned that Judith and Julia would leave, or that Sander would die, I might have been more careful not to grow so fond of them.

The cunning woman had seen some of what lay in store for Sam and Sal Pavy and me. Perhaps there was more. Though she had warned me that it was not wise to examine the future too closely, I was willing to take the chance. I was sick of being tossed about by the winds of chance. I wanted some star to steer by, however faint.

When I found La Voisin, she was taking down her tent. Though she had shed most of her woolen scarves, she kept one wrapped about her head and face—to conceal the warts that disfigured her, no doubt. She gave me a suspicious glance. "I suppose you've come to complain."

"Nay. To ha' me fortune told."

"Again? Most of my customers find that once is quite enough. In fact, a number of them have come to demand their money back. That's why I'm leaving."

"Your predictions for them didn't come true, then?"

"Oh, they came true right enough—just not in the way they may have expected."

I grinned ruefully. "I ken how that is."

"Yet you've come back for more?"

"Aye. I'm weary of being Fortune's fool. It seems to me that any glimpse of what's ahead, no matter how brief or how blurry it is, must be better than fumbling along blindly."

La Voisin sighed. "Well, I suppose I must oblige you, after you gave me money for coal." She sat at the table and drew her scrying ball from a pouch at her waist. "Had you not, I might have been forced to burn this, to keep warm."

"It would burn?"

"Of course. Though it may be carved and polished, it's still a lump of coal." She uncovered the black ball and peered into it.

"I was hoping you might tell me—" I began, but she cut me off.

"I do not make fortunes to order. I see only what I see. Now be silent."

Meekly, I took a seat on the other stool and waited, scarcely moving a muscle, until she finally spoke again in that ominous, otherworldly voice. "You will tell a great many lies," she said.

I blinked at her, then at the ball. "What sort of prediction is *that?*"

She spread her wart-speckled hands, palms up. "I do not interpret, I only see."

"But—but I've been doing me best *not* to lie. Now you tell me that I must keep on?"

The cunning woman wrapped up her scrying ball and returned it to its pouch. "I never said you *must*. I said you *would*."

"Oh. Well, that's certainly a comfort." I rose from the stool. "Perhaps I was wrong. Perhaps it's best to fumble along blindly after all. God buy you."

As I walked away, La Voisin called after me, "We are not truly Fortune's fools, you know."

"Nay? What are we, then?"

"Her instruments. You imagine that there's no use struggling against Fate, that she will always have her way, no matter what we do. But don't you see? It's our very efforts to cheat Fate, or to change it, that make things come to pass in the way they were meant to."

At first, this explanation of hers seemed to me as baffling as the prediction she had made. But the more I mulled it over, the more I came to see the sense in it. It was easy to conclude that since we could not hope to alter Fate, we might as well not try. But that was like saying that since the plague struck down whomever it chose, there was no use trying to prevent it. It was like saying that we players should not bother rehearsing so hard, since the audience would either like the play or not.

It was true that most of my own efforts of late had failed. But what might have happened had I not made them at all?

Pulling Sal Pavy from the river had not prevented his death, only delayed it—but long enough for him to say farewell, and to forgive me. If I had not helped Tom Cogan arrange his escape from prison, he would have taken the truth about Julia's parentage with him to the grave. If I had not been so eager to impress Judith and to raise money for Julia's passage, I would never have written my play.

Of course, the world would have been no worse off without *Timon of Athens*. Still, creating it had been satisfying, in a perverse sort of way. It was rather like the satisfaction I had once gotten from being able to lie so convincingly. It was very much like it, in fact. I had always thought of acting as a form of lying; after all, we players habitually posed as someone we were not, and spouted sentiments that were not our own. But, though we were not the people we pretended to be, we were at least people. Plays were nothing but a lot of words on paper, attempting to give the illusion of life. What more outrageous lie could there be than that?

Though I was well out of sight of La Voisin's tent by now, I turned and gazed thoughtfully in that direction. Perhaps I was making the same mistake I had made before, the very mistake that the cunning woman's other clients had made—taking her predictions at face value. She had said that I would tell a great many lies. But might she not have meant the sort of lie that players and playwrights tell, the sort that the audience knows is untrue but chooses to believe anyway?

Well, even if that was not what she had meant, I could choose to believe that it was. If it was my fate to be a liar, then I would revel in it. I would write the most real and riveting lies I could concoct, lies that theatre companies would delight in telling and that folk would pay to hear, again and again.

I quickened my pace. Before long the sun would be down and I would need to head home, where the boys would be waiting eagerly to harness me and turn me into Banks's horse, and Mr. Pope would want to hear about all I had seen and done that day, and Tetty would ask me to tuck her into bed. And I would not, for all the world, have had it otherwise.

But for the next few hours my time was my own, and I meant to spend it in a quiet booth at the nearest tavern, where no one could find me, writing down as many lies as I could think of, in hopes that one of them might turn into a play. I would need paper, of course. I reached into my wallet and drew forth a dozen or so sheets. Though the fronts were filled with my lines from *Measure for Measure*, the back sides were invitingly empty.

I glanced at my part, feeling a bit guilty. We were to start rehearsing the play the following afternoon, and I had not yet learned a single line. Well, perhaps I could go over them for half an hour or so that evening, before sleep claimed me. After all, none of the other players would have their parts down yet, either, particularly not the new prentices and hired men the company had taken on. They would be as uncertain as I where they were to stand and what they were to say.

It occurred to me, then, how nearly real life resembles the first rehearsal of a play. We are all of us stumbling through it, doing our best to say the proper lines and make the proper moves, but not quite comfortable yet in the parts we've been given. Still, like players who trust that—despite all evidence to the contrary—the whole mess will make sense eventually, we keep on going, hoping that somehow things will work out for the best.

I could not be certain what sort of part Fortune had written for me; all I could do was to play it out to the best of my ability. I had the feeling that it would prove to be rather like the script for *Timon of Athens*—far from perfect, but full of promise.

Though *Shakespeare's Spy* is obviously a novel and not a history text, I did my best to make it as accurate as I could. Sometimes, for the sake of the story, I did take a few liberties with the facts, or indulged in a bit of speculation. For example, I'm not certain that the Thames actually froze over in the winter of 1602–1603. But the river did freeze several times during Queen Elizabeth's reign, so solidly that celebrations called Frost Fairs were held on the ice.

I also put in a number of people who, as far as I know, didn't exist. Widge is my own invention, of course; so are Jamie Redshaw, Julia, Tetty, and Tom Cogan. Nearly everyone else in the story is based on a real historical character—though again, I did sometimes fudge the facts a little. La Voisin, the cunning woman, practiced her art in the 1660s and '70s, so, unless she lived to an unusually ripe age, she probably wasn't around in 1603.

Frances Vavasour was one of the queen's ladies-in-waiting, and she did marry Thomas Shirley; there's no evidence that she had an affair with the Earl of Essex, but it's not at all unlikely, considering how numerous his conquests were. Sal Pavy may never have acted with the Chamberlain's Men, but he did act at Blackfriars. And, though there's no record of the cause, he did die at the age of thirteen.

Shakespeare had not just one daughter, but two—Susanna and Judith. In 1603, Judith would have been seventeen or eighteen. At the age of thirty-one, she married Thomas Quiney, the shiftless, alcoholic son of one of Shakespeare's friends.

Father John Gerard's career contained far more danger and daring than I could fit into this book. Luckily he wrote his own, *The Autobiography of a Hunted Priest*, which was reprinted in the 1950s.

King James's wife, Anne, really did fancy herself an actress. She and her ladies-in-waiting regularly performed in expensive, elaborate masques at the court. But it wasn't until 1660, when King Charles II took the throne, that women were allowed at last to appear on the stages of public playhouses in England.

The cast of characters is not the only thing based on historical fact, of course. Most of the big events—the plague, the queen's death, the closing of the theatres, James's accession to the throne—happened more or less the way I've presented them. Some of the smaller elements in the book are true as well. As you know if you've read *Shakespeare's Scribe*, Widge's "swift writing" was an actual system of shorthand invented by Dr. Timothy Bright in the 1580s. And the cyphers Henslowe uses to communicate with his spy are part of a code devised by Queen Elizabeth's secret service, whose job it was to uncover Papist plots against Her Majesty.

Like all the other plays mentioned, *Timon of Athens* is the real thing. It's even still staged occasionally. But because the script is, if not exactly putrid, at least not top-notch, many Shakespearean scholars think that someone besides the Bard had a hand in writing it.